ALSO BY KYRO DEAN

- The Pharaoh's Curse

- The Earl's Assassin

- Glister

- The Covenant of Shihala

- The Seal of Sulayman

- The Haunting of the Immortal Killer

- Eve of Fyre

THE BARON'S GHOST

—•—

ROGUE ROYALS: BOOK 1

KYRO DEAN

EIGHT MOONS PUBLISHING

To Writer Josh – What can I say? Without you, this book wouldn't even exist.

The Baron's Ghost Table of Contents

J OIN MY MAILING LIST for updates and free reads:

ONE

Christina's mother had always clung to a truth said to be known only to the gentlewomen of upper Avendale: that a soft, kid-skinned glove could protect against dust, get done what must, and earn people's trust.

Armed with this seminal knowledge, she spent most of Christina's childhood challenging, "What more could a lady need?"

While her mother had long since passed (cholera doesn't give a pinched farthing about kid-skinned anything), Christie took the heart of her wisdom everywhere she went. Even now, as she secured a thick, black pair of gloves around her wrists and tightened the grip on her gun.

Her objective was simple: steal the delivery schedule from Thorton and Blackwell Shipping Co. without being seen. Or, as her commander suggested, get in and out alive, no matter the price. But she preferred the first method. After all, killing was a thing that darkened the soul, and hers was dark enough.

A deep bellow echoed long before the silver tip of an airship emerged from the smog, its teardrop nose reflecting green in the lights of the shipping dock below. It would be all hands on deck until the airship landed. That gave her thirty minutes to get the job done. Close, but doable.

She waited for the crack of grappling hooks before sprinting over the iron tracks that marred the ground like veins. The heels of her boots dug into the gravel with each crunching step. She crossed the trainyard, flitting between pools of darkness, then slowed her pace in the shadow of the shipping office. Drunken yells sounded from the housing projects on the other side.

She would have to be careful; there was nothing louder than a slobbering drunk, and she couldn't afford anyone sounding the alarm.

In the safety of the shadows, she eased her shoulders against the rough slats on the side wall of the office. Her coat slid along the splinters as she pressed herself into the wood. She glanced around the corner and into the dusty street.

All clear.

She slunk around the corner and into the dark recess of the office door where she tucked away her gun and reached up for her aigrette. The small barrette was the same one her mother used to keep her hair back when she was a girl—with a few deadly upgrades. Its brass top contained five metal feathers that mirrored her fingers in size. She slipped out the smallest, a flat-ended piece, and inserted it into the bottom of the lock to hold the tension. Then she grabbed the middle one whose end was bent in a peculiar pattern, dipping it into the tiny hole. The gears churned with each twitch of her hand, their chattering muffled within the door. Her pick caught and the lock clicked.

She glanced at the street before tucking her feathers back in and slipping inside. The room was spartan in decoration, with a few chairs and a rudimentary desk with a lamp on one corner and a bottle of ink on the other. Christie rubbed her chest; the black, sticky liquid was an all too familiar reminder of the darkness she lived in after her parents died. After she was forced to marry. She had only been seventeen, those many years ago. But she was not a child anymore.

Christie pulled her eyes away, scanning the room for hiding places. She needed to focus and complete her objective so she could get paid. Her future mattered, not the rotting bones that littered her past. Neither her parents nor her husband could touch her from their graves. And all the better for it.

Tattered maps and a picture of an airship hung askew on the back wall. Christie rounded the desk and ran her glove across the smooth surface. Two drawers sat on each side with a wooden chair gracing the hollowed-out middle.

She traced her fingertips down the drawers and along the underside of the desk, feeling for any catches or nicks in the wood. Nothing. She knelt down for a better look, breathing in the scent of pine. The thin framing bowed with her touch. Pick the lock? Or just smash the thing? Though the locks would take more time, picking them would conceal any signs of forced entry. Then again, the lock's tiny gears would be much harder to coax open than the door's, and she didn't have time to waste. Smashing things was more fun, anyway. At least the yelling from the drunken circus outside would hide the sound of shattering drawers.

Christie froze. The yelling had ceased. A rush of blood filled her ears as she strained to hear something. Anything.

Her hand slid down to where she holstered the Good Baron. The heavy, double-barreled pistol had been a gift from her late husband, and while she hated the man, she loved the gun. So much so, she had another made, which she called Rudy and kept strapped to her thigh for when situations got tight.

But this was not an emergency. Not yet.

The creak of a floorboard splintered the silence.

She froze. Or maybe it was . . . .

Her left hand crept toward Rudy. So much for sneaking in and out with no one noticing. She gripped both guns and took a deep breath.

One.

Two.

Three.

Christie jumped up from behind the desk, extending her arms and locking her trigger fingers. She pointed four barrels at a man whose face hid in the pall of a black-rimmed hat. His brown-gloved hand pulled the rim of the hat further down, showing off a single, brass bird ring on his pinky finger that looked annoyingly familiar.

"Don't move," she warned.

The man tilted his head up just enough to reveal a haughty grin and the shadow of a mustache. The dim light streaming through the window reflected in green sparks off his straight teeth. "Christina Rushing. It's been a while."

The timbre of his voice sent chills down her spine. Her chest hammered like a steam-pushing piston, but her aim remained steady. How did he know who she was? And why was he using her maiden name? The airship's foghorn bellowed and docking hooks blasted from their cannons in the background. The man's familiarity nagged at her like a shadow at the end of a hallway. Christie raised her right hand and fired.

Bullet tore into wood just above the man's head in a perfect warning shot. He flinched and released his hat. The dim light flickered across his slack-jawed expression.

"Charlie?" Christie lowered Rudy, though she kept the Good Baron locked in place. She hadn't seen him since the night he betrayed her. The night he left her heartbroken, a victim to the dark. The thrill of memories flushed her cheeks and the heat of old wounds simmered anew. That lying blackguard and his flippant smile.

He cocked his head to the right. "There were rumors you went off and got yourself into trouble after you were widowed, but seeing it for myself . . ." He let out a low whistle. "And how might Thorton and Blackwell be of service to you? You're not trying to steal from us, are you?"

She swallowed, thickness coating her throat, and raised Rudy back up. "Afraid so, Charles, ol' boy. I have orders."

The left corner of Charlie's lips tugged up into a grin that pinched her heart. "You, taking orders? Nonsense. The flame-haired girl I knew would shove an apple down someone's throat before she did something she didn't want to." He smoothed the wrinkles from his cravat and waistcoat, along with the ones from her memory.

"The girl you knew died with her parents." Christie let off another shot by Charlie's foot. He yelped and jumped back.

Charlie put his hands up in a show of surrender. "Alright, alright. The fire's still there. Any chance you'll put the guns down and chat with me civilly?"

Pain-soaked memories broke free from her heart in the hardened edges of a laugh. "And what has civility ever done for me? Besides rip me from my home and toss me to a wolf I was forced to call husband."

Charlie's hands sank a little. "Fair enough." He paused. "Listen, I know you think you were dealt a rough hand, what with Baron—"

"Don't say his name!" Her guns trembled for the first time. She took a heavy breath. She was here for the shipping documents. Not to take lip from some boy she used to know.

His smile fell. "I'm sorry, I didn't think—"

"Open the drawers." She pointed Rudy toward the desk. "Now."

He eyed her for a moment. Then, with wide steps, he cleared the floor to the desk and took a keyring from his breast pocket. She stepped back far enough for him to get by, moving the Good Baron to the center of his back. The faint whisper of cinnamon teased her nose, and she sniffed hard to free herself from it.

"Easy now," he said.

She pushed her gun into his coat. "I'm waiting."

His hands worked steadily, despite the pistol in his spine. Hers still held a tremor.

"Over there." She pushed him back out from behind the desk. With one eye on him, she rifled through the drawers. Quills, an ink bottle, buttons, a pocket square, and a small vial of snuff. "The Devil take it."

"Problem?" Charlie's cocky smile crept back into place.

Her lips tightened. "Where is the shipping schedule?"

"Ah, so that's what you're after."

"Disappointed?"

His hand slid lower to scratch his cheek. "Perhaps."

"Stop moving." Christie's ears pounded. Something in his voice oiled the pistons in her heart. She refused to be manipulated like a machine.

His finger stopped mid-scratch as he trained his eyes on the barrels of her guns. "You didn't think we'd keep paperwork like that in some unguarded drawer, did you? Not with governments, shipping competitors, and anti-industrialists out there trying to sabotage everything we do? My question is: which one do you work for?"

Charlie grabbed his top hat and flung it at Christie. The brim spun with the rigidity of a metal disk. She plummeted behind the desk. The razor-thin edge sliced into the wall just above where she crouched, and a lock of her copper hair flittered to the ground.

"Sam Hill in bloody blazes," she cursed under her breath.

She peeked over the desk. Charlie shot at her, chipping the wood into a dozen splinters with a smoky *crack*. She ducked back down and grimaced. Man alive, she was in for it now.

She leaned against the desk to steady her shaken nerves. That two-timing backstabber. She should have known better. Charlie Blackwell would never let his guard down long enough to get caught in a pinch. And he'd never leave the house without his gun. The only reason she still breathed was because he had missed. He never missed. And his blarney face had gotten her to reveal what she was there for too. She had let his presence rattle her, to make her weak, just like he used to. But no more. Her priority was finding a way out of this mess.

"Come now, Charlie," she called over her shoulder. "Wouldn't you like to help out an old friend?"

Footsteps scuffed around the side of the room, and Christie scurried to get to the narrow end of the desk before falling into his sights. She twisted herself around the corner. The air cracked with the acrid scent of cordite, and another bullet buried itself in the floor where she had been sitting.

"So, that's a no to my request."

She could not keep this up for much longer; there was only so much desk she could hide behind. She needed something to distract him.

She spat out the first thing that came to mind. "I heard you've not yet married. That you don't even have a prospect."

Heaven to Betsy, why did she say that? She stifled a groan. Marriage and Charlie were the last things she wanted to think about.

She soldiered on. "What an awful shame. I know your daddy expects an heir to carry on the Blackwell name. Why is it you're still single, again?"

The heavy thud of Charlie's footsteps slowed. "I'm running a major import/export company. I don't have time to coddle a wife at the moment."

Christie forced a laugh but choked on her own bitterness. She coughed. "And here I thought it was because you're a heartless scoundrel incapable of love. Either that or the fact that your company's record is as black as charcoal and even Britannia wants nothing to do with you. Awfully lonely, that: working so hard for work alone."

"A scoundrel? That's a little harsh." Charlie almost sounded hurt. Too bad she knew he was a bunkum snake. "Besides, we're only twenty-five, you and I. I've got time. Why so curious, anyway, Christina? Interested in applying for the job?"

One of the boards beneath her sagged. He must be directly opposite her. With a deep breath, she tucked Rudy back into her thigh holster so she could feel the ground better. She placed her palm on the floor and held her breath. The thick fabric of her gloves muffled some of the vibrations. The wise choice would be to take them off. But when was she ever wise? They stayed on. Always.

The rough board to her left sank a titch, and her chest tightened.

Push to flee right, or face him head-on?

"Oh, you don't want me." Her voice wobbled just enough to make her hate herself for it. "I'm a terrible wife, remember? So bad, my husband died of shame." She didn't mean to, but the last few words pushed their way through a locked jaw. Apparently, the hushed whispers of the gentry weighed more on her than she thought.

"Ah. And all this time I heard he'd been poisoned." The end of Charlie's words jumped up sharply.

Christie sprung up to meet his attack.

She swung the butt of her pistol into his jaw. He cried out, and she pushed past him. She ran for the door. Charlie caught her arm, twisting it to the side. Streaks of pain enveloped her shoulder.

He grabbed the Good Baron, but she clung to the gun. Her free hand darted to her thigh. He blocked the move, stepping forward and grabbing her waist. That blasted smirk appeared on his lips again. Heat radiated between them, and she pushed back against his ribs. He grabbed her wrist from off his chest and forced it upward. Her fingertips brushed the metal feathers of her aigrette. She grasped the tallest one and bit back a cry as the metal tines pricked through her glove. With all the force she could muster, she swung the quill-end down and into Charlie's shoulder. He yelped, releasing her hand but refusing to give up the gun.

It didn't matter. All she had to do was wait.

Charlie's eyebrow drooped on the right side. His firm grasp loosened.

"What did you—" His eyes jumped to hers, betrayal glistening in his ocean eyes. "Poison?" His grip gave way, and his knees landed on the floor with a thud. "It was poison . . . after all," Charlie slurred and sank onto his stomach.

Christie holstered the Good Baron and nudged Charlie with the toe of her boot a bit harder than necessary. This time, she would be the one walking away, and he better not forget it. Now to search him for secrets. She flipped him over, digging in lint-filled pockets for anything she could sell. A few banknotes and a pocket watch later, she flapped open his coat.

Holding her breath, she ran her hands down his chest. His muscles were hard and soft, warm and firm, like he was still a bare-chested seventeen-year-old climbing trees. But what did that say about her? She hardly wore the form she carried so many years ago. Not so soft, so delicate. Not so rosy-cheeked nor wide-eyed.

Not that it mattered.

She bit her cheek and pressed on, pushing her fingers over his spiced skin and shirt to search for anything hidden. Thank goodness for her gloves. Add "preventing lust" to her mother's list of what the kid-skinned layer of protection was good for.

This search was going nowhere, she needed to dig deeper. She popped open his top button, then the next, and next, until . . .

There. At last.

A tuft of paper protruded from a discrete pocket. She pulled out the sheaths, and with a flourish, opened them up like an accordion. The document smelled of heat and vanilla and a hint of Charlie's spiced cologne. The ink's black contrasted darkly with the sand-mottled parchment.

The schedule. By Jove. If its price tag was any indication, the scrawled letters must hold a powerful secret.

She scrunched the papers back up and sucked in her stomach so she could shove the bundle in the bodice she wore over her shirt. If only the rib-staving thing would go in. She crammed it in piece by piece, tearing the corner a bit as she worked the paper in past the fabric. At least it would stay put as she slunk her way out of the shipping yard. Now to get back to Commander Austen before the docks came alive with the bustle of freshly unloaded cargo.

Christie stepped over Charlie's limp body, forcing herself not to look back at him or give in to the memories stirring in her belly. She couldn't linger. And he didn't deserve her presence, anyway. No one did. She swung the door open and pushed her way out onto the porch when a thick hand wrapped around her arm and yanked her back into the room.

Two

—•—

CHRISTIE TOPPLED BACKWARD AND fell to the floor, unable to see her assailant through the tumble of curls across her face.

"Awfully cruel of you," a deep voice said, "to leave him there to die."

Christie shifted onto her hands and knees, and her hair parted like a river of lava around solid earth. A thick waist. Square shoulders. Familiar balding head. Her heart eased its racing.

"He won't die." She lifted her chin sharply. "Just be numb for a couple of days. You're paying my current bill, and you said to spare him if encountered."

Mr. Thorton's face remained smooth except for a downward twitch of his lips. "Yes, well, I was rather hoping you wouldn't encounter him."

"Wasn't that *your* job? To get the papers from him and into the desk?" Christie brushed off her legs and hopped up.

"He's much more devoted than I expected. I think he'd bathe with the schedule if he could. I paid a girl to lift the papers off him, but that clearly didn't work."

"I'd say not." Christie pursed her lips into a scowl. "He almost shot me."

"Hazards of the profession."

"I'm charging you double. It's the price of the schedule now for you not doing your part."

Mr. Thorton's frown twisted into a grin. "Of course. Does that mean you found it?"

"Does a watch have cogs?" She patted her corset where a tuft of the parchment stuck out the top. "There's a reason I charge what I do."

"Good girl." Mr. Thornton said, the patronizing tone in his voice practically dripping off his lips. "Now, don't you have somewhere to be?"

"Ah, yes. Reporting for duty to Oceana's Commander Austen. Wouldn't all this have been easier if you just made the shipping schedule yourself and sent it to me in a letter?" She nodded her head in Charlie's direction. She tried to hide her rising curiosity, but gears were already churning within her mind. "Why are you, a Britannian, paying me to rob your own company under the guise of Oceana, anyway?" It didn't make sense.

Thornton stroked his chin slowly, narrow eyes walking up and down her body. "Technically, Oceana's paying you to steal it. I'm paying you to do it my way. I noticed some discrepancies in my company's dealings lately and wanted them investigated. But I can't have my partner thinking I'm out to get him. The only reason I came here at all was to inform you that the papers weren't in the desk, but it seems you've managed to acquire them regardless."

Christie mulled over his response. With how many jobs she'd done for the oily businessman over the past year, she'd bet her gloves his intentions were anything but altruistic. Not that he would admit otherwise. And not that she cared, as long as the money came in and she didn't get caught.

"So, what do you want me to tell Oceana's government?"

"Use your discretion. The proper channels will hear what they need to hear either way."

"Should I mention Charlie?"

Mr. Thorton narrowed his eyes and took a step forward. "Charlie, eh? I wasn't aware you were still on such friendly terms."

Christie plastered on an air of nonchalance and kicked Charlie's shoe. "I just poisoned him and let him fall on his face. 'Friendly' doesn't fit the bill. Though it would have been nice to know that the Mr. Blackwell you referred to meant *him* instead of his father. I thought all I had to do was outrun a fat man in his sixties, not spar with a healthy, young man and his gun."

"Minor details," Mr. Thorton said with a wave of his hand.

Not to her. There was a reason she had tried to leave everyone from her former life behind. Why she was trying to start a new future by herself, devoid of any baggage. And yet, here her past was, toppling over and spilling her dirty memories everywhere. Memories of summer sun and afternoon teas. Of freezing rain and lonely winters. She stuck out her hand, palm up.

Mr. Thorton looked at it for a moment before digging into his pockets. "Exacting your extortion payment while on the job? I'm disappointed in your lack of professionalism." He dropped several notes and coins into her waiting hand.

She smiled wide and kicked the door back open. "I'll live."

It took an hour to sneak her way back to the remote outcropping designated as the rendezvous spot. The beach was more stone than sand, and twice she felt the poke of sharded rock make its way through her boot. Both times hurt less than the indecision rippling across her abdomen.

It wasn't too often she had the opportunity to be paid for the same job twice. It was even rarer that the two parties involved were both major players in the world market and incredibly well-funded. It meant her pockets were happy, bulging when often lean and going a long way toward her island. It also meant trouble. And Thorton's ambiguous suggestion that he was only up to good sat worse in her stomach than three-day-old porridge. If he was willing to pay for the circuitous acquisition of the schedule and Oceana was willing to pay for the retrieval of the same pieces of paper straight up, who else would be willing to pay for it?

Even more pressing: *why*? Cargo airships filled the skies above the oceans between the three major powers, Britannia, Americana, and the man-made nation of Oceana, all the time. What was on this schedule that made it any more special than the tobacco and silk, cotton and salted pork that soared above her head even now?

"Ahoy, Christie!" Commander Austen called.

Her eyes refocused, pulling away from the blurry reverie she had been walking through to see him with one foot resting upon a craggy stone. She rounded a small boulder the same grey as the choppy waters and hopped into a salty puddle in front of him, splashing his pants with dark droplets.

He scowled and tucked one hand into the pocket of his polished uniform so his built chest bloomed out like a V at the shoulders. His darkly tanned skin and sharp, brown eyes were imposing and stately as ever. The opposite could be said for the steamarine he stood beside.

The round, metal ship *tinged* in protest as each lap of water nudged it against the stony shore. Its frame was unimpressive: a semi-circular window nestled between square sheets of soldered copper. Two cylinder-shaped tailpipes moved the ship forward with expelled steam through a screw propeller, and bluish-silver circles of zinc rested in the center of each square as anodes to prevent corrosion. All in all, the outside of the hull looked more like a drowning spider than a vessel.

Thank goodness the hatch's giant corkscrew and rubber edges stood as a reminder that the beast was, in fact, a machine. Despite its foreboding appearance and hefty price tag, the steamarine was barely functioning junk.

Not only that, underwater travel was Christie's least favorite part of the job. She hated feeling trapped.

In the dark.

Breathing in tired air that smelled of desperation and poppies.

Christie lifted her hand in response and scaled the last few rocks to where he stood. The green dock lights reflecting into the clouds shifted to a dark emerald, and heavy raindrops smattered her leather coat.

"Everything go as planned?" he asked.

"As much as could be expected."

Austen cracked a wry smile. "Kill anyone?"

"I didn't get the chance," she said, though she wished she had disobeyed Thorton's orders and done Charlie in. Or not. Or yes. She could not know. And she wasn't sure she wanted to. Her conversation with him bounced around in her head, distracting her from what was important: her future. Not her past. Either way, she wasn't telling Austen. He was a government agent, a man beholden to someone else's whims. No, the grave was the only place she'd share her secrets.

"Get the schedule?"

Christie met his eyes before flicking them off to the side with a lick of her lips.

"And what would you do if I didn't?"

"String you up by your toes and whip you dead. Then sell that pretty mat of curls you call hair and pull your teeth to see if we could get anything off them."

Christie grinned, then dropped it to a grimace when Austen's smooth face and matter-of-fact air refused to budge.

"Death seems a little extreme for a little old shipping schedule."

Austen's eyes narrowed as he turned and scanned the horizon. "Not this time. There are a few more strings attached to this job than usual."

Christie scoffed and slapped his shoulder as she checked his back. "I don't see any strings on you. Nor have I the entire year we've worked together."

He smirked. "You wouldn't. Now, hand it over." He stuck out his hand and raised his brows.

"You don't know I have it." She folded her arms and shrugged, a strange reluctance to hand over the goods staying her hand and trying her commander's patience. If she could find another buyer . . . .

Austen released a sigh as heavy as the waves crashing against the shore. His brows drooped and a pained look crossed his face. "If you've failed, Oceana will string us both up."

The queasiness seeping into her organs caught fire. She rubbed her elbow and turned away from the wretched look on his face. It had taken so long for her to trust anyone after the Baron that even the tenuous balance between her and Austen was a rare novelty that had taken years and countless life-threatening adventures to form.

Besides, even if she could make more from selling it to someone else, she would lose the steady work Oceana provided for her. It was economically wise to hand it over. And if Austen was spared pain because of it . . . fine. Whatever. Happy coincidence.

Christie sucked her stomach in, gripping the dry paper. She wrenched the document free, but the corner furthest down caught, and the bottom strip tore off completely. Commander Austen shook his head.

"Sorry." She offered a sheepish grin. "I'll give you the piece that ripped when I change tonight. I'm afraid they're tucked into the folds of my shirt at the moment."

"How is it you became our best spy?" he asked and rubbed his eyes, but the relieved smile that relaxed the lines on his face released the tension in her own gut.

"Through discipline," she sang the second word in a gravelly voice, imitating the captain.

It worked. Austen's exasperated pucker softened into a grin. He grabbed the schedule and held it up to the moonlight like it was his lady lost.

"You've been away from your wife too long." Christie smirked. "You need to get home."

Austen folded up the schedule and eased it into his pocket. "You can say that again. I spend more time babysitting you than anything else. And, trust me, I'd rather be doing literally anything else."

He shot her a grin and hefted her over the railing of the steamarine and down into the cockpit. Shadows filled the inside, the meager amount of light coming from a set of bulbs the steam-powered motor churned with converted electricity. The seats were made of oxygen tanks, and the feel of the cold metal seeped through the fabric of her pants when she sat down.

She ducked her head, careful to avoid the whirring vent that sucked the carbon dioxide they breathed out into a pipe where it mixed with other gases and chemicals and heated water for their steam. She moved over to make room for Austen and patted the seat next to her.

"You can take those off if you'd like," he said pointing to her gloves. "The air in here will warm soon enough."

"No, thank you." She tugged them on tighter. She wasn't taking her gloves off for anyone. "I don't want to get my hands dirty if I have to end you later. A spy can never be too careful, you know."

He breathed out a deep chuckle. "Very practical of you. Perhaps I should put on gloves in case *you* get out of hand." He winked.

She grinned and pulled her aigrette loose so her messy hair fell in a sheet between them. She liked to make him laugh, but she didn't want to get too close. She had grown far too comfortable with him, and the fact that she had already betrayed him sat like needles in her throat.

They were heading straight for Oceana's headquarters, and she still wasn't sure whose side she was on. Or if she even wanted to be on a side at all. She had to play her hand just right when acting as a double agent. She walked a fine line between a bag full of money and a belly full of lead, a secure future where she could choose to be alone and a dangerous one where she would be forced into solitude if she could stay alive at all.

And at the center of it, the peculiar shipping schedule, a piece of which she still had tucked against her ribs.

THREE

—·—

CHRISTIE SHUT THE DOOR to her small room located on the outer ring of Oceana's barracks. After the door's lock clicked, she leaned her head against the knotted wood, shrouding her face in hair. It was a safe space. The one place that felt normal—that she felt normal—while she traveled around as a spy-for-hire. In all the places she'd lived, none felt like home. No place containing people ever would. Not after she had been married off to—

Christie punched the door. Here she was thinking of *him* . . . *again*. She had successfully confined him to her nightmares for months, and after one chance encounter with an old, backstabbing acquaintance who tried to shoot her, she couldn't shut the memories out.

With a steadying breath, she slipped her gloves off one finger at a time and tucked them into her pocket. She was safe in here. Everything was fine. Her hands fell to her waist and began unbuckling her corset. The thick leather straps all met in the front so she wouldn't need help. From anyone. Ever again.

She slid each brown strip from its brass buckle and breathed deeply as the pinch loosened. She tried to go without the suffocating contraption her first few weeks of widowhood, but soon found it was the only thing holding her together. What better way to fight pain than with pain?

With the buckles undone, the corset fell and a slip of paper drifted to the ground at Christie's feet.

The schedule.

She bent down and untied her boots before grabbing the ripped piece of parchment. Using only her feet, she pulled off the heels, then sat down on the lumpy bed. The strip that tore off was folded in the familiar accordion style, and she opened it up. She wasn't supposed to read anything she stole or passed along; she was just a highly trained, assassin pack mule. But when had she ever heeded rules?

That was the reason she became a spy in the first place. To be free from society's bloody expectations. And to do that, she needed a significant boost to her fortune if she was ever going to buy one of Oceana's private, man-made islands—if she was ever going to escape people and the guilt-ridden memories they stirred within her.

Two lines were scrawled along the bottom in smudged ink. The first line she could barely make out:

Lord Sheffield, Earl of Portsmouth—not someone she was familiar with, though Portsmouth was just west of the manor where she had lived after she had married.

Then her eyes found the second name, and her throat ran dry.

Lord Ravensworth, Baron of Seaford.

Christie's world spun. Her lungs refused to work.

How could he—

Why was he—

Why was her late husband's name on an active delivery schedule?

She let the paper fall to the floor and screamed into her waiting hands.

Footsteps rushed down the hallway. A heavy hand knocked.

"Christina? Are you okay?" Austen's voice came muffled through the door, thick and syrupy.

But it was enough. Enough to slow her spiraling thoughts. Enough to remind her where she was: at an Oceana steambase in the middle of the Atlantic. Not in a dark room with her hands dripping in poppy-red blood. Her eyes flashed open, and she flipped her hands over and back and over and back just to make sure they were clean.

Like they ever could be.

She ripped her gloves back out and hastily shoved them on. She had been foolish to take them off.

She pressed both of her feet into the ground. "Yes?" her voice wobbled. She cleared her throat. "Is something the matter, Commander?"

"We thought we heard a scream. Is everything all right?"

Christie allowed herself a tiny smile. Austen hated emotions and "women stuff," which, while infuriatingly vague and misguidedly misogynistic, did make his attempt to check on her almost endearing.

"I'm fine, Commander." She got up from her bed and opened the door a crack. It wouldn't take much to get rid of him. "Just the red devil taking his pitchfork to my belly if you know what I mean." She said the words casually, topping them with a wink.

Austen's cheeks flushed pink. "I see. Well, that's . . . unfortunate . . . or not. I mean, it's not unfortunate to be a woman, I just mean . . . the pitchfork?"

Christie relaxed her lips into a sloppy grin and tucked her visible hand on her hip. "I'm glad you understand. Need anything else?"

"Seeing as you're trimming down for the night, I, er, don't suppose you have, you know . . . that torn scrap of paper?" The rose color in his cheeks deepened to a crimson.

Christie narrowed the opening in the door, grateful her body blocked the room. The paper sat in full view on the floor behind her, but she wasn't about to give it up. Not until she figured out what it meant.

Christie tilted her gaze downward. "Sorry, Commander, it wasn't salvageable. Just a bunch of damp, twisted paper. I thought it would be sturdy enough to survive being tucked under my bosom," she trailed the last word and glanced up at him, "but I guess—"

"Of course, I understand. No need to blather on about the details," he said, backing down the hallway. "It's past curfew, get to bed."

Christie closed the door, too preoccupied with her dilemma to laugh at Austen's awkwardness. She turned to the side like a screw through hardwood, afraid to face what waited for her.

The piece of paper hovered in her periphery, tangible proof of the Baron's ghost.

FOUR

— • —

THE SALTY AIR SMELLED like freedom and kelp and whipped her hair into coiled snarls as she traveled down the narrow, waterlogged road. Every rickety bounce allowed her a better view of the rocky cliff face to her right. And with every little bump—briefly, temptingly—Christie thought to jump, to escape into the whirling breeze and follow the ocean to the solitude she so desperately sought. But if the Baron had truly died, her own death would only bring her nearer to him.

If, that was. *If* he had died.

Could the pall of her husband still lurk on? The horrifying thought renewed her fervor to slay the ghosts that haunted her so she could move on for good. And to beat the devil, she had to face him. To dig the Baron up and make sure he was really dead.

Or, at least, that's what she told herself as she gazed upon Ravensworth Manor in the early morning light. The original builders meant it to be a refuge from the summer heat, but the Baron had chosen to live there full-time, despite the bleakness of winter. Most of the cheery yellow paint had given way to a motley brown, and even in full sun, the house clung to the shadows. No wonder the Baron's only male relative—a cousin twice removed—declined to contest her ownership of the manor in the Baron's will. In its current state, it was far from an asset.

But she never wanted it. And the Baron knew that. Just one, last cruel test of her limits.

The final and only time she had set foot in the house after the Baron's death was to grab what she could carry of her dowry and burn the Baron's portrait that sat over the mantle. Her only other plan to return to the place had been to haunt it when she died.

Now she was wasting her precious, dangerously-earned wages to hire a coach to bring her back. Fate was a blackguard.

Christie trudged up the seven stairs to the door and tugged on the bell. The fog in the air swallowed the hollow ringing, and she wondered if Ana had heard it. Not that Ana could hear.

The door lock clicked, and the rotting wood creaked open. Two red eyes showed in the darkness ahead, and Christie felt the chill of home.

Curiosity fought with fear, the one a lantern searching for truth, the other blackness with teeth. The dark reached for her, filling her with dread. Her feet moved forward one thud at a time. The door slammed shut behind her.

Christie gave Ana a wide berth as the anamaton headed to the kitchen. It had been here since before she first arrived, its haunting, scarlet eyes a permanent fixture in her nightmares. She despised everything about it, from its two-meter stature to the claw that stood in place of its right hand. Ana's clumsy feet clunked about with the grace of a peg-legged pirate, and its rust-pocked coating needed to be polished. She had hoped Ana would have given up the robot ghost by now, but the jobbernowl was diligent in refueling its steam-powered motor.

The library would be the first place the Baron would go if he were still alive, and the last place she wanted to be. She stood in the doorway, the thick french doors on either side like jaws about to snap. Knees knocking, she forced herself into the room. The ceiling-high curtains had a thick coating of dust. She had always wanted to fling them open when she lived in this dreary place, but the one time she had tried, the Baron had become consumed with one of his raging fits, and she had never dared search for the sun again.

Surely, the light would draw him out of the shadows if he lurked nearby. She dug one hand into the fabric—thank heaven for her gloves—and used the other to cover her face. On the count of three, she ripped the drapes open to let in the sun.

Christie turned to face the room. A barely lingering whiff of tobacco filtered in with the dust. The library looked different in the light. Empty, bereft, like the trunk of a tree with no foliage to shade it. She walked to the Baron's desk, standing in front of it like she had always done when called. A black stain splattered the faded rug just below her feet. She tried to will herself onward, to focus on the search, but memories ensnared her. Mesmerized, she froze as a rawness crept up her spine and his voice filled her ears once more.

You failed. Again.

The words were etched into her soul.

Pots clanged back in the kitchen. She jumped and shook loose her clenched fist. What about inside his desk? He had always kept his planner and other necessities in the heavy cedar drawers. But it was too much, too personal. She searched for an out, a way to avoid the menacing dark. The bookcases loomed behind her, and she took to rifling through the shelves like a mongrel for scraps.

The silky wood, covered in layers of disuse, held a smattering of first-edition collections. Toward the bottom were rows of atlases and technical manuscripts about the intricacies of flight. She knew them well; one of the thickly bound books was always tucked under the Baron's arm. His cruelty was even more exacting given his intelligence. He was always one step ahead. Always thinking, not feeling.

She trailed her pointer finger along another shelf; a dark line followed her touch past pictures and albums, some painted and others in the new black and white photographs that captured a glimpse into people's souls. She picked one up, leafing through it. All pictures of the Baron. All worthless. She tossed the album back on the shelf where it fell open to a picture of the Baron standing on an airship covered in mechanical birds. A few other trinkets lay strewn about on the slick wood. She piled them all on top of the album to search through what lay behind. Nothing but dust.

No matter where she stood in the room, the presence of the Baron's desk weighed upon her mind. She had run out of places to search. Did she have to see what was inside? Blood coated her tongue. She had bitten her lip again, this time too hard. She squeezed her hand, rubbing the leather fingertips of her glove together. No. There was no need to open the desk. She turned her back to it. If she didn't know what was in it before, she wouldn't be able to discern if he had touched anything recently anyway. A search would be pointless.

More sounds of clattering came from the kitchen, setting her on edge.

"Ana, would you quit it already?" she called before dropping to a mumble. "Bloody devil machine."

Searching the house stirred far too many memories. None of them pleasant or even fair. If the Baron had left no trace in the library, the odds were good he was stiff in his grave. Unfortunately, unless she knew for sure, her nightmares would only get worse. She had to do it. She had to unearth his body and stare into his loathsome face once more.

Christie ran to the garden house out back. The serene tangle of plants was exactly as she left it, as it should be; this was the only place on the estate Ana would not come. And it was the only place on the estate Christie could tolerate.

The garden grew wild and free from constraints, filled with colorful plants perfect for poisonous tinctures. A hoe and a rake caught the slant of sun filtering in through the garden house windows. She breathed more easily in the untamed freshness and lifted vines in search of a shovel. Then she spied what she needed; a large spade—as tall as she—lay against a wall near a large pot full of red poppy blossoms. Christie seized it and burst out the rear door.

The Ravensworth family plots sat under a giant silver birch tree with broad leaves that clung to droopy branches. The Baron's plot lay nearest the front edge. He had staked it out years ago as the place where he wanted to rest.

A waste, since rest wasn't an option in hell.

Christie stood at the foot of the grave. She stabbed his headstone with her shovel. The metal scraped against the granite before thudding on the ground.

Her hands trembled and her stomach squirmed, but it had to be done. It was time to face the Baron again.

FIVE

CHRISTIE PUSHED THE SHOVEL into the damp soil. The blade grated against stones in the sand and twisted her nerves. She leaned against the handle. A thick mass pulled up from the earth, tearing grass and dirt that wriggled with worms. She heaved it to the side with a grunt.

With all the Baron had put her through, it seemed only fitting that this would be how they met once again: her working until she broke, while he laid by and watched. She speared the ground again, stopping only to wipe sweat from her brow in the chilled evening air.

Why had this been her lot to bear? She threw the dirt to the side.

And what if he *was* alive? Shovel.

What would he say? Throw.

What would he do? She swallowed hard.

Spit stuck in her throat like sap down dry tree bark.

Would he suspect it was her? She panted, resting against the handle. He couldn't. There was no way he could know.

She continued, scooping and discarding the dark soil. She barely noticed the sun race across the sky or the rumble in her stomach. She ignored the ache in her muscles and the ghostly hand that squeezed her heart and told her to run, the glass shards of his phantom voice that told her she was *nothing, nothing, nothing.*

The tip of her shovel thunked against the top of the wooden coffin. Drenched in the musty smell of earth and sweat, she stared at the worm-covered lid. The sun set in front of her, burning her eyes. But she didn't look away. What if his cold, white hands emerged to take her under?

The Baron never did wear gloves.

The bonds of death did nothing to break the horrid spell he held over her. She continued to stare, transfixed, as the crimsons and sallow yellows smearing the sky turned into the black and blues of midnight. The moon made its way overhead and still she stood, petrified at the thought of what lay below her. For of one thing she was sure: the closed box held what haunted her. Whether a body or a ghost, it was still the man who tormented her like a devil, first in life, then in her dreams.

The softer pinks and purples of morning's sunrise shone light on the dewy grass, each droplet twinkling with bursts of color. The freshness of daybreak woke her senses and she, at last, emerged from her nightmare.

She could not do it. She could not face the Baron again. Not yet. Not when the thought of an empty box was far worse.

She threw the shovel into the hole. She could find out who the mysterious Earl Sheffield on the shipping documents was instead. Maybe he would know about the Baron. Or what the list meant. She raised her chin up in prideful denial and headed back inside the house. If she was going to neighboring Portsmouth estate, she would need a different pair of gloves.

She would deal with *him* later.

Christie yanked the brass doorbell pull of Sheffield Manor as the clouds cleared and the storm gave way to sunshine. The rope reached the end of its mechanism and the faint ring of a bell tinkled within the manor. She was, at once, grateful she had changed into the one dress she carried around with her on jobs. Britannia's gentry would not appreciate her long leather coat and black, buckled pants. They were even less likely to welcome the Good Baron and Rudy, especially in female hands.

For a dress, it was tolerable: a light-fabricked thing, decent for running, with deep pockets stitched on the inside. But the thin cotton and delicate lace did little to keep out the chill in the damp morning air. She rubbed the soft lace of her gloves over her arms to stay warm. Their delicate, respectable nature rarely found use in the blood-soaked world of spies, but they would do nicely for this job, despite the bite of cold. A balding butler opened the door just as she tucked her hands under her armpits.

"May I ask who's calling?" he asked with an arched brow.

She blushed and yanked her hands free. "Christie—" She stopped herself. Why was it she could steal state secrets but not remember her manners? "I mean, the Dowager Baroness of Ravensworth to see Lord Sheffield of Portsmouth, please."

The butler hesitated a moment before bowing her in. He left her in the middle of the foyer and disappeared up a winding staircase.

Cavernous ceilings topped walls lined with family portraits and pastoral paintings. A sparkling chandelier shot rays of light across the room, illuminating every corner as the soft whir of a motor spun the crystal diamonds in a slow swirl. The roving patches of luminescence spiraled down the wall to where the black bustle of a maid's skirt disappeared and a cracked door closed shut. The grandeur made her miss her parents. Why had they gone off and died from some common illness? They had been weak. *They* had been, but not her. So why was she left with nothing when they died? And all because she was a woman.

Christie glanced up the stairs before surreptitiously removing her boot. She walked over to the nearest painting and smeared the mud from her sole onto the back of the frame. Satisfied with the boggy mess, she pushed the frame against the wall, enjoying the squish. She knew it wasn't the Sheffields' fault the gentry had forsaken her, but her soul required vindication, and this seemed as good a way as any to obtain it. Every good spy knew there were secrets hidden in the cracks between wall and frame. This one now held hers.

She had just slipped her shoe back on when the butler reappeared, regarding her with sharp eyes. "His Lordship is not taking visitors at this time. You may return and try your luck in a week or so."

"Not taking visitors?" Her parched tongue struggled to form the words.

She could not bear to stay in Ravensworth manor one day longer than she had to. She had to talk to Lord Sheffield and find out why his name shared a spot on the shipping schedule with the Baron's. He was her only lead. Her only light to keep the blackness at bay. And no butler was going to keep her from wielding it.

"No," Christie said firmly, straightening her posture.

"I'm sorry?" The butler's eyebrows raised.

"It is of the utmost urgency that I speak with Lord Sheffield today. Immediately."

The butler squirmed like a filk who'd just been caught. "I can't help you, my Lady. He is simply indisposed."

"And what could be more pressing than meeting with a concerned neighbor?" She tried to sound like the other ladies she'd heard bossing servants about.

This time the butler met her eyes. "He is unwell, my Lady. I ask that you return again when his health has improved. I'd be happy to send a letter to inform you as soon as he is taking visitors."

Christie's shoulders softened. Illness. It was selfish to think, she knew, but it always seemed to cause far more imposition on her than the individuals whom it infected in the first place. That was certainly the case with her parents. They were free to move on to the next life together while she remained alone to sludge through this one. The territorially crossed arms of the butler promised this would be the case with Lord Sheffield too.

"I see," she said, trapped by vazey convention. "I look forward to your letter."

With that, the butler shooed her back onto the porch and shut the door. She scuffed her boot on the stairs and ran her hands through her wind-blown mane. Lady Christina was getting nowhere. Time to play by Christie's rules.

She leaped off the porch and across the lawn, taking care to duck below the windows until she rounded the corner. The servant's entrance lay halfway down the side. She could not risk anyone noticing her; there was no justifiable reason a lady would be skulking around the house of an earl. Especially not in her formal white gloves.

She made her way closer, dodging behind a thorny bush. The servant's door opened. A cook waddled out to a basket sitting on the ground next to the entryway, scooped up several milk bottles, and carried them back inside.

With the click of the door, Christie dashed past, grabbing a bottle as she went. After all, her stomach reminded her, she had had nothing to eat since yesterday morning. By the time she made it around back, she dropped the empty bottle in the shrubs next to the back door. She scanned the gardens behind her for signs of people. The coast was clear. She opened the back door and sprinted in.

Christie collided with an imposing chest and stepped back onto her dress, tearing the hem with the heel of her boot. The young man reached out and grabbed her arm. Instead of helping her find her footing, he dragged her outside and dropped her in the muddy grass.

"Care to explain why you're robbing my estate?" he asked. Piercing eyes adorned his straight nose, peeking through wisps of chestnut hair. Polished buttons graced a crisply pressed suit, and his shoes shone in the morning light. He was a regular brow-beating stuffed-shirt, the picture of societal perfection. She hated it.

Christie righted herself and brushed the grass off her dress. Streaks of rusty brown smeared her gloves. Mother would have been mortified at the filth. The red. She itched to remove the lace and wash it clean but now was not the time. She forced herself to let them be.

"I am no thief," she said, tossing her head back.

"You've got something there . . ." His pointer finger and thumb stroked the smooth skin just above his upper lip. "And . . ." He looked around a moment before spotting the bottle in the bushes. He lifted it up and tilted it toward her in a toast.

"I brought an afternoon snack for my journey to see your father."

"I watched you take it from an upstairs window," he said flatly.

She folded her arms. "Would you let a lady die of thirst?"

"You are no lady."

"How dare you? I am the Lady Christina Rushing, daughter of the Earl of Avendel, and Dowager Baroness of Ravensworth. As such, I am a lady twice over."

"Hmm." He tilted his chin up and looked down his nose at her. "My apologies. I assumed by your tattered appearance and petty thievery that you were a huckster area-diving for trinkets."

"As I recollect, the tattered state of my appearance is your fault. And if I wanted to rob you, you wouldn't know until I was done and gone."

"The true words of a lady of means." He smirked.

Snobbery was getting her nowhere; he had far too much of that himself. Christie changed tactics. "I'm here on very urgent business with the Earl of Portsmouth."

"Mhm."

"So, I need you to take me to him, presently."

"Of course, of course. Why didn't you just say so? Please, right this way," he said, offering his arm with a wink.

She glued her elbows to her waist as they walked around the side of the house, but with a disarming nudge, a smile, and a leisurely conversation about the weather, he finally convinced her to tuck her elbow into his. What was the harm? The tight-laced man looked as soft as gentlemen came and was his fair share of dashing. And he seemed to have come around to her way of thinking.

Christie reluctantly slid her arm across his wool coat and briefly, alarmingly, relished the warmth. She regretted pinning her hair up for the visit. The tools in her aigrette were wasted on these mincing fops, and she needed someplace to hide.

"I'm Phillip, Viscount of Portsmouth, by the way," he said. "I run the majority of this estate and—" His cheeriness hardened into stone. " —am the gatekeeper to my father."

His words emptied her lungs. She had been too hasty in accepting his arm. Too quick to assume he posed no threat. She tried to pull herself free. He held her elbow tight as they walked, not toward the front door, but back the way she came.

"You see, my widower father is very ill, and I can't have nosy, young dowagers trying to catch him off-guard while he's weak."

She yanked her arm hard. Her hand slipped free, but Phillip grabbed her shoulders and bent down a head's worth to stare straight into her eyes.

"I know who you are and what you do. And my father will not be your next victim." His words fell on her ears like the broad side of a dagger.

Christie dug her boots into the dirt and leaned her head forward, toeing her way toward him as she struggled to control her breathing. When their noses nearly touched and her eyes were boring into his, she hissed, "You know nothing."

She rammed the steel heel of her boot into the insole of his foot and ducked under his outstretched arms. He turned around and limped toward her, but he was easy pickings now. His arm swiped out to grab her. She snagged his shirt and pulled. He lost the balance of his one good foot and dove headlong into the soggy earth.

Christie pranced just out of his reach.

"See? If you knew anything, you would know that I love to see men fall face-first on the ground. Especially when they're being rude." She grinned. Lord Flippant looked much less imposing with a dirt-filled mouth.

Phillip pushed himself off the ground and wiped the mud and grass from his face. "Just stay away from my father, understand?"

"I'm afraid I can't do that. He has information I need."

Phillip cleaned his hands off on his pants, clearing debris away from his ring and the brass bird that sat atop it. "Information. Money. Marriage. A title. It's all the same to you black widows, isn't it?"

The sun glinted off the bird's metal beak, a match to the one Charlie had been wearing. "Is that your ring?" She reached out to touch it.

He pulled his arm away from her. "You're not listening at all, are you? Just picking out what to take for when you become my father's widow too."

"I would rather be a widow than a wife," she said through pursed lips. "But I'd rather be dead than either. Now, where did you get that ring?"

Phillip brooded for a moment before answering. "It was my father's. When he became ill, he gave it to me to keep it safe. I've worn it ever since."

Why did both Phillip and Charlie own the same creepy bird rings? And why did the brass ravens look familiar?

Phillip straightened his collar. "You promise you're not trying to marry my father?"

The ridiculous remark pulled her from her thoughts, and she barked with laughter. "I've had my fill of marriage to last a lifetime. Trust me."

"Trust a spy?" Phillip asked, his rigid lips taking on a grin.

Christie stiffened. How did he—It did not matter. She needed to get him off her trail. "First I'm a thief, then a gold-digger, and now a spy? You're utterly paranoid."

"I know it's true. I mean, there are a lot of rumors out there about what you do: assassin, mistress, juggler, spy . . . ."

"Juggler?" She coughed. "Who in the world have you been talking to?"

"The point is, I know the spy one is true. I heard you introduce yourself at the front door, and I had my suspicions. I'm sure you can agree that the rest of your actions here speak for themselves. And now, if you'll give your word that you'll let my father be, I have a job for you, if you're willing."

Christie stared into Phillip's storm-grey eyes and folded her arms. There was no way she would stay away from his father, but he didn't have to know that. And agreeing to work with him would buy her time to find another way in. But how much time did she have? If the Baron was alive, she'd most certainly suffer, while the dead lie still forever. If only she could face the coffin and find out if he haunted more than her dreams.

She sized him up one more time, then tilted her head with a raised brow. "Fine. I give my word."

"Do you want to know what the job is before you agree?"

"It won't make a difference. All jobs are the same." Christie shrugged.

Accepting his job meant certain trouble, but they always did. No one would pay someone else to handle their secrets if they weren't ensconced in danger. And she loved secrets. Especially when they gave her an excuse to avoid the disturbed earth behind Ravensworth Manor.

"The real question is, are you paying?"

He nodded, cool eyes fixed sharply on her face.

"Then I'm willing."

Six

PHILLIP INSISTED HE WALK her home across the windswept cliffs, past the back of the manor, and up to the front porch. If he noticed the piles of dirt in the cemetery, he said nary a word. Maybe the darkness lingering there stretched only for her?

"I'll pick you up tomorrow night at six o'clock sharp," Phillip said, refusing to take the last step onto the porch.

His firmly-planted feet prickled her. Why shouldn't he take the last step up? She was being perfectly respectable. That's what he valued, right? *Respectability.* And why did it bother her so? He was nothing but a pampered ninny.

And yet . . . .

The weight of the manor pressed upon her. The only thing she wanted less than being in the house alone with Phillip was being in the house completely alone. She'd have to change tactics once again. His tight-buttoned facade was harder to peg than she had originally thought, but he was still a red-blooded male, right? Maybe a bit of old-fashioned seduction would do the trick.

"Are you sure you don't want to come in?" she asked, fluttering her eyelashes a bit too heavily.

Phillip cleared his throat and took a step further down. "I walked you home for the sole purpose of making sure you wouldn't try and break into my house again."

Christie's cheeks warmed. He must think the worst of her. It wouldn't matter normally, except for the darkness still looming in the house. She slid her hand across her chest and looked up through her lashes. "Are you sure? I can have Ana make some tea . . . ."

"I'm sure. Get some rest. It's clear you haven't been among respectable society in quite some time. You do have something suitable to wear, don't you? Something less . . . dirt-covered and ripped?" His gaze fell to the tear in her skirts.

She pulled up her hem only to reveal muddy boots. Pistons and poppets. She flapped her skirt back down. *A soft touch of the glove and a hint of wrist would lure him in,* that's what her mother would have said. But even her creamy whites were filthy, just like the hands underneath.

"Why don't you come in and help me look?" She offered a forced smile.

"Right. A black widow, indeed. I'll be off, then. Make sure you're ready on time; it's of the utmost importance that we get there by seven."

He turned and walked down the last five steps into the night. Christie fought the urge to call him back. To plead with him to stay. But he was right, that wouldn't be respectable, and she needed to get into character. Who knew what devils she'd run into at the ball tomorrow. Only monsters lived around these parts.

Christie creaked up the stairs and down the dingy hallway to the room she used to stay in. Everything lay exactly where she had thrown it the day she'd left: dilapidated books dumped in an open cedar chest, sheets spread about the floor in dusty pools of sandy white. She crept through the minefield and into her closet, making sure to step exactly in the middle where a triangle of light kept back the shadows.

Three gowns hung near the front like the abandoned sails of a ghost ship. She rubbed her thumbs across the pads of her fingers, so the dirty lace caught just so.

She was solid.

Real.

Palpable.

Not adrift in a nightmare with red-stained hands. She exhaled and lifted the sleeve of a mauve dress she had worn before she was married. Little holes punctured the taffeta like a sieve.

Moths.

She sighed.

A storm-blue dress with a high collar and black clasp around the neck hung behind it. Close inspection revealed the same culprit had ravaged this gown too. The third, a wool dress in dark green, hung limply on its hanger. Her hand fluttered to her clavicle, and the grey shadows of the closet deepened to a black. Her trembling finger reached out and hovered above a dark stain that ran down the front.

A thud on wood. Christie's eyes grew wide.

A shuffling to her left.

She turned.

Devilish eyes stared at her from the doorway. She screamed.

Ana remained steady, a tray of tea balanced between hook and metal hand. Christie's limbs shook. What was the matter with her? Why hadn't she finished what she'd started and opened that ruddy coffin?

"I'm not taking tea this evening, Ana," she snapped. The adrenaline was seeping down her neck in droplets of sweat, and she took the napkin from the tray to dab at it. "I was trying to find something to wear, but my gowns are in tatters, so thanks for your terrible house cleaning. A maid with a hook, what a ridiculous contraption."

Ana trudged backward and bent to place the tea on a side table. Steam whirled and hissed from the robot's joints as it straightened back up and once again darkened the closet with its shadow. It thrust its hook out. Christie flinched. But the curved metal was not for her. It moved upward, above her head to a chest on the shelf. With a jerk, it grabbed the handle of the case and brought it crashing to the floor.

"Ana!" Christie stepped back. "You could have killed me."

Red eyes stared blankly back.

"It was very rude of you."

Steam released in a puff from Ana's shoulder joint.

"Well *phhffff* to you, too. Don't you have something to not clean somewhere?"

Silent as the dead, Ana's crimson eyes turned, and she hobbled out of the room.

Christie's hands moved to tuck themselves into the sides of her corset in search of comfort, but her fingers failed to find their mark. Hades in a steamarine. Now that she was back in polite society, she had to put her pain-sealing bodice underneath her clothes. She kicked the trunk instead, forcing it out of the closet and by the bed. She sat down and a cloud of dust furled around her. She coughed. With a wave of her hand, she cleared the air, then unsnapped the locks. She clenched her eyes shut as she opened the lid, only daring to peek when the hinges stopped their groaning.

On top lay the mourning dress she wore the day she celebrated her freedom. It was a macabre and lacy piece that had no place at a ball. Unless she wanted people to think she was still grieving for the Baron a year after his death. Which she did not. Why had Ana put it away so carefully? She pulled the piece out and laid it on the bed. Underneath, wrapped pristinely in tissue paper, lay the exact opposite. The vibrant dress she wore the day she lost everything.

Her wedding gown.

Christie lifted the creamy satin. The rustle of the fabric awakened the only light in the house. Soft, pink chiffon flowers danced about the organza overlay, teasing the white satin underneath. It was the most beautiful dress she had ever seen. That's what she had told her mother when she saw it in a shop on her sixteenth birthday.

At the time, her mother had "tsked" her dream away, disapproving of the low neckline and shoulder-draping sleeves. As they marched away from the store, Christie thought she'd never see anything so lovely again. But to her surprise, the next night, the dress was waiting for her in her room beside an elegant pair of white lace gloves. The very gloves she wore now. Her mom had hugged her and told her she wanted Christina to feel her family's love the day she gave her love to another.

Only that never happened. She had been alone, unhappy, and bereft of love the day she wore that dress.

Her fingers trembled, dimpling the silky fabric. Part of her wanted to rip it up, but she could not bring herself to do it. The delicate flowers never wronged her. *He* had. No. *They* had. Her parents. For dying and leaving her alone. Her heart stung with guilt, and she clenched her teeth to help bear the pain. The feeling passed with a sigh. She held up the dress in the rays of light that peeked through the window.

She puffed out her cheeks in a serious inspection. The fabric was fancy enough to fit in at a ball, but the overbearing white screamed jilted bride. She lifted the layer of see-through organza. It could come off entirely if she removed the belt. She smirked. She knew just how to give this dress new life. Only . . . only she'd have to take off her gloves. She splayed her fingers out. Crunched them back into a fist. Private islands were expensive commodities, and she wasn't exactly swimming in banknotes. It didn't help that the Baron's tastes were so eclectic; the manor full of oddities and baubles was worth more as tinder. In short, she needed Phillip's money.

She could take off her gloves for a few minutes, an hour tops. She had to do it. She had a job to get done.

The clock chimed six and Christie was still in her knickers washing red down the kitchen sink. She scrubbed harder and harder, unable to discern between what was skin and what was not. The more crimson water splashed off her hands, the more vigorously she scraped to get it off.

She had been here before.

She had done this before.

The rim of the sink dripped with the blood of dead poppies.

She had to get it off.

She had to get it off.

She had to get it off.

She scrubbed harder at her skin.

She would never get it off.

A hand rattled the window behind the sink. Christie jumped, casting sprinkles of scarlet water in dots across the glass.

"What on earth are you doing?" Phillip asked through the glass. His voice sounded tinny, like it was trapped in a cookie jar.

The room crispened into focus. She peered at his distorted nose through the pane. What had she been doing? She remembered working through the night and turning the clear water on in the morning, but the sun was once again moon. Her hands, covered in raw color and slivers, stung. Several places wept a pinprick of blood where her nails had nicked skin. She grabbed her leather gloves from the counter and pulled them over shaking fingers. She should not have taken them off. She should not have risked it.

"Why aren't you ready?" He jabbed at the window. "I told you timing was essential. Are you a spy or not?"

Christie ripped her gaze away from her hands, from the red water, and back to Phillip.

"I'm a spy."

"Then move. We need to leave." Phillip pointed sharply toward the front of the house. Despite his apparent frustration, he still refused to come inside the house to find her. Was she that awful?

She squeezed her hands shut. Open, then shut.

"Go." Phillip pressed his face close to the glass so his mouth gaped in darkness.

"I'm going," she huffed.

But she was not. Whatever had held her mind drifted back into the corners, leaving her awkwardly aware that she stood in her underwear. She waved her hand at Phillip, but his mouth only tensed. She pointed at herself with a scowl. His hunched brows grew tighter before bouncing up. He dropped his head, managed to keep his shoulders back as he tripped on a bush and strode out of sight.

Served him right.

She crept to her room, still squeezing her hands open and closed. Already the cloth between them felt better. She had lost herself back there. She never wanted to do that again.

In front of the window hung her dress, the satin now a rosy pink from the poppy dye she had made in the garden house. She hurried over to where the dress hung and reached out a finger. Hesitant, she swiped the fabric.

Dry. Thank goodness.

But then . . . how long had she been washing her hands?

Ignoring the pain in her knuckles, Christie pulled down the dress and stepped into the top. She cringed as the still-wet red on her undergarments dappled the inner lining. She pulled the bodice up and buttoned it closed with some effort. Next came the overlay. With tender fingers, she slipped it on and cinched her waist with the white Satin belt from the original dress.

Time for the final touch. She plucked up a bag by the dresser and pulled out her brass feather aigrette and freshly-cleaned lace gloves. She tucked her curls up with bobby pins and adorned the messy bun with the feathers. What was a spy without her toolkit? And what was she without the memories it held? Of her mother. Of her old life and who she used to be.

She slipped off her leathers and hastily slid her hands into the lace gloves. Red skin showed through, glimpses into the rawness this morning had left behind. A small snag ran along the inside of one of her pointer fingers, but it was hardly noticeable. They would do nicely.

After all, *a hint of skin lets curiosity sink in, and that's how you hold a room*. Her chest tightened as she thought of her mother. Silly sayings like that were all she had left of her, her fine wisdom reduced to nothing but kitschy phrases a young Christina could remember.

She breathed in deep and held the air in her lungs, then stepped out into the hallway. She couldn't help but smile coyly as she waltzed down the steps to the front atrium. This would teach Phillip to call her a tattered huckster. She swung open the door, her eyes diverted demurely to the ground.

Silence.

She stole a glance upward.

Phillip stared.

Over her head and into the house.

"I've never seen an anamaton in person before. Your butler is horrifying. You know that, don't you?"

"I . . . uh . . . yes?" The cool breeze of evening slapped the heat blooming in her cheeks. Was that all he had to say?

"Good. Let's go. You've got work to do."

SEVEN

T HEY ENTERED THE GRAND ballroom complete with glistening gas
lamps and ceiling sconces filled with twirling crystals. Christie clung
to Phillip, not because she wanted to, but because she struggled to keep up
with him.

She had operated in pants for so long, wearing a full dress and crinolette
was like wading through the ocean. If she had wanted to march this much,
she would have joined the military. Twice she performed an exaggerated
side-step to catch the back of Phillip's shoe out of spite, and twice the action
solicited just the scowl she was looking for.

She dipped for a third, but Phillip tucked his foot up and caught hers.
She grasped his coat to stay upright. Warmth, like the summer sun on a
blooming field, spread out from his chest and up her neck. She could even
smell the dry grass, tinted with a hint of savory tobacco. She swallowed the
allure and pulled away as soon as she found her balance. She looked up
through the red of her brows, but instead of a smirk, Phillip's face remained
placid. A woman just draped herself across him, and that was his reaction?
Jaded toff. Did he trip her on purpose, or was she just imagining things?

He continued to pull her along in a clipped stroll across the room.
"Upper balcony, furthest room back," Phillip spoke in hushed tones as they
made their way across the floor. "That's where the meeting will take place."

Christie nodded. "So to be clear, you don't know who I'm supposed to
be spying on, or what I'm supposed to learn?"

"Correct. But you'll know it when you hear it."

"Right." She gathered a fistful of skirt to give her legs more walking room.

The assignment didn't bother her, she often went into jobs blind. Her question lay in Phillip himself. What was such a stickler for the rules doing hiring a spy? Unless it was all an act.

She peered at him from the corner of her eye. His broad shoulders were framed in a slim-fitting jacket that buttoned in the front, and was tipped with sleek cream gloves. The all-black outfit gave him an intimidating, dandified look that she would be jealous of if she hadn't learned better. If she showed the same kind of power, she would get caught. But if she appeared like a doting princess in a fabulous dress? She could look amazing and get away with murder, as cliché as that sounded. In her irony-filled gown, she blended right in. Clichés were all that populated this gentrified ball.

She slipped her gaze past Phillip, away from her still tingling hands, and above the scornful glares of former peers. She refused to make eye contact or let her face flinch. She had more pressing problems. The biggest obstacle of the night lay right before her.

"Phillip," she used her rusty honey voice. "You're going to help me up this giant staircase, right?"

"Hm?" His face was stoic. "Oh, no. I want to see a spy at work. Up you go. And don't trip. That would be mortifying."

Christie gave him a scathing glare, but the statuesque turn of his nose was his only reply. She couldn't tell if he was having fun at her expense or if he was just a wretched addlepate. Either way, he'd pay for it with a kick in his shins once she was back in pants.

Taking one dainty step at a time, Christie struggled to sashay up the steps. She threw her head back and hoped the red of her hair didn't exaggerate the rosy blossoms growing on her cheeks. After far too long, her booted foot found the last stair. Thank goodness she had refused to slipper her feet. Heels would have made the journey impossible.

She took a right and opened her ears as she ambled toward the back room, a smile plastered on her face. A dotty teen who was too young to respectably attend the party fanned her faint frame. An older woman complained of the noise. A young man held onto the sash of a woman hurrying ahead. Nothing requiring a spy-for-hire. Nothing requiring any attention at all.

The ruffles of her gown brushed the thick, oak door that marked the end of the hallway. Pretending fatigue, she leaned against the smooth wood. Gruff voices tickled her ear. So there was a meeting after all. She bit her lip. Phillip had been right; she would already be in place if they had arrived on time. If she had not become lost in the maze-like dark of her broken mind.

What had ensnared her so?

She clenched her hand until it numbed. She did not want to know. There was no helping it now anyway. She ran her fingers along the door crack. Entering the room now could not be done without notice. Perhaps there was a servant entrance in the adjoining room she could make use of.

She pulled cheek off wood and fanned herself with an exaggerated wave. With a sigh, she flopped her back onto the neighboring door. The third and fourth tools in her aigrette should be the right fit for this job. She slipped her feathered lock picks out and snuck her hands behind the folds of her dress to work on the knob. Within a moment the door handle turned.

Success. These snobby dotards and their measly locks made this job all too easy.

She gave the hallway another cursory check. Not that anyone there noticed anything but themselves. She had never stopped looking for the Baron over her shoulder, and she could not afford to stop now. Not when he might actually be alive.

She pressed herself against the door and it swung open, but the starched crinoline of her hoop skirt caught in the door frame. The woman who was still being pursued by her sash-holding man-pup crinkled her brows as she passed by down the hall again. Christie sucked in, bending her body so her clavicles protruded like shells in sand.

What was she doing?

Her waist was not the problem. She pushed the puff around her hips down and twisted back and forth. At last, the fabric popped through, all of a piece, and she tumbled inside, shutting the door behind her.

She took a moment to rest her forehead against the damask wallpaper. Gold imprints caught the light over the Agony in Red background, but it was just a foil. Like everything else in society. From her cage of a dress to the aristocratic veins running the length of the curtains, it all meant nothing. And she was done with the nothingness wrapped in judgment. She needed to finish this job and get out—of this room, of society, of everything—for good.

Christie tucked the feathers back in her aigrette and ran her hands along the shared wall between this room and the one she needed to get into.

There.

A slit? The tiniest crack. She bent behind a chair to try and find the catch. The door to the room opened behind her, and Christie crouched lower as feet shuffled into the room. She scurried to scoop up stray folds of her dress and tuck them under the half-dome that held up her skirt. She hid behind a grey chair that was wide and overstuffed, like a beached walrus she had seen as a child. Hopefully, its girth was enough to hide her. She was tired of making excuses.

"This is not where we agreed to meet," a baritone voice whined.

She stifled a groan. She hated snivelers.

"It's close enough, Dobson. Sit down," the second man replied.

Christie's ears perked up. If someone had secrets, Mr. Thorton *would* be in the thick of it. She peeked around the side of the chair. Her tall, sometimes-employer lit up a cigar and took a seat on the green velvet couch in the middle of the room. His eyes darted to her corner, and she ducked her head.

Had he seen her? Heard the rustle of her skirt? She held her breath for three, four, five seconds, then let it go in a silent stream. That was too close. No more sneaking peeks. She would have to suffice herself with listening in.

"Sorry if I'm not as cavalier as you are when discussing matters of a sensitive nature," the man called Dobson said in a squirrely voice.

"You're a black-market arms dealer. When are you not discussing sensitive matters?"

"Keep it down, will you?" Dobson said.

"Relax. This will only take a minute. Come, sit," Thorton coaxed in a voice slick enough to grease a universal joint.

"Does this mean you have the shipping information for the cargo?"

"I do," Thorton said.

"I want proof."

Shuffling followed by a flap. Blast caution, she needed to see what Thorton pulled out. Instead of popping her head over the right side like last time, she bobbed left and looked between the wooden slats of a small side table.

Christie caught her breath. The shipping schedule. How did that end up back in his hands? She puckered her lips. Better question: Who was backstabbing whom? Thorton or Oceana? Or was Thorton's connection to Oceana much deeper than she suspected? Thorton had made it clear he had tipped off Oceana, but it seemed like an awful amount of trouble to go through for a shipment of illegal weapons. And for goodness' sake, why did he put her through all that trouble of stealing it when he was just going to end up with it anyway?

Christie balled her fist, crushing one of her gown's flowers. She bit off the beginning of a cry and gently opened her hand. The lovely petals sat crumpled on her palm. Another thing ruined. She pinched her arm to keep her focus on the conversation.

She peered back through the slats of the table, the shiny wood framing the two men like they were pictures on the walls of Phillip's house.

"You're sure about this?" Dobson asked, his brows knit tightly together. "There's a piece on the bottom missing."

"Of little consequence. I assure you."

Christie's fingers brushed another flower before retracting and clenching upon themselves. How could her supposedly late husband's name on a current shipping schedule be of little consequence? That was like saying Bell's electric speech machine did not matter, or that Babcock and Wilcox's non-explosive boiler made no difference to steam engineering. She pinched herself again, this time for the absolutely boring references she had just used thanks to years of being drilled by the Baron.

"And you're sure you want to go through with this?" Dobson stopped his fidgeting. "There's no going back once I leave this room. I will be in blackout mode until the goods are delivered."

"Oh—" Thorton leaned back. "I'm sure." He stretched his legs out, his head sliding behind the slats of wood that framed her view before popping back forward.

"The twenty-third, right?"

"That's the day." Thorton handed Dobson a wad of banknotes held together with a gold tie clip.

Christina nearly choked on her spit at the sight of the bulge of money. Maybe she should try arms dealing. She'd never been paid that much for any job.

Dobson fanned the notes with a deep sniff. "I'm on it," he said, then left the room.

Christie had to wait another thirty minutes while her legs fell asleep for Thorton to finish his cigar and leave. Hazy smoke filled the room and smelled of musty cedar and a sick bed. Her tongue stung with bitterness and her throat parched. She would be sick up to her knees if she had not suffered through similarly smoke-filled rooms with the Baron. Even with that previous acclimation, queasiness nipped at her stomach, and her beautiful dress now smelled awful, seeped in the stench of tobacco refuse.

Though Thorton had only just left, she bustled out of the room, refusing to wait one moment longer. She shook her dress to air out the smell. The faint teen retched as Christie passed. Poor simpering thing. Thorton's cigar could fell a pig.

At last, the stairs came into view. She scooped up her skirts, lengthened her stride, and bumped into Thorton himself.

EIGHT

— · —

Eyes wide, Christie looked up past the thick shoulders of the brick of a man. Should she run from Thorton or play it off?

Run.

She ducked her head and bolted around his side, but a strong hand grabbed her elbow. Holding tight, Thorton spun her around and forced her to descend the stairs with him.

"I almost didn't recognize you." His voice was deep and sing-songy. "You look lovely."

"Just doing a job. In and out. You know how I work," she said, brushing imaginary dust off her skirt.

"You smell lovely, too."

Christie's muscles tensed. Did he know? She fought the instinct to pull away and stab him with her aigrette. If she were anywhere else . . . but she wasn't.

"It's a wonder you can smell anything over the odors streaming off your coat." She scrunched her nose for effect. "Let's see, molding grass with a hint of sweat. A cigar, I presume?" She twitched her lips and stared straight ahead.

He chuckled, a deep coarse rumble. "Indeed. And here I thought you were enjoying the finer things in life. Alas. It is only me."

She bobbed her head with a breathy laugh, letting a ringlet of hair fall between them. It wasn't much of a curtain, but it was better than nothing and was all she had.

"You know," Thorton continued, "it worries me to see you so near when I'm not the one paying your bill."

"Likewise." She scanned the room for Phillip. Thorton was playing nice, but something was off. If he knew she had eavesdropped, what would he do? And if he did not, why was he asking her the worst questions possible?

"May I ask who's bankrolling you today?" Thorton asked, his tone even and playful.

"I'm afraid not," she said. *Where. Was. Phillip?* "Client-spy privilege. Something you've been known to appreciate yourself."

She had to find a way out before he accused her of eavesdropping. Or worse. She would have to leave with or without Phillip. It was the only way.

"Indeed. May I at least ask—" A cough scooped up his words and hacked out their consonants.

A group of bustled ladies passed, blocking her escape. She ground her teeth at the missed opportunity.

Thorton again found his voice. "My apologies. As I was saying, may I ask when your work will be done? I've an errand I need you to run."

Christie turned all her attention back on Thorton as they neared the bottom of the staircase. He had another job for her? All those questions . . . and he was hiring her again? She unstitched her brows. So, he was clueless. And having just heard one of his own secrets, the next job was sure to hold more pieces of the puzzle.

"I can start at your earliest convenience."

"Excellent," he said. "Though, you'll need to change. The task I have in mind doesn't involve frilly dresses." His wide mouth broke into a grin.

"Even more of a reason to get started."

Her boot found the rug at the bottom of the stairs. Thorton released her elbow and grabbed her hand, kissing the top of it and tucking a slip of paper into her palm.

"Until next time." He nodded and left.

A breath of tension escaped her lips. That had been close.

Christie circled the room three times with no sign of Phillip. She had a mind to leave, but it was raining, and she did not want to damage the dress anymore. It was already a red-speckled, sewer-scented gown at this point.

What if the wet caused the dye to run? She would be left scrubbing the crimson off for days, once more immersed in darkness.

"Christina? Christina Ravensworth?" a tinkling voice came from behind.

Christie turned. *The cassocks take me.* She should have run. "Harriet Spencer," she muscled out. "It's so . . ." she fished for a word, " . . . to see you."

"Likewise," Harriet responded. She looked over Christie with a critical eye. "Look ladies," she called to a group of pampered pinheads nearby. "Christina Ravensworth has returned to society. And in such a lovely gown. I'd kill for a dress like that." She shot Christie a look through lidded eyelashes. "Did you?"

The gaggle of women chortled.

"Yes," Christina replied.

The giggles died out.

"You shouldn't be here," Harriet continued, smoothing the folds of her emerald dress with lavender gloves. *Gaudy*, her mother would have said about those gloves. Like an ostrich who thinks it's a peacock. "You've fallen a long way these many years. What a shame."

"I have a right to be here." Christie's shoulders tensed. How dare this sanctimonious pigeon suggest she was less than. "Same as you. If not more. As I recollect, you were born to a viscount, and I to an earl."

Harriet sneered. "Yes, but you married a Baron. A stodgy, kooky, old one at that. A perfect match, if you ask me. And now you don't even have him. You're just a dowager with no family. A burden to society."

Christie crushed another flower between her gloved fingers.

"You deserve what you got in the Baron, you know," Harriet went on. "You were always misbehaving, always so unruly. We were all hoping he'd wear you down. Teach you how to behave. I think he saw you as a challenge. Why else would he have offered to take you on? No one else wanted you."

Christie ripped the flower off her dress.

Harriet continued, "I daresay, your parents even went so far as to die to get away from you."

The gaggle snickered.

Harriet smirked. "And then your husband went and did the same."

The girls broke into laughter. Christie dropped the flower. She swung her hand back so she could bring it forward with the force of a crashing wave, but another hand caught hers. A hand dressed smartly in brown gloves with a bird ring over the top.

"Christina, my darling, there you are." Charlie's voice quieted the women. He had always been able to hold the attention of a room full of idiots. And her mother had always been impressed with his gloves. "Thank you ladies for talking to my dear old friend while I attended to other business." He leaned forward and took Harriet's hand in his. Harriet's shocked eyes melted with a blush. "I ever so appreciate it." He kissed the top of the witch's wrist before taking Christie's arm in his. "If you'll excuse us." He nodded and ushered her away.

"You didn't need to save me. I was fine." Christie yanked her arm away the second they were out of sight.

"Save you? Silly scrumpet, I was saving poor Harriet." Charlie grinned at her. "I know what happens when your hand flies back."

Christie's cheeks warmed. She should have poisoned him with something stronger. Something that would have numbed his tongue forever. Why was he smirking at her like that? What sort of revenge was he plotting?

"Then you knew I had it under control. Harriet Spencer deserved what was coming to her."

"Perhaps, but you don't want to make a scene in a place like this. You already stick out like a sore thumb."

Christie scowled. "I was behaving respectably up to that point."

"I was referring to how radiant you look all cleaned up and in your gown. Your mother would have loved what you've done with the old thing."

Christie looked away, swallowing back the lump in her throat. She couldn't remember the last time someone brought up her parents since they had passed, at least non-derisively. And how did he know about her dress? He wasn't at the wedding. Was he?

Charlie continued, "But now that you mention it, I wonder how respectable you've actually been." He took a step behind her and leaned over, resting his chin on her shoulder. The whisper of his lips tickled her ear. Her neck. She stifled a shiver. His hands held a loose grip on each of her arms, the bird ring glinting to her right. "You stole something from me."

Her spit stuck in the back of her throat. "Your pocket watch?" She forced herself to swallow, ignoring the heat rising in her cheeks. "You made it easy to."

He breathed a sigh into her ear, and she swatted him away. He always used to do that. Come up from behind and whisper into her ear like they had secrets worth telling. But they were not sixteen anymore, and their lives were riddled with genuine secrets. Like the bronze he wore on his finger.

"Say, Charlie, I don't remember seeing that ring growing up. Did you pick it up from a dead uncle's inheritance?"

"Oh, this old thing?" Charlie flashed his ring along with a smile. "How about I tell you the fascinating history of this piece in exchange for the document you so forcefully borrowed the other evening."

Christie sucked air in through her teeth and tapped a finger on her chin, pretending to deliberate. "No."

Charlie's smirk tightened. "Come on, Christina. No one knows the master copy of the schedule is missing yet."

"Then you're off scot-free," Christie said. "Just make another one, and no one will know the difference."

A tall man in a black suit passed. *Phillip?* She grabbed his coattails. A mustached man turned and huffed. She let go. Where was Lord Flippant? She needed to leave before she fell into Charlie's trap. Whatever it was.

Charlie sighed. "I have already made a new one. The company can't function without a schedule. But that's not what I'm worried about. Who did you steal it for?"

Christie scanned the room, looking for an escape. Harriet and her hoard corralled the west wing. Thorton stood with his back turned and in her way on the east. The stairs were to her back and Charlie to her front. Her hands once again trailed her waist, searching for her corset.

"I stole it for myself," she said distractedly. "A trophy to signify your failure as a friend and a person in general."

Charlie's grin collapsed. "*My* failure as a friend? You broke into my office, stole my document *and* watch, as you just reminded me, then shoved a poisoned quill into my neck. We're not children anymore. This is serious."

"I'm very aware of the serious nature of the situation. And I only poisoned you because you shot at me."

"But I missed. You know I never miss."

Christie's feet squirmed under her dress. "Don't flatter yourself," she said, but he was right.

She had never seen him miss a shot. Not in all the horseplay and tournaments he competed in growing up. Not in all the times he humored her whims as they strolled through the sparse woods outside her home while their fathers tended to business. A branch, a fence post, a leaf blowing in the wind. He was the one who taught her how to shoot, and her shooting skills were the reason the Baron had given her her gun.

She cut off the memories and closed her heart. "If you're not going to tell me about the ring, then just go, Charlie. Leaving is the only thing you're good at."

His face crumpled like one of her dress's flowers. "Please, Christina, I'm being as honest as I can here."

"I am too." Her attention snapped back to Charlie's boyish face. A hint of a mustache darkened his upper lip. It looked ridiculous. "You abandoned me. Left me when I needed you."

"It wasn't the appropriate time," he said in a forceful whisper.

"No, it wasn't the appropriate time for me to get married to a monster. I agree. But I didn't have a choice. You could have helped me."

"How?" Charlie asked, his voice rising along with the color in his face.

Christie's pulse washed any coherent thought from her mind. "Just, somehow. That was your job as . . . as . . ."

Charlie took a step closer to her, so the tips of his shoes hid under the hem of her skirt. "As?"

Christie pushed him away. "As a decent human being, Charlie."

A few feathered heads turned at her raised voice.

Charlie ran his fingers through sandy-brown hair, his blue eyes shadowed underneath matching brows. The whole effect made him look like the ocean come alive, a crash of emotion before he would undoubtedly disappear once more.

"See, Christina. That has always been the problem."

Christina glared, but her retort was cut off.

"Hey, ho," Phillip said, bursting in through a crowd of men to their left. "What's going on with you two? Do you know each other?"

"Not anymore," Christie spat, folding her arms. "Let's go."

Phillip looked back and forth between her and Charlie for a moment. "As you wish. I've had the carriage pulled up for some minutes yet. They'll be relieved to see us go. Charles," he said, nodding. "Are you still good for our meeting on Monday?"

Christie stopped pouting long enough to listen. A meeting? Between two bird ring bearers?

"Absolutely." Charlie shook Phillip's hand. "Thorton and Blackwell Shipping Co. strives for perfection in all our dealings." He turned and gave Christie a half-bow. "Lady Rushing. It's been interesting, as usual."

"Shave your mustache shadow, Charlie. You look awful," Christie said sweetly, dipping her head with exaggerated politeness.

"Charles." Phillip clipped his feet together and bowed before turning.

He offered Christie his arm. She hesitated, looking between the two men. The waning smile on Charlie's face was enough for her to slip her gloved hand over Phillip's stiff coat. Serves him right. She flashed a smile at Charlie, turned, and left.

"I wasn't aware you had a past with Charles Blackwell," Phillip said as they approached their carriage.

"It doesn't matter. It's in the past."

"Perhaps." Phillip nodded. "Though him calling you by your maiden name is highly inappropriate."

"Is it?" She sighed. "My old name is the one thing from my past I wouldn't mind coming back."

"Fortunately for you, then, I have found that history has a way of being more circular than we'd expect." He offered her a hand up, and his ring caught the light, flashing at her like a beacon. "Things from our past often pop up until we take the time to address them, gnawing at us until our brain finally realizes why."

Christie stopped listening. The glimmering bronze reflection illuminated her mind, and only one thought echoed within her.

The ring. The ring. The ring.

She remembered where she had seen it before.

NINE

M ORE THAN ANYTHING, CHRISTIE wanted the carriage to move faster. Infernal beasts, horses. So slow and filthy. Why the gentry still used them when they could zip around with steam was a mystery to her. The ruling class had always been slow to change, especially when they thought the alternative machinery was *dirty* and *crass*. But now that she remembered where she could find the ring, she could focus on nothing else.

Not one, but two answers haunted the cold cemetery behind the Manor.

"Lady Ravensworth," Phillip's sharp tone called her back to the present. "Are you even listening?"

She was not, but his questions had been the same for the last twenty minutes. "I told you not to call me that. My name is Christie. Christina, if you must. And Thorton is shipping some illegal cargo. I don't know what it is." She looked out the window to conceal the half-truth. Why were they not at the manor yet?

"And that was it? Nothing else?"

A bump jarred the thoughts rattling about in her mind. "I don't know, Phillip. I did what you asked. Will you just pay me, please?"

The shadows in the carriage extended his frown so it looked larger than his face. "You're a terrible spy," he muttered and pulled out a bag.

He held it out, and Christie opened her hands expectantly. That was a dandy sum of money, and the bulge of coins helped her stay in the present. He tilted the bag, but instead of dropping it, he tipped it upside down and poured half the contents into her hands.

"You leasing-monger." She clenched her fist around the tinder in her hands. "That's not the price we agreed upon. You're trying to rob me while I'm sitting right here."

He would regret stiffing her. Especially once she found out the secret to the bird looped around his finger, mocking her.

"Your information was terrible."

"And you're swinging the stick. You—" She bit her tongue and threw the coins into her lap.

Christie rubbed her hands through her hair, knocking out several small pins that held it back and stopping short of her aigrette. What was she to do now? She needed all of the money. She needed to escape. To get away from stupid questions and lurking shadows. A sum like that would go a long way toward her freedom from society. From Charlie and her past. From the creepy bird rings. On the other hand, she needed to avoid Thorton's bad side or she would be dead before she could even escape. Which meant she could not reveal too much to Phillip.

"Remember anything now?" he asked, his voice deceptively pleasant.

"That you're lucky I'm wearing a dress." Christie glanced at him sideways, but he gave her nothing. Blast his stoicism. Did he feel anything, ever? "Fine, fine." She sighed and pinched the bridge of her nose. She now owed him two kicks in the shin. But without revealing the weapons deal to Phillip, what was there left to say? "He also . . . offered me a job."

"Excellent. I'm coming with you," Phillip said.

"No way." She forgot she was in a carriage and stood up, bumping her head on the roof and spilling her coins about the cabin.

He leaned forward and out of the shadows, picking up each coin one clink at a time. "Why not? You clearly need help."

"Not from you," she mumbled under her breath.

"I disagree. I mean, do you plan anything ever or just go in full charge and make things up along the way?"

"The second, if you must know. And you're the least qualified person in all of Britannia to be giving advice on how best to break the law. Go home to your daddy and leave me be."

The carriage clattered to a bumpy stop in front of Ravensworth Manor. Christina swiped the coins from his hand and flung the door open. She scooped up her skirts and alighted in a puddle of mud with a cringe. She would never get the filth out of her dress now. She would never be clean.

Her hands clenched and loosed, clenched and loosed, the lacey fabric between them offering a hint of calm. She focused on the brass of a bird ring to keep her grounded in the present. It would take all of her to finish the job she could not execute the other day. The one waiting in the cemetery.

"Wait." Phillip leaned out one of the windows. His right hand *chinged* with the bag of money that rightfully belonged to her. "If you want this, I come."

Christie's vision blurred with rage. Or rain. It didn't matter. The heat of her temper burned through both. "Fine by me. But I'd make your funeral arrangements before we go. There's no way a stuck-up lord like you will survive it."

The corner of Phillip's mouth tucked up into a grin. "There's a good girl. I'll stop by Monday afternoon then." He flicked his wrist out the window, and the carriage lurched forward. "Oh, and don't bother disappearing on me," he called back at her. "Or I'll send Charles Blackwell to find you."

Charlie? Christie's fists punched at her sides. She slammed the manor's front door behind her. He would send *Charlie?* She marched past the stairs and straight out the back door. *Charlie Blackwell?* Like he's some sort of watchdog? A hound with her scent? Her breath puffed in the cool air. Charlie could not find her if she were a button on his lapel. She marched toward the cemetery.

Enough nonsense. It was time to visit the Baron.

She stomped across the grass and straight to the Baron's grave. Her anger crushed any feelings of trepidation, and she grabbed the shovel from off the ground. Her sopping white gloves stood in stark contrast to the dark wooden handle. She should not ruin these. Not again. Surely, the rain would wash her hands clean. She shoved the spade into sinking earth and grasped the fabric on the pinky of her left hand. She tugged each glove off one finger at a time, then folded them neatly and tucked them squarely in her sash.

See? She was fine.

With all the strength she could muster, she wedged the shovel's blade under the molding lid. She positioned her weight low down on the makeshift lever and heaved. The coffin lid splintered and cracked, a mirror of the lightning-shattered sky above. Her boots slid down into the grave. The mud smeared the hem of her dress a russet brown. But not even worry over her dress could stay her rage. It was too late for the creamy chiffon, anyway.

She slipped through the muck and found footing on thin rims of wood. Twice she hoisted the lid, and twice her skirt caught and ripped. She gathered the fabric in a sopping ball and twisted it behind her. Once again, she lifted, and the lid fell to the side with a soggy crash of hinges.

The Baron.

She stood over him, one foot on each edge of the coffin. Lightning cracked above, illuminating his corpse.

Blackened skin clung to his face. Her hand shook as she covered her nose and mouth to keep back a scream. His clothes had started to give way to decay, and his shriveled limbs were darker than the night. But she knew it was him. His cruel teeth still smirked in his jaw.

He was dead.

She shivered, unsure if she felt better or worse. Gusts of wind whipped through her hair, parting clouds and ruffling her dress. A flower tore free from her gown and settled on the Baron's hole-pocked lapel. A ghostly chorus of wind played tricks and set her heart on edge.

You failed, again. His voice hissed in her ears. *You will never survive.*

A cup of tea. A whiff of flowers.

His teeth reflected moon and memory. She raised the shovel and jammed the sharp blade into the bones of Baron's neck.

The coffin shifted. Christie held her breath. Everything settled. Even surrounded by solid earth, he still left her off-kilter. Why else would a box half buried in earth rock her so? He was dead. Of that she was sure. But she had come for something else.

The brass ring rested on his blackened finger, ensnaring the light of the moon. She shifted her weight, held her breath, and reached for the metal bird. Twice she pulled back, the rotting corpse of the man she hated too much to bear. The third time, her fingers pinched the sides of the ring. The casket groaned beneath her.

She froze.

Then plummeted through coffin and earth and into darkness.

Christie awoke to radiating pain and a splitting headache. She groaned.

Where in bloody blazes was she?

She lifted her head. A heap of splintered wood shifted on top of her. Freeing herself without further injury would require gear-like precision. She eased her head back and rested it on the dirt. First, she needed to assess the damage. Cuts and bruises covered her face, her arms, her chest and side, and the twisting pangs shooting from her ankle coalesced in her forehead as a headache.

Dusty light filtered through roots, soil, and what remained of the rotting wood of the coffin a meter above. The beady eyes of the Baron's bird ring glinted in the soft glow on the ground next to her, still encircling a blackened finger.

She wove her bloody and bare hand through the wreckage until she found a good hold. With the rest of her strength, she heaved bones and planks off her hips and legs. Nails tore at her dress. One sleeve hung by a thread, and a gash in the fabric revealed knee and thigh.

She shifted under the weight of the coffin's cracked lid, twisting her torso. Her arms flailed for support. A rough board sliced her hand. She gasped.

The Baron's skull slid into view, and she cried out. She thrust her head upwards and scrambled to free herself from the pile of decay. Her body quaked, and she brushed the splinters from her clothing and hair. But she was not done with him yet.

Placing her boot on the wrist bone, she ripped the ring off his finger; the forearm shattered and fell to pieces with the force. She squeezed her eyes shut and breathed, but found little comfort in the smell of earth and rain and blackened flesh.

Why did the Baron have to make everything terrible? She kicked his skull away for good measure. And where exactly was she? For all his lies and love of darkness, she could never have imagined the Baron possessed hidden caves beneath the manor.

Why had he chosen the spot for his grave directly over a mysterious tunnel? Was it coincidence? Doubtful. Everything the Baron did—every word, every gesture, every scornful sneer—held purpose. Her chest tightened. Had he meant for her to come for the ring, to dig him up and find this? Was this a pit for her to die in?

Preposterous.

Bonkers.

And so like the Baron.

But she would not die so easily, not after everything he had put her through. She would prove him wrong and survive.

Christie reached out in all directions, stumbling over roots and finding only damp air. Though the light was bright directly beneath the fallen grave, anything outside the circle hid in deep shadow. Damp earth met her fingertips, and she clung to the rough wall. Up and down she traced the crevices and bumps until, at last, her fingers lighted on a diagonal protrusion. She gripped the piece, and it switched downward.

A gentle hum filled the cavern, and deep within the blackness, a light flickered on. Then another, and another, down the line like gas lamps on the boulevard in London at the onset of evening. With each clicking flash, lights brightened the dank walls around and on past her, down a hallway that branched out in every direction. She followed the bulbs, one burst of light at a time. The muffled crash of waves sounded from a distance.

She turned a corner, and her breath caught.

She stood in the mouth of a giant cavern nearly three stories high. Large gears hung from the corners farthest back, and churning water fell from a crack in the wall to a deep pool below. A massive airship clad entirely in black hung from the ceiling in the center of the room.

All its railing shone ebony in the flickering lights, the planks of its deck a lustrous dark cherry. The oval balloon netted on top ran its entire length and beyond and shimmered with silver. Several thick, metal tubes hung out of the hull on the bottom like the legs of a crawfish. A wooden set of stairs hung on chains from the rough ceiling and led up and over to the decking.

Crank a shaft and pull a piston. Christie shook her head in awe and instantly regretted how it aggravated the pounding in her skull. What was a blooming industrial-sized airship doing underground?

Christie crept up the steps that curved along the front of the bow. Certain pieces of the airship stood out to her from the books the Baron used to read: the mooring lines and spindles, the air valves and scoops. But there were other complicated mechanisms she could not fathom, including a set of copper and brass gears that interlaced on the side of the hull. They lay in an intricate pattern that resembled the flight of a flock of birds. Or beasts. She could not quite tell.

She paused and cocked her head, taking it all in. The metal birds must twirl and spin magnificently when activated. Their chattering would be a ghostly call in the fog of the skies. A design of brilliance. A mark of the Baron. Her fingers lighted on the closest gear, lingering a moment with the chill of the metal. She slid her fingers off and pushed ahead. There, the bowsprit jutted out straight, the end of it curving downward where it would normally lay flat. She stepped back a few paces on the makeshift bridge to get a better look.

There, awash in the yellow light of the bulbs overhead, stood the figurehead. She held up the Baron's ring. They were a perfect match.

Ten

I T HAD TAKEN A great amount of effort stacking the carnage of the coffin in just the right precarious configuration so that she could pull herself up from the hole, but like all things she set her mind to, she had accomplished it. And with a few more tears in what no longer resembled a dress and a thick smear of dirt on her cold cheeks, Christie burst out of the grave and into the boggy heat of midday.

She ran all the way to the Sheffield Estate in a hobbling gallop, wincing every time her foot struck earth. She couldn't stop. She had too many questions gnawing at her insides, and she needed answers.

Phillip had his meeting with Charlie right around now. Hopefully, that meant he was out of the house.

She approached the manor and slowed to a jog. Break in? Or try the butler again? She headed toward a window but veered last minute to the front door and up the steps. As much as she hated to admit it, Phillip was still too much of a wild card, his intentions and motives still convoluted with his station. If she could get in through the main entrance, he would have less reason to be furious if he found out. Which would then give him less of a reason to side against her in whatever game they were playing.

The brass lion head clunked against the oak door, and the butler appeared. His pleasant demeanor melted into pursed lips when he saw who it was. This time, he did not invite her in.

"I'm sorry, is there something you need?" he clipped the words.

Why was he being so unpleasant? Christie fabricated an amiable smile. "I need to see Earl Sheffield. As I mentioned before, it is very urgent."

The butler's thin brows knotted in the middle. "I'm afraid he's still unwell. You'll have to come back another day."

He stepped back to shut the door. Christie stuck her boot in the frame and blocked the way.

Her boot.

Bully.

She was still in the skeletal remains of what she had worn to the ball: a shredded gown and muddy boots. No wonder he wouldn't let her in. Incoherent consonants flooded her mouth. The drafty tears in her dress let in far too much breeze. She patted her sash down and pulled out her still-wet gloves as if they could save her. How could she be so careless?

She slipped them on and struggled to form words. "Yes, you see, I . . . I have this thing—I mean a ring. With a bird?" She gave up and thrust the brass bird into the butler's face.

The downward wrinkles on his forehead bowed upward, and his white-gloved hand shot out. "Where did you get that?"

Christie pulled the ring back to her chest. "Ah. Ah. I want to see the earl."

The butler's right cheek twitched as he stared at the ring. But her request won over. "Let me see if he's awake."

A minute later, the butler returned and stepped Christie through the door. The folds of her gown trailed behind her, leaving a murky trail along the marble and carpet. She had a mind to feel bad about sullying the white, but neither her mother nor anyone else was around to scold her. Her ring seemed to keep the butler's tight lip at bay, and the intrigue in that pushed her forward, despite the mess.

"I didn't get your name." Christie tried small talk to calm her nerves. "You look like an Alfred to me. Are you an Alfred?"

The butler ignored her, led her up a flight of stairs, and opened the first door at the top. She stepped inside a dark room, and the door clicked shut behind her. Thick silk curtains hid the windows, and the air smelled stale and sick.

"Who are you?" a voice crackled from the belly of a four-poster bed.

Christie tiptoed closer. "Lady Christina, Dowager Baroness of Ravensworth."

Beleaguered breathing pocked the silence. She made her way to the side of the bed. A shell of a man lay propped up on silky, red pillows, his skin sunken and shallow despite bright eyes. Grey eyes. Like Phillip's.

"Ravensworth?" The earl coughed. "So this is what he's left with? The heir to his fortune a mere girl, like you? And it looks like you're barely that."

"I'm not the heir to his fortune," Christie said. She took shallow breaths to avoid smelling the sour air in the room. The taste of cottonballs and incense was thick on her tongue. "I was left with nothing."

"No?" the earl asked. His thin arms pushed into the cushioned blankets, and he turned to face her. His eyes lingered on the rips in her dress. If nothing else, her attire should convince him of the truth in her words. "Do you have the ring?"

Christie held it up so he could see.

"And the manor on the cliffside?"

She nodded and sat on the edge of the bed.

"Then, my dear, you have it all."

His words broke off in a fit of coughing, and Christie searched for a way to help. A bitter-smelling tea sat on the bedside table. She reached for it, then pulled back. She could see a hint of her reflection in the brown liquid. But his coughing moved her past the image, past her hesitation and the grip of memory. She picked up the cup and offered it to him. He took the tea with shaking hands and slurped unceremoniously until the fit subsided.

He took a rattling breath and continued, "You're here about the ship, I presume?"

Christie's pulse picked up. Finally, she was getting answers. "I know there is a ship," she gave a measured response. "And I know it has something to do with this ring." She toggled the brass beak side to side. "But I've come to you for the rest of the puzzle."

The old man barked out a sickly laugh. "All his talk of survival and the code, and he didn't even tell you what it was for."

Christie rubbed her chest. Her heart beat unevenly. She knew why the Baron never told her. She was a failure. He told her *that* every day. "Can you tell me, then, why there's an airship under the manor?"

"The *Ol' Bird*? Why, she's a smuggling ship. A pirate ship, if you fancy adventuresome nomers."

"A smuggling ship? Whatever for?"

The earl's bright eyes dulled for a moment and wandered about the room.

"Lord Sheffield?"

His gaze flitted back to her. "I'm sorry my dear. Who are you?" His skin had grown a shade paler since they'd started talking.

Did she have to start all over? How often was this going to happen? He was her only source of information. Her only lead. He could not be a dead end too. This time she would keep things simple.

"I'm Lady . . ." The name clung to her throat. "Ravensworth."

"Ravensworth?" Lord Sheffield sat straighter on his cushioned throne, though his eyes stared somewhere past her. "How is the ol' man?"

Christie opened and closed her mouth a few times. While true, 'dead' did not seem like the right answer at this moment. Maybe if she convinced Lord Sheffield the Baron had sent her, it would hold his attention longer.

"He's well, my Lord."

"And you're his new bride?"

She nodded.

"What a basket of oranges, you are. You landed a winner in the brains department. Must have married him for his brilliance."

Christie's smile twitched. "Of course. He has sent me here on important business."

"You?" Lord Sheffield wheezed the question.

Christie held her eyes firmly on the Lord's face. It would do no good to roll them now. "Yes, my Lord."

"Ha!" He cackled. "Ha, ha! Blackwell owes me a bucket of sovereigns."

Christie fidgeted. Was he laughing at her? And which Blackwell was he referring to? Charlie didn't have a farthing to his name, though his name was worth quite a sum.

"I'm sorry," she prodded gently, "I don't understand. What have you to do with Blackwell?"

His mirth melted into an awful hacking. After a long, guttural-soaked minute, he cleared his throat. "We had a wager on who would break whom. If Ravensworth is letting you handle important business, it means you must have softened him up, won over his trust, that old moke."

Needles marched up her neck and into her forehead. The only thing she had won from the Baron was his loathing, and he hers.

"And Blackwell?" She shut her eyes for the answer.

"He thought Ravensworth would run you down and out—no offense, mind you—that one of you would kill the other before long."

Christie blanched at his words.

"He said he had an ace in the bag, knowing you so well from your acquaintance with his boy, Charles. Ha. Delusional ol' kook."

Christie clutched the smooth bedspread that slipped against the cloth of her gloves. Her breath was as raspy as Lord Sheffield's. "Yes, well, to business, shall we?"

"Is this urgent business good news?" The wrinkled brows of Lord Sheffield danced. "An exciting announcement perhaps? That seems like a job you would be right for."

He couldn't mean—

She bit the curse on her tongue. "No, nothing like that."

And in all the darkness there was that light. For all the Baron's horridness, he never once touched her like that. No romance. No lust. No rooms or beds shared.

Lord Sheffield patted his glossy, red sheets. "Come, now. You're telling me there's not a bundle of joy on the way? I know Ravensworth is in desperate need of an heir. And with you being the looker you are . . . ."

No matter how she heaved, air refused to enter her lungs. She released the crimson of the sheets, trying to shake the color off her gloves. Her hands. She stood up as Lord Sheffield fell into another coughing fit. This had been a terrible idea. To pretend the Baron was alive, that she was . . . anything to him.

Because she was not.

Just a tool for his delusions. And even as she thought it, her chest tightened and bile rose from her stomach. For all she had hated him, why *had* he not wanted her? Why had her presence not even tempted him a little?

She needed to go.

Lord Sheffield's discomfiture perturbed the air behind her, and his rattling persisted. She pulled her hand back from the doorknob. Her parents had sounded the same way right before they passed. She could not leave him in such a state. She returned and reached across the bed to offer the earl some tea. Lord Sheffield's skeletal hand darted up and caught her wrist. She froze. The clouds in his eyes cleared, and the crispness of reality settled into grey moons.

"Lady Ravensworth? What are you doing here? Or have you finally come for our secrets?"

Were they back to the first conversation or on a third? Had her chance once again returned? She needed to ask better questions before his mind wandered somewhere she could not reach.

"I have come. It is my right." She held up the ring. "Now, tell me, who was part of the original smuggling operation?"

His eyes narrowed and released. "Why, just the three of us. Ravensworth. Myself. And Blackwell. Ravensworth built the gadgets; he's cruel, but brilliant, as I'm sure you know." The earl nodded in her direction. "Blackwell provided the shipping routes of major companies within Britannia and Americana, so we could smuggle undetected."

"And what did you do?"

"I provided the goods and managed the money. That is until we started shipping sand for Oceana."

"Shipping sand for Oceana?" Christie tugged against his surprisingly forceful grip. "In Britannia, that is treason." Though there was some justice in the idea that the Baron had helped build her future private island. "Are you sure? Oceana swore they stopped building islands half a decade ago."

"You don't really believe that, my dear, do you? Why else would they hire smugglers?"

Christie pulled on a stray lock of hair. Was Oceana lying to her? They swore to her and everyone else they were honoring the treaty they had made with their threatened neighbors and were no longer building islands in the middle of the Atlantic. That's why she had been working so hard; she needed to snatch one of the few private properties left before they were all gone.

"You know," the earl rasped, pulling her back to the conversation, "that's what led us to quit the smuggling bid and what drove your Baron bonkers—no offense. We weren't expecting such treachery when we started."

Heat shot from her heart and into her limbs. "Sand smuggling led to treachery? What happened?"

The earl opened his mouth, but his eyes clouded again.

"No!" Christie cried. "Earl Sheffield? Please. I need to know what happened." She shook his shoulders, but his gaze found the distance. Wherever his mind had ventured, it was not here.

The door crashed open, and she jumped. Phillip stormed into the room.

He crossed the gap between them in three murderous steps, grabbed her one clothed shoulder, and tore her out into the hallway.

"How could you?" His voice boomed in the vacuous house.

She pulled her tattered hem out from under her boots and straightened up. "It's not what you think."

"Oh, no? Because it looks like you're talking to my father after swearing to leave him alone, and in those ridiculous clothes, nonetheless. I've never seen anything so inappropriate."

Christie tried to side-step her way to the stairwell "I told you I needed answers."

"You are so selfish. Is there anything you've told me that hasn't been a lie?"

Inner fire pricked her skin. "You're one to talk. You're the filthy son of a pirate."

"And you're a—" Philip paused, his mouth open and his finger hanging indignantly mid-air. "What did you say?" He steeped his voice in threat.

Christie clamped her mouth shut and glared at him. She should not have said that.

"Never in all my years—nay, never in all the history of my family—have we ever been called filthy. Or pirates. And yet you dare to call me both in my own home? Alfred!"

Christie couldn't even gloat about getting the butler's name right. Not with flippant Phillip and his snotty asides calling for help. "Don't try to deny it. I know it's true. And to think you act so self-righteous all the time. Your father was a smuggler and a pirate. He just admitted so himself."

"How dare you prey on him when he's weak and delirious."

"I didn't prey on anyone. Your father offered the information willingly because I had this." She held up the ring. "And don't act like you don't know all about it."

Phillip's fingers darted to his right hand where his bird ring still glinted. "Where did you get that?"

Christie smirked. "Turns out I'm more than just a Dowager Baroness. I'm also a Dowager pirate. Who would have thought we'd have so much in common?"

Alfred appeared at the bottom of the stairs. "You called, my Lord?"

Phillip glared at her before shifting his gaze to the butler. "Nevermind, Alfred. I'll deal with her myself."

Alfred raised an eyebrow. "Very good, sir. But if I may, your four o'clock has just arrived."

"Blackwell," Phillip cursed.

Christie put the ring on her finger and waved it in his face. "It all makes sense now, you meeting with Charlie. You're in it together. The newest generation of pirates. Well, you can't cut me out. Turns out all the gear is mine."

Phillip took hold of her elbow and led her down the stairs faster than she could travel them safely. She tripped on her hem and nearly fell, but he pushed her on.

"Lower your voice and stop talking nonsense. You're unhinged. Just like the Baron. You had years alone with the old lunatic. It makes sense you'd come out damaged."

Christie stopped struggling and fell silent. Unhinged? Damaged? But she was nothing like the Baron . . . was she?

His voice dropped to a gruff whisper. "Charles Blackwell and I are legitimate merchants who are meeting to discuss business. I don't know where you got a ring to match mine, but I'm sure it's just a coincidence."

"Oh, yeah? Charlie has one, too," she whispered back. She was not mad. There was proof. "Charlie has one, too," she insisted.

"Nonsense."

"If you're certain you and Charlie have nothing to do with pirates, let me join in on your meeting."

"Absolutely out of the question. If anyone sees you here . . . No. I won't have it."

"What's wrong with me being here?" Indignation flamed her cheeks.

"Just look at you." He swung his hand up and down in front of her. "In the same dress as last night, all ripped up, and you spilling out of your clothing." His eyes met hers then looked away. Roses bloomed on his cheeks "People might think—No. I'm not doing this. You will leave. Now."

Christie stomped her foot, tearing more of her dress. "I am not leaving without answers. If you won't let me get them from your father, then I deserve to get them from you. I'm part of whatever this is, whether you like it or not. At least let me listen in. No one has to know. I'll stay hidden the entire time."

"Why are you always so obstinate?" Phillip stopped her in front of the door, turning her sharply to face him. "I owe you nothing. My answer is still no."

"Why?" Christie demanded. He was being utterly unreasonable. Downright dodgy, in fact. "Do you have something to hide? Something an upstanding viscount might want to conceal? Say, a pirate ship and its stolen booty?"

Phillip's jaw twitched. "Of course not." His determined eyes burrowed into hers. "I've never touched booty in my life."

"Oh, I bet you haven't," she said with a smirk.

He glowered at her, face twitching.

"Let me listen."

"No."

"Let's make a deal then," Christie offered, holding out her hand.

Phillip crossed his arms. "You didn't keep our last deal."

"If Charlie has a matching ring, you bring him into the parlor where I get to listen. If he doesn't, Alfred here—" She tilted her head to where the butler waited by the door. "—can drag me out by my hair."

Phillip's chin jutted out, a sharp cliff topped by grey skies. "And you'll stay out of sight?"

She nodded.

"Not a peep, not a peek, not a breath from you?"

She nodded again. What was he so afraid of? So she was a little ratty, it's not like her presence could ruin his reputation that easily. There had to be something more to what was going on, some sordid connection between him, the rings, and Charlie.

"Fine," Phillip growled in an exhale. "But if you go near my father again—" He paused and lowered himself so they were eye to eye. "Your time with the Baron will seem like heaven."

Christie smiled and rubbed her arm to keep the goosebumps at bay. "Deal."

ELEVEN

T HE GRASS AND MUST-SCENTED curtains tickled her nose and threatened to make her sneeze. She had originally picked a lovely hiding spot, tucked to the side of a bookshelf within hearing distance and with ample room to run if the situation went south. But Phillip had moved her. Had said her berth was too wide and her breathing too loud.

It was horridly rude of him.

Like he would know what a proper hiding spot looked like anyway. He wasn't a spy. He was probably just worried she would snoop through the personal letters tucked between the blue dictionaries on the third shelf. Which she absolutely would have. That's another reason she had chosen the spot.

Then he had gone and shoved her into the old curtains that lined the windows at the back of the room. The fabric left her uncomfortably hot and nearly out of earshot. She officially moved Phillip onto her "if-I-don't-get-my-island-I'm-coming-after-you" list. But her time would come as soon as she could prove he and Charlie were in cahoots.

She shifted slightly so both eyes could see out of a fold in the drapes, keeping her shredded skirts tucked behind her. Despite the heat of her breath against the fabric, all the tears across her bodice allowed goosebumps a chance to paint her skin.

"Come in, Charles," Phillip said from across the room. "Thank you for moving our time back and coming to meet me here. I had a pest problem I had to take care of."

She scowled, but the two entered the parlor and moved to the burgundy, high-backed settee in the middle of the room. Charles flung himself on the cushions and draped his arm across the back, his brass bird catching the light.

At least Phillip proved to be a man of his word, allowing her to listen because she had been right.

Charlie's easy smile tightened her throat. "Of course, Lord Sheffield. Anything for our clients. It ended up working well for me too. Turns out there's been a bit of trouble in the skies."

"Oh?" Phillip glanced back to where she hid.

Christie rolled her eyes. What a novice. He needed to keep his eyes on his guest. Especially since that guest was Charlie.

"A few of our vessels have been attacked by air thieves over the last couple of evenings."

Phillip cleared his throat. "That is unfortunate."

Charlie shook his head. "They've made off with a significant portion of your recent inventory. Of course, our insurance policy will cover that, but it will take some time for all the paperwork to go through. I thought you should be informed in person, considering our history."

Christie leaned forward to hear better, poking her nose out of the embroidery.

"History?" Phillip laughed. "I wouldn't call our fair and legitimate business dealings a history."

Charlie cocked his head. "I suppose." He stood up and trailed his fingers along the back of the couch. "You don't seem too upset by the news."

"There's nothing I can do to change it, and I trust your company will honor the agreement."

"The thing is . . ." Charlie paused. "I think it's an insider job."

Phillip cleared his throat and tugged at his collar. "Nonsense."

Christie fought the urge to slap her hand to her forehead. Phillip was a terrible actor. She was right; the stuck-up snob would never survive the spy game. His nervous twitches were so obvious, he was beginning to implicate himself in everything.

Charlie paced in an ever-widening circle, each pass drawing nearer to where she hid. "I hate to use the word because it sounds so juvenile, but *pirates* play by their own rules, and betraying a company with an inside man . . . ." He reached the corner of the bookshelf where she'd originally planned to hide and snapped his head to the side. "Well, that's exactly the kind of filthy trick they'd try."

She grimaced. He was definitely on to her. And Phillip had been right about that ruddy spot. She pulled her nose back into her fabric lair.

It was only a matter of time.

Phillip sprung up from the couch. "I agree. Is there anything I can do to assist you? We can leave right now." He swooped around the side to cut Charlie off and circle him back, but he was no herd dog. Just a clumsy pup tripping over his own paws.

"I think you've done enough," Charlie said.

His fingers dipped into the fabric of the curtains. She held her breath. He ripped them open, and a flurry of dust filled the air. Only one set of curtains lay between her and Charlie now. She needed a plan.

"Where is she?" Charlie kept his tone light.

Her free hand grasped her thigh. The Good Baron. Rudy. She had left them on her bed for the ball and had forgotten to pick them up when she'd emerged from the caverns. What a daft move. Without her barking irons, she only had one choice. Her fingers walked up her body and toward her aigrette.

"Hm?" Phillip said, his signature aloofness coming back into play. Where had that been earlier?

"Chri-sti-na." Charlie punctuated the syllables. "She stole something from me the other day."

Phillip picked at his nails, looking bored. "Sorry to hear that."

"Right after she poisoned me."

Phillip froze.

Charlie burst open another set of curtains. It was almost time. She reached her brass feathers and tugged the fifth, poisoned one, free. She hadn't had time to refill the metal tip since the last time she'd stabbed him, but maybe the threat alone would give her some leverage.

"You see, I've suspected an inside man for some time, but I couldn't figure out who it was. Then Christina robbed me, and I knew it had to be someone with funds. So I went snooping at the Sterlings' ball, and lo and behold, not only is she there, but you carry her away on your arm."

Charlie stood right in front of her now, his back turned so he faced Phillip. His words rang bitter, but his attention seemed to have shifted away from the curtains. Maybe luck was on her side, and he wouldn't find her after all.

"Are you accusing me of intrigue and deception?" Phillip's placid tone took on a hint of anger. "Or of having a lovely, titled young woman on my arm at a ball?"

The feather in Christie's hand pressed cold into her skin. Charlie would not take well to Phillip's words. His family was self-made, and had always felt slighted by the gentry.

Charlie's muscled shoulders tightened under his jacket. "If you're asking me to believe that Christina went to a ball willingly with anyone, much less you, I'm going to have to stick with intrigue and deception."

"How dare you?" Phillip took a step forward.

"Ah, ah." Charlie stuck out a finger. "How dare *you*?" He whipped around, and his brown leather gloves slid into view a few centimeters in front of her nose. "Hello, Christina," he said and flung open the curtains.

Christie thrust the end of the quill under Charlie's chin, pressing her body against his so he could not escape. The shared warmth of their past burned hot and threatened her concentration. She poked the quill so it nipped his skin, and he jabbed cold metal into her side.

A gun.

She had been so flustered she'd forgotten to scan him for weapons.

Every time.

Every time Charlie was around, she made mistakes.

"Hello, Charles ol' boy." She tilted her chin up and offered a dapper smile.

The corner of Charlie's mouth tugged upward. "If we keep running into each other, people will start to think there's something between us."

"There is." She batted her eyelashes. "A whole lot of air."

"Enough." Phillip grabbed hold of Charlie's shoulder just past her nose. The stiff fabric of Charlie's coat dimpled under each fingertip.

Christie eyed him with parted lips. Aside from when he'd caught her trying to talk to his father, this was the most emotion she had seen from him.

He took a measured breath, and this time his voice came out steady. "Let's everyone calm down. I think there's been a huge misunderstanding between all parties involved."

"What's there to misunderstand?" Charlie tipped his chin upwards and away from her quill. "You had her steal the schedule and are now robbing me to collect the insurance money on your own property."

Phillip's cheek moved a hair, the first drop in a storm. "That's incorrect information, I'm afraid. I hired Lady Ravensworth here because I also suspected foul play among our colleagues. I needed a spy to listen in on a clandestine meeting I stumbled upon."

Christie cringed at the mention of her married name.

"It's true." She locked eyes with Charlie. "Phillip is not your insider. But we won't tell you who is until you answer a few of our questions."

Charlie grinned and poked his gun into her ribs. "And why would I agree to that?"

"Because if you don't," she said and touched the metal tip of her quill to his skin, "I'll poison you and roll you over with my steel-toed boots. Again."

Charlie's eyes narrowed. He pushed the gun farther into her side, and Phillip's knuckles whitened with tension. Then, Charlie released her.

He stepped back, swept his eyes across her frame, and nearly choked. "What is happening with this?" He waved the gun up and down at her lack of attire. "Why are you here . . . in that? Right now? All the ripping? I mean, I like it. I mean, I don't." He rubbed the barrel of the gun on his temples. His cheeks burned rosy. "You didn't actually attend the ball together with Phillip, did you? Like *together* together?"

She twirled her brass feather and bent her knee so the dress slipped off her thigh. Seeing Charlie flustered was a gift. Maybe she could still make him run hot? Get him to confess to a life of piracy and bird rings while he was distracted? But before she could say anything Phillip spoke up.

"Of course not. Despite how it looks, nothing inappropriate has taken place. Especially not between me and Lady Ravensworth." He shook his head determinedly.

Christie scowled. Did he have to make it sound like the worst thing in the world?

"In fact," Phillip continued, "she originally came to see my father."

Christie winced at the implication. "You're an idiot."

Charlie raised a brow and holstered his gun. "Is that so?" A faint smile teased his lips. "So . . . older men? That's your thing?" He slunk over to the couch, plopped down, leaned back, and propped his feet up on the table. "It all makes sense now."

Christie yanked the fabric back over her leg. They had embarrassed her enough today. "I believe it's our turn to ask you questions, not the other way around."

"All right. Not that I believe you, but ask away. I'm an open book. Especially considering, well, *our* history." He looked at her and fluttered his eyelashes.

She cleared her throat and averted her eyes from Charlie's mocking gaze, finding Phillip's instead. He stared at her, stoic and formal. Though a hint of pink colored his cheeks. What had he to be bashful about? She was the one spilling out of her dress.

Phillip broke both their gaze and the silence first. "Christina, here, believes you're a pirate."

Charlie's grin cracked even wider, his light eyes dancing with mischief. "I didn't realize she thought so highly of me. I'm flattered." He brought his hand to his chest and bobbed his head.

"Oh stuff it," Christie shot back. "I know what that ring on your finger symbolizes. Don't turn this into one of your games. Answer straight."

Charlie scratched the underside of his chin. "All I know is I won this ring from my dad in a game of poker when he was sloshing drunk, and he's been too prideful to ask for it back."

Christie analyzed every move he made. Unlike Phillip, he was an easy read. And he was telling the truth.

"I'm not crazy," she said, squaring her shoulders.

"Interesting how that's the first defense you jump to," Charlie said.

Phillip spoke up. "I'm sorry about all this, Charles. I called you here today to tell you what we've learned, not to ambush you. Lady Ravensworth has just been insistent that our rings make us part of some secret smuggling operation."

Charlie's lips tightened slightly in the corners. "Not to worry, I know how persistent she can be." He gave her a wink. "What I didn't realize was how much of a hold she has on you."

Christie snorted and glanced at Phillip, who was locked in a staring contest with Charlie. He did not move. Not even a twitch of the lips. Of course not. But he did not refute it either. And that made her stomach twist.

She needed to change the subject.

"I have proof," the words tumbled out of her mouth.

Phillip and Charlie both turned to look at her.

Maybe she did just wing everything without planning. Her snappy responses were causing more trouble than good. Oh well. She was in it now. Besides, if they tried to betray her, she could always poison them and lock them in her secret cave forever.

"I can show you."

Charlie popped up from the couch and into a deep bow. "Lead the way, madam pirate."

TWELVE

ONCE MORE CHRISTIE STARED down into the grave of her late husband. Though this time, she did it with a faint shadow of hope. And Charlie and Phillip.

"Down you go. Mind the rotting bones at the bottom. They'll leave a mark on your trousers."

Phillip leaned over the hole and said nothing. Charlie, however, was less pleasant.

"You think I'm going in there before you? No way. For all I know, this is the place you bury all your past lovers."

Christie stiffened at the word 'lovers,' which she considered neither him nor the Baron to be. "Get down the hole, Charlie."

"Not a chance."

Before she could argue further, Phillip crouched and lowered himself down. Unlike her, he was tall enough for his head to poke out of the opening when standing on her make-shift pile of rubble. He glanced toward his feet.

"You undersold the disgustingness of what's down here. This is very unpleasant," he said before disappearing.

Christie folded her arms and smirked at Charlie. "Scaredy cat."

He shot her a dirty look before jumping into the grave. A thud and a string of muffled curses emanated from the depths. Christie gazed into the dark, considering Charlie's suggestion. She shook her head. Burying them was unsustainable. She had never seen the Baron descend into secret tunnels while he was alive—she would have relished the sight of him entering his grave early—which meant there had to be another way in, and therefore, out. She could not lock the two men or her secrets down in the cavern forever. Not yet. She sighed and lowered herself into the hole.

She landed securely, her feet only sliding a little on the pile of debris and rot at the bottom. Now to find the light switch. If she remembered correctly, it was to the left of the hanging tree root. Her hands waded through darkness and met scratchy fabric. A shirt pulled tight across a firm chest. She pulled back and waited for Charlie's snarky comment. Silence. It must have been Phillip. A tall, surprisingly strong Phillip. She bit her lip. At least he couldn't see how much he had surprised her. But what to do? The wall was definitely in that direction.

Tentative, she reached through the dark until her fingers again brushed the wool. This time, Phillip's hand met hers. Her heavy pulse thrummed in her ears. He intertwined his fingers with hers, guiding her through the black and over to the wall behind him. When her other palm touched soft earth, he released her. Despite the cave's cooling shadows, his warmth still kissed her skin.

"This way." She coughed, lingering a moment to let her face cool before turning on the lights.

Rough, rock-faced walls revealed themselves on each side. Little scraggles of root punctuated the grey dirt with their white tendrils.

Charlie whistled. "We may be pirates after all."

Christie led them down the hall to the main cavern and under the red, outstretched wings of a mini flying machine. The *Ol' Bird* cast its shadow across the dripping stalactites and web of chains that crisscrossed the ceilings and walls. Even Phillip grunted in surprise as they approached the gear-covered airship.

But it was chatterbox Charlie who spoke up first. "It's a cross between the C-Stars and Dirigible Class Seven. She's a beaut. Oh man, I've flown a C-Star before, but it didn't have the engines this baby does. I wonder what the pipes underneath are for. They look like they deliver right to the hull."

"What kind of cargo could be sucked up like that without taking significant damage?" Phillip leaned over the closest railing to get a closer look at the *Ol' Bird*.

"Interesting question. Nothing in crates, they'd get stuck in the shafts." Charlie said. "I daresay it would have to be liquid or something else with a low, semi-fluid viscosity. And look at those smaller airships. I've never seen anything quite like them." Charlie pointed to two mini machines.

One of the airships stretched out red glider wings and could fit two, maybe three, people in its cockpit. The other was double the size, with a mini balloon and black rutters, almost as if the *Ol' Bird* had a baby with a fish. Or . . . Christie smiled. A steamarine.

Charlie ran to the steering wheel while Phillip disappeared below deck. They were like giddy school children free for the holidays. That only confirmed they were telling the truth: neither of them had known about this beforehand—or at least Charlie hadn't. Phillip was still too hard to read.

So, what was she supposed to do now? She had shown them the caverns to get answers and ended up with two more man-sized problems and a slew of questions. Maybe she could start a spy ring? Bring in additional revenue? She had the tools, but the two bumbling bunnies would surely be more trouble on a job than they were worth. On a job—

"Argh," Christie cried. She had forgotten about Thorton's job. She had lost track of time, and the last ferry to Oceana had most likely already left. That would set her back an entire day. Mr. Thorton would not be pleased with the delay. Her paycheck would reflect that.

"You going full-on pirate?" Charlie grinned over the railing of the ship, completing the schoolboy image.

"You need to get out. I've got to go. I have a job."

Phillip appeared back on deck and descended the staircase. "I think you mean, *we've* got to go. You heard the lady, Charles. Out you go."

"Whoa, whoa." Charlie jumped over the railing and down onto the wooden planks in front of Phillip. "You guys aren't leaving me behind while you go have some adventure. It's not like you can lock the front door to the caves. I can come and go as I please. Why is Phillip going anyway?"

"I'm going so I can help Christina. And because I got her the job in the first place."

Christie grimaced. He should not have said that. She knew what Charlie would say next and tried to head it off. "He won't pay me for my last job unless I let him come on this one. It's a courtesy gesture at best and one I'm rather sore about. As soon as we get back, we can confirm who your insider is, and you can get on with your life. There's no point in dragging along more deadweight, especially since you're paying me nothing but a pig's whisper."

Phillip's lips twitched, and he folded his arms. Was he enjoying this?

"I think you forgot to add in my winning smile." Charlie beamed at her. "Priceless, that."

"Not happening."

Charlie glowered at her. She had him beat. But instead of skulking off, his signature smirk returned. "So, uh, where are you headed?"

Christie sealed her lips and braced for the siege. She was not revealing a drop more of information than necessary.

She jumped when Phillip touched her arm. It had been many years since she had last been the recipient of such a casual touch. Coming from Phillip made it all the more jarring.

He cleared his throat with an apologetic grimace. "I do need to know that information. I can only plan ahead if I'm aware of where we are going and what we are doing."

How could two men always at each other's throats collude so conveniently against her? Her shoulders sagged. "We are going to Oceana's command base."

"To do what?" Phillip and Charlie chimed in together.

She deepened her slouch. "To change the destination coordinates of two of Oceana's airships. I swear, if you two set back my plans in any way, you will pay with your blood." The price of freedom was starting to pinch. Which was exactly why she hated dealing with people.

Charlie tucked his hand in his pocket. "You know what the best way to Oceana is, right?

"Probably the ferry," Phillip replied, though Christie knew where Charlie was headed.

"Either of you know how to fly or drive a steamarine?" Charlie notched his eyebrow.

Christie chewed on her lip. This whole thing was turning into a disaster. Maybe she should give them the slip down one of these dark tunnels and do the job on her own. She'd lose the rest of Phillip's extortion money but keep her sanity. Her lip popped out from between her teeth, and she sighed. Without Charlie flying, she'd never make it in time to figure out what Thorton was up to, and her intuition told her it was big. She couldn't miss an opportunity to gain such a valuable secret just because two bumbling glocks wanted to tag along.

"Fine. You can come. But we're going by air." She could not handle being trapped elbow to elbow with those two beneath the crushing weight of the ocean.

"I knew you'd come around," Charlie said with a giddy sparkle in his eye.

"So we take the main airship then?" Phillip asked.

"She's called the *Ol' Bird*," Christie said. "And no. I think we better take the small one. It will be faster and easier to avoid detection." She pointed to the red wings. "Can you fly it, Charlie?"

"Do apples have seeds?" He waggled his brows.

"Yes," Phillip answered. "Though we do have a tree in our orchard that produces the plumpest apples which are completely devoid of them. It's a scientific oddity, but extremely delicious."

Charlie shot a heavy-lidded stare first at Phillip then at her. "Yes, I can fly it."

Christie nodded. "Good. Now, how do we get it down?"

Behind them, a faint hissing echoed from the darkness, and two crimson eyes appeared.

"Haunted trainwreck," Charlie gasped. "It's a bloody ghost!" His hand flew to his holster.

Phillip stepped back and put a hand on Charlie's arm. "Don't shoot. That's her butler."

"Yikes." Charlie's hand released the grip on his gun. "No wonder she hates it here."

"Ana?" Christie's mind churned.

She had implored the Baron to get rid of Ana repeatedly, but he insisted nothing would run without her. Yet the house was always a mess, and all the anamaton seemed to do was make tea that smelled of sweaty socks. Maybe the Baron meant nothing *down here* would work without the machine.

"Ana, we need the small ship. Get it down for us," she commanded.

Ana's scarlet eyes burned blankly for a moment. Its metal joints whistled and hissed and its clunky feet turned. On the wall, fifty paces down, hung several levers wrapped in rope. Ana moved near the middle one and looped her hook through a knot in the braided cord before jerking the lever downward. A series of clicks and thunks echoed through the cavern and the rope unwound rapidly, only stopping when it reached the end. Ana's frame jarred, but held firm, its hook looped through the now-taut cord. So there *was* a purpose to that fish-fileting hook after all.

The red wings shuttered, and the cords holding the flying contraption pulled it toward the cave wall on the far side. The stairwell clattered and bounced. Christie caught hold of the railing, stumbling as the wooden planks rotated her and the others to create a path that now led to and under the small airship, like a mini runway.

The ground rumbled. Christie caught Charlie's shirt as he tripped past her, pulling him into the crook of her elbow. Phillip hung onto the wooden rails. The cave shuddered, and the farthest wall yawned open. Salty mist mixed with the steam spewing from two large engines tucked away on either side of the cavern. The outer cliff face pulled inside on enormous hinges powered by black-greased gears and thick, clanging chains.

There was no way she could have missed the Baron going for a pirate ride while she lived in the house. The treachery that had ended their smuggling business must have happened before they married. That meant seven years. Seven years she had suffered through the torturous training of the Baron while the means for freedom hung from chains beneath her feet. Another cruel joke of his, no doubt. Another ember fueling her drive to be rid of people forever.

The setting sun splashed the cave with hues of pink and orange and the ocean lapped in the distance, a navy blue that shimmered with white. She had watched a sunset like this with Charlie before. Back then, the heat had left the sky and settled in her cheeks. But back then, she had a home, and her life was filled with light. This time, the sun kept its warmth as it dipped lower and lower below the horizon, leaving her cold.

"Well that was easy enough," Charlie said. He leaned into the arm Christie had used to catch him. "Care for a fly through peach-colored skies?" He slipped his arm around her waist.

She shimmied out of his grasp, ignoring the burn rising in her cheeks. Maybe it hadn't been the sun sharing its warmth all those years ago. Maybe it had been Charlie. She brushed the thought off along with his draping arms. "Let's focus on the task ahead."

"Yes," Phillip stepped between the two. "Let's."

Thirteen

CHARLIE HAD OVERSOLD HIS flying skills, that much she knew as they hurtled uncontrollably toward the water for the third time. With each wind-whipping plummet, the engine churned with a *kwa-cha-cha thwop,* and the red wings shuddered with the updraft. Christina clapped a hand to her flipping stomach as he righted the airplane with a sharp pull. This was the most alive she had felt in a long time. Funny that it would be with Charlie and Phillip over the Atlantic Ocean.

Steam puffed out the back of the flying machine in a contiguous stream that smeared the early evening sky in white streaks, broken only by two rapid bursts of sputtering every few minutes when the machine purged excess water from its pipes.

Phillip clung to the plane on her right, his skin a few shades paler than normal. Every time they dove toward the water, she wound her fingers through his jacket and leaned over him to let her fingers glide through the mist of splashing waves. For what it was worth, he didn't seem to mind. Or maybe he did but was too sick to say.

Charlie, on the other hand, sat to Christie's left, cursing up a storm as usual, though his swearing had taken on an admirably nautical flare more appropriate for their circumstances. She studiously watched him manage the controls so she would never need to rely on a favor from him again, but the switches and knobs all looked the same. It might as well have been needlepoint or a farm full of hogs for all she understood of it.

His flying gloves were spectacular though. Thick, tan leather with pinched seams running along the top of each finger. She snuck a feel on the next tumbling descent. Even through her own standard spy glove, the kid-skin of his glove was soft and smooth, an exquisite pair of hand-wear.

"Nice, aren't they?" Charlie's voice pitched with the wind.

"What?" Christie shrugged in forced apathy. Why had she risked swiping a feel? Charlie was all about the lady's touch. Of course, he would notice.

"The gloves," Charlie said. "Go on, give them another stroke. I don't mind." He winked at her.

She folded her hands tightly together and pinched her lips closed.

"They were a gift from your mother, you know."

His words blew her defenses away with the wind. "My mother?"

"Your father must have mentioned my interest in flight to her. When I came to call on you one day, she had them ready for me. Told me the right pair of gloves was the first step in making dreams come true."

A lightness brushed Christie's heart. That was just like her mum.

He held his free hand open to her, inviting her to come and visit the superb fashion sense and sweet memory of her mother. She relented, laying her hand lightly on top.

"That had to have been eight or so years ago. You've held onto them all this time?"

"They're important to me."

"Because of your dream?"

"Because of you." Charlie's ocean eyes ensnared her own. She should look away, fight the eager flap of wings in her stomach and the way her body wanted to lean into him. But his familiar spark pulled her to him with the strength of the tide.

"Eyes to the front if you don't mind." Phillip's terse words cut through the wind. "Or I'll make sure I vomit on you next."

Christie ripped her hand away. Ana take her to the devil's own lair. She had to be more diligent in guarding herself. Charlie was far more dangerous than she'd anticipated. She could not let his disarming smile and sugared words erase what he had done to her. Her suffering had been partly his fault, and she should not forgive him so easily.

The *lap, lap* of water was their constant companion as they headed southwest. Like the ridges of a clam, the ocean broke over a man-made shoal that protected Oceana from large waves. Tiny islands dotted the horizon. Some of the sand sported tropical and luscious plants, all imported, in the form of lavish gardens. Others held mini fortresses replete with cannons and "trespassers will be shot" signs.

Others, yet, were empty; blank canvases waiting for the inspiration of whoever could afford them next. Waiting for when *she* could afford one next. There were only a handful left, and their barren shores and remote location were perfect. The sight plucked at her pain as they passed by. Not much longer. If she could just do this job and one or two more, she would have enough.

A large island, quadruple the size of the others, rose high above the hefting waves. "There," she yelled and pointed.

Goggles obscured Charlie's eyes, but the downward pull of his lips said enough. "You want to fly straight in?"

"It has the most room for landing," she yelled, straining to be heard over the wind.

"It also has the most people for shooting. At us." Charlie shook his head.

Christie turned to Phillip. "What do you think?"

His normally straight lips dipped at the corners, and he clung to the metal sides of the flying contraption. "Whatever is . . ." His eyes grew wide until he managed to swallow. "Fastest."

"That's the vote, Charlie." She turned, elbowing him just enough that the plane took a small dip. "Take her down."

Charlie muttered something under his breath, but the whirling air sucked the words away before they reached her ears.

They landed with force. Christie leaned away from Phillip, afraid he would lose more than his composure as he plastered his hands to his mouth. Her hair almost bounced free of its tether, and she clasped one hand on her aigrette to make sure it stayed secure. The jarring pops slowed to rhythmic bumps, and the wings gave one last shudder before they came to a stop.

Christie stood and stretched her back. The other two remained firmly seated.

"You boys coming?" she asked, unable to keep the tease from her voice. Of course, they would struggle with basic spy work, but seeing it for herself was a gift.

Phillip opened the side door and slunk out, puddling into a crouch. Charlie shook off the ride and hopped out, stumbling as he found his land legs.

"I told you I could fly anything," he said, though he would not look her in the eye.

"Indeed," Christie said, nodding cheekily. "Seeing as you two are fairly incapacitated, I'll head on alone, and you can wait for me here."

Phillip stood and freed his mouth. "I'm fine. Let's proceed." He staggered forward with heavy feet but managed to keep his shoulders taut despite the sweat beading on his upper lip.

"Me too," Charlie said. His footsteps jerked in tiny jumps.

His body was probably still running off the adrenaline from the landing. She had better hurry before whatever fumes were feeding him ran dry. He used to get like this after shooting tournaments: hyper and giddy before he crashed, utterly useless, on a settee for three days straight.

"Fine," Christie sighed. "You two go make a distraction while I sneak in and make the changes."

"But—" Charlie started.

"There's no way to do this without a distraction. I need Oceana's guards to be wherever I'm not. If I'm caught, I'll be court-martialed and tried both here and in Britannia for who knows what. And Charlie, you'll never find out who's betraying you. And Phillip, you'll—" Why was Phillip here? To pay her? That wasn't a convincing argument. To find more out about Thorton maybe? "You'll . . . Oh, whatever. If you want to help, then help."

Charlie brooded.

"We can handle it," Phillip said. "What level of dire magnitude would best fit this situation?"

"How big can you make it?"

Voices echoed from over the sandy slope ahead of them.

"Hide!" she whispered hoarsely. "And stay here until the coast has cleared. Then follow the plan." She pointed them toward the red wings.

Phillip eyed the contraption warily but obeyed. Charlie was already climbing for cover before she started talking. Christie, however, remained. She recognized the baritone giving commands.

"Stay where you are," Commander Austen yelled as he came into view over the ridge.

Christie placed her hands on her hips. "And when have I ever done that?"

Commander Austen's raised eyebrows were just the answer she was looking for.

"Back so soon?" he asked, eyeing the flying machine.

She patted his arm when he stopped in front of her. "What can I say? I missed you."

Austen's gaze shifted between her and the mini airship.

"And I need money." She made an effort to visibly wince.

"Ah." Austen's military stance slackened. "Blown through your earnings once again?" He slapped her on the back, knocking her a step forward. "I think this must be record time."

Christie shrugged. "A lady has needs. And mine happen to be expensive."

"Are you talking bows and shoes? Or whiskey and guns?"

"A little of both."

Austen put his arm around her shoulders and led her over the dunes like comrades heading home from battle. "Soldiers, fall in line. Leave the spy's odd contraption be. Who knows how she might have booby-trapped it."

She glanced back at the ship, relieved to see that Austen's men were giving it a wide berth. Her reputation once again preceded her, though in the spy game that was a good thing. Maybe they had heard about what she had done in Bangladesh and Aegyptus. Or, at least what she had told people she'd done in Bangladesh and Aegyptus. The Baron's training had given her more than the ability to survive in combat and subterfuge. It had given her a wide array of information with which to construct outlandishly dreadful tales.

Austen's arms draped heavily over her, pushing her feet into the sand with each step. "Formalities aside, my clumsy spy, what would you like to do for Oceana?"

"Isn't it your job to tell me that?"

"You arrived so suddenly, I presumed you had business in mind."

She took two sand-scuffing strides for every one of his. The metal doors of Oceana's military compound loomed near the bottom of the next shifting dune. Despite Austen's willingness to trust her, she did not usually drop out of the sky for a visit.

The pinch growing in her stomach was from more than her corset. She should have known he'd be suspicious of a drop-in, or at the very least presume she had come with a purpose. And of course, he would assume her intentions were benign, just like she told him. He trusted her. And that was the worst part of it all.

Austen led the way into the compound and turned her toward the barracks. But the blue-walled sleeping quarters where she had learned of the Baron's ghost were the last place she needed to be. Her job was to change the shipping logs. Those were kept in the command center. How could she manipulate Austen into taking her there?

"Listen, commander, there is a reason I came back so quickly." She slowed her steps to a halt.

"You mean, aside from being broke?"

"I've got a secret." She rocked back on her heels.

"Let's hear it then."

"Ah, ah. I want to tell Captain Barnes myself. I get so little recognition for the dangerous work I do."

"I thought you preferred your recognition in the form of banknotes." Austen rubbed his thumb on the pads of his gloveless fingers.

She crossed her arms. "I tell the captain or take it to my grave."

His left eye squinted, and his lips puckered. "Still a no."

"Commander," she protested—as close a plea as she could muster—and hated it.

Pleading was a sign of weakness the Baron would have demolished with a bone-breaking regiment and three days in the dark, and she couldn't bring herself to do it. She also didn't want to seem too eager, though she needed this job to go right. Normally, she was spying *for* Oceana, not *on* them.

"Unless it's something of significant import, the captain has better ways to spend his time. Now, if you tell me what it is—"

"Which I won't."

"Then I can't help you."

Christie pulled her arm out of his hold. Why was he being so difficult? He usually let her have free reign. Christie grabbed his arm and looked up, her eyes as saucer-like as she could make them. "Please?"

"No."

"Pretty please?" She stroked his arm with her fingertips. She didn't usually resort to such sloppy tactics, but she was running out of ideas.

He shook her loose and straightened up. "Woman!" He backed away. "Secret or no, protocols must be followed."

Christie bent her knees to make ready a pounce when a brigade rounded the corner in two lines, their shiny black boots like army ants. In the center marched Captain Barnes.

Christie pulled her hands to her hips. This would either go really well or bally badly. Barnes never had liked her. He was always finding ways to make her life hard, like insisting she take the steamarine for every bloody mission or making her eat with the cleaning staff instead of the soldiers.

A knife's edge is made of tiny, sharp ridges; after all the barbs he had put her through, she just needed him to turn his back.

He halted in front of her. "What's she doing here? I thought our little spy was attending to personal matters."

"Yessir," Austen barked, swiping his hand to his head and back down. "She just showed up today. I was taking her to her barracks before coming to inform you, sir."

"You know the rules, commander." Barnes' voice was sharp. "No known spies on the premises without express permission and constant detail."

"Yessir," Austen said.

Christie glowered. So much for being friends. "I don't need a babysitter, captain," she said. "I work for your side."

"I thought you worked for the highest bidder," the captain sneered. "Isn't that what you told us when we tried to recruit you full-time?"

She had said that.

And it was true. She could never become military personnel, with all their saluting and strictly obeying orders.

"Then let's hope you're the highest bidder right now." She raised her chin. "Because I have a secret I think you'll want to hear."

Barnes seemed to consider her answer before snapping his finger. The detail of men surrounding him marched off, leaving him alone with her and Austen.

"Out with it," he demanded.

"Not here. It's not safe," she said, darting her eyes about them as if someone were listening.

The captain waved her words away with his hand. "Nonsense. Our facility is highly secure."

"Then why did a spy waltz right in the front door?" She felt bad throwing Austen under the bus, especially after he had let her in, but it had to be done. She had to get into the command room.

Barnes' eyes became slivers beneath hooded lids. "My question exactly. If your intel doesn't pan out, Austen here will pay for it."

"Yessir," Austen dipped his head. "May I suggest the command room? It is the securest place in headquarters."

Barnes nodded and turned, waving for them to follow.

Her shoulders relaxed, and she shot Austen an apologetic look. While she normally relished burning bridges between colleagues, the creases in Austen's face hurt her chest. Especially since he had unknowingly helped her toward her goal.

The command room faced north, its view expanding over the islands and out into navy blue waters. Sun shot across the glass on its westward trajectory, streaking shimmering white bands across the panorama. The last of the day's light was nearly gone. Good. She was far more familiar with working in the dark. Barnes cleared the room and shut the door behind them.

"There. The safest room in the house. Now, what is your precious secret?"

Christie tightened her lips. She hadn't actually thought about that part in her scramble to make it into the command room. Which she was now in.

With no plan. Drat Phillip and his dulbert need for plans. She never used to worry about this stuff. She just trusted her gut and went with the flow.

"Miss Rushing? The secret, please." Barnes tapped his fingers on the desk.

Christie took a breath and cleared her mind so she could hear her gut again. "I was recently privy to a secret meeting between a representative from Thorton & Blackwell Shipping Company and a black-market arms dealer."

Barnes' fingers stopped their tapping. "I'm listening."

Where was she going with this? She wasn't even sure she could trust Oceana after hearing what Lord Sheffield had to say.

That gave her an idea.

"I couldn't hear what they were saying, but one of the men—" She left out Thorton's name. "—had the shipping schedule I stole for you."

"Nonsense." Barnes' tone was sharp, and his eyes shone with the dull gloss of boredom.

"It's true. I recognized it by the tear on the bottom corner."

"You mean, the tear that happened when you were in charge of its safety?"

Christie glanced at him sideways. "Yes. *That* tear. It was the same schedule, I'd know it anywhere. If stealing it was for investigational purposes, why is it being used in an illegal arms deal? Your ship is leaking, Captain. So you tell me. Who in your ranks is a traitor? Or is all of Oceana in on the double-crossing?"

Barnes slammed his fist on the table. "How dare you accuse Oceana of misdeeds. I should have you tried for treason, right here."

"I'm not a citizen of Oceana," she spat back.

What was she doing? The last thing she wanted to do was to fight with the captain, especially since he governed her future home. But she needed to buy time. Where were Charlie and Phillip? Where was their distraction?

Barnes sneered. "You're right. I don't have to try you at all."

Commander Austen cleared his throat. Both Christie and the captain snapped their heads in his direction. She had forgotten he was there, hovering in uncharacteristic silence while in the presence of his superior.

"What is it?" Barnes asked him.

"Her careless accusations won't be taken seriously by anyone, sir. It's not worth the scandal, especially since our treaty with Britannia dictates we release all prisoners back to their home country for trial. You do not want to invite the scrutiny of the other major powers."

"Oh, cross the treaty," Barnes snapped.

"So you are traitors." Christie smirked.

The captain raised his fist, and the entire room burst with a blinding orange light. The ground shook beneath them, and papers and trinkets fell off the desks in a clatter.

"What the devil?" Barnes stepped closer to the windows. "Commander Austen. Deploy the troops! We need medical and the fire brigade on the ground floor immediately! Our ammo stores have been hit."

Christie peered out the windows. Down below, a building burned with red-hot flames, belching brackish plumes of smoke. Barnes grabbed her shoulder and steered her towards the exit. She went willingly, jumping ahead to open the door so he could head out first. She exited the room and followed a few paces. Barnes jogged down the hall, barking commands at any soldier in sight. When she was certain he was distracted, she doubled back, catching the door as it was about to lock shut.

She slipped inside.

The windows now gazed upon ashen skies, the flicker of fire consumed in puffs of grey. Christie could smell the acrid chemicals from here. She grinned. She had to give the boys a hand. They definitely went big.

Tendrils of pollution seeped inside the command room. She coughed and pulled out the coordinate books for Oceana's airships. Thorton had been secretive with his directions, probably to prevent her from snooping too much before the job. But that just fanned the flames of her curiosity.

She opened the page for Oceana's *Harpee Seven*. She found the twentieth line down and mentally added one degree north and eight degrees west to the numbers already listed. She erased and rewrote the new number. Then, she flipped to the page for Oceana's *Majestic*. She followed the same process, only this time, after adding one degree north, she subtracted nine degrees west.

The ruckus outside was still at a peak. After a glance at the door, she studied the large map that hung on the wall. *Harpee* and *Majestic* were military ships that patrolled Oceana's borders. The new coordinates she had written down would put them well into the protected waters of both Americana and Britannia. Why did Thorton want to push the borders? And, once again, why did he need her assistance if he was working with Oceana? If her whole job was altering their logs, could they not have just changed the coordinates themselves? She was missing something. She had to be.

The door clicked.

Christie dropped to the floor.

Her throat ran dry, and not solely because of the smoky air. If someone caught her in here, she was certain she'd be thrown into the raging fire below.

FOURTEEN

C HRISTIE CROUCHED IN THE middle of the floor near the back wall of the command office, completely exposed. She held her breath as feet scuffled about near the front. Moving for cover might draw attention, but staying exposed was begging for it. She had to take the risk.

She crawled forward, knee to hand in deliberate slides to hide behind the nearest desk. Drawers opened and closed, and someone talked to themselves in hurried whispers. At last, the door re-opened and the footsteps faded. Christie loosened the grip she had unconsciously wrapped around the Good Baron. She stood up. The door swung open again.

Christie flung herself to the ground once more. What the hazy fog were these people doing? Didn't they see the giant fire burning down their fortress?

This time there were two pairs of feet. She squeezed under the desk, making sure to pull in her boots. What was the point of completing her mission if she would never live long enough to see the reward?

She cringed when she heard Barnes' voice. "Where are the traitors who did this?"

"We're searching every nook and cranny, Captain," a soldier's voice tinned. "We'll find them."

"I bet it's that devil spy's doing. She shows up and the base erupts in flames? It's not a coincidence. I want her brought to me the second she's found; she owes Oceana her blood. And seize her flying contraption so we can melt it down over her corpse."

"Yessir," the soldier said before his boots clipped out of the room.

Blood rushed to Christie's head, leaving her limbs cold and her stomach woozy. All she wanted to do was to escape society, not have it chase after her with gun-loaded zeppelins.

Captain Barnes remained as thick smoke filled the command room. Christie's throat burned, and she covered her mouth to fight back a cough. Her gloves—she would never get the charred smell out of them. At this rate, finding out this blasted secret would be the ruin of all her gloves. Things looked as bleak as the air in the room, and the early evening light certainly didn't help. Her only hope was that the boys made it back to the flying machine before Oceana captured them.

She pressed herself into the corner of the desk she was hiding under just as Barnes' pressed pants walked by. He headed toward the back of the room, coming into full view. If he turned around and saw her, she'd be strung up and tortured.

He took a key from his breast pocket and opened a cherrywood cabinet. Christie eased herself forward for a better look. Maybe her traitor talk had rattled him. Maybe he was the head of the snake. That would explain his desire to find her. Or maybe there was no snake, and she was just being paranoid. Thorton was always up to no good; that's why he was her constant benefactor. But something about the whole thing still sat funny with her. Barnes was her other steady employer, and he never hired her to work with others, only to spy on them for Oceana's gain. Oceana, in general, rarely colluded with foreigners, especially Brits.

Barnes' hands shifted out of sight. Her confidence faltered. Maybe she should actually plan ahead like Phillip suggested. If she was quiet, she could skirt out of the room without him noticing. Then she could meet the boys at the rendezvous point. But if he turned . . . .

She shook her head, tucking back furls of loose hair. This wasn't planning ahead, it was her thinking about the impulsive thing she was about to do, which was just wasting time. Besides, if she was going to do something impulsive, it would be to stab Barnes with her poisoned feather and make a run for it.

She worked her fingers through frizzy tangles of hair to get to her aigrette. She tugged on her poisoned feather, but the entire barrette slid loose. She swiped it into her lap before it clattered to the floor.

Freed curls fell across her face and tickled her nose. Rusty lugnuts, this wasn't going right at all. She scooped up a handful of hair and tugged it back, combing the aigrette back into place. It was still a little loose, but she managed to slip the poisoned quill out without the rest tumbling free. She splayed her spare hand on the worn, wooden floor, waiting for her chance to jump up and bolt.

"I know you're there," Barnes' voice chilled her blood. His back was still turned, but his shoulders straightened into a wall.

How had he known? What would happen to her now? Her right hand tightened around the cold metal of her feather. Tines poked their way through her glove.

"You didn't have to set the camp ablaze in my honor," a gruff voice said from behind her toward the front of the room.

Sweat trickled down the back of her neck. Barnes wasn't talking to her. She recognized the ample dose of honey coating the words and ducked her head as if it would help conceal her.

"Ah, Thorton, you flatter yourself." Barnes turned his head to the side.

Her stomach squeezed. What in bloody blazes was he doing in Oceana? A few degrees more, and she would need more than her aigrette to get away. Should she put the feather back and abandon all spyish pretenses? The Good Baron would clear her a path through the command room, but clutter the hall with suspicious soldiers the second its muzzle clapped.

"I thought I told you to stay away from the base," Barnes replied coolly.

"And how could I with the fifty-foot homing beacon you've made of your ammo stores?"

Barnes turned again to face the wall. "It was your ruddy spy who did that."

Christie bent lower to the floor. If only she could ghost her way through it and off to safety. The men in the room were gasoline and fire, and her hair was already crisping. Intel may be her livelihood, but she couldn't collect payments if she were dead.

Thorton's boots scuffed at the front of the room. "I see."

Was he amused? Did he know she was here? And if he did, would he help her escape or kill her himself? Either way would keep his secret safe. That is if there was a secret to keep safe. Barnes and Thorton were talking quite comfortably. Were they both in on the real purpose behind stealing the schedule?

"What do you want?" The commander tucked his chin over his shoulder.

"To return this," Thorton said. A papery thwump hit a desk several yards away. "The schedule was enough to assure our mutual friend of our seriousness."

Barnes turned. Christie braced herself. But he only had eyes for the bone Thorton had tossed his way.

"The shipping schedule? Why would I need this back? I already copied all the information I needed from it lest more of its pieces were inexplicably torn away." Barnes shot an icy glare across the room. He stepped past her with heavy thuds.

Goose pimples crawled up her arm.

How in Sam Hill had he missed her? She bit her fist. Things were much worse than she had expected. Barnes was definitely working with Thorton in whatever shady deal they had going on. But did that mean whatever Thorton was planning had the backing of an entire nation? Or was Thorton playing a bigger game than even Barnes knew? Because when it came down to it, both men had paid her for the same thing that now sat between them at the front of the room.

Thorton's voice yawned. "I told you I had nothing to do with that. Things happen. The piece that is missing is of no importance. What is important is that your men don't get suspicious when a stolen schedule disappears."

Barnes shot off a laugh. "Too late for that. Your spy was already asking after it in front of my first officer, saying she saw it in a secret meeting. It's a writhing rat's nest, this whole thing."

A thump rattled a nearby desk.

Christie winced in her hiding place. She needed to get out of there, especially now that Barnes had outed her. Thanks to his flap jaw, Thorton knew she had been eavesdropping at the ball. She'd have a corporate bounty on her head before nightfall, and that was on top of the one Barnes already had out with his men. She should run as far as she could and hide in the darkest hole.

But how could she? She had lost both of her steady benefactors in a single blow. Her hope of finding solitude on an Oceana island was sunk. This secret had just become personal.

The cogs in her mind churned into overdrive. Something wasn't right. If Oceana backed what Barnes and Thorton were doing, why would a missing schedule worry Barnes' soldiers? Barnes had to be acting on his own, wielding an entire army for a dirty side business. She just had to figure out what that bit of dirt was and how to use it to her advantage.

Maybe if she could catch them red-handed, she could bargain with Britannia for safety. Or blackmail Barnes into giving her an island. It was the only play she had left.

"Get control over your rogue agent," Barnes growled and opened the door. "Because if I find her first, I'll bleed every one of your secrets from her lips."

"Trust me," Thorton's rocky voice shoveled out the words, "I will."

FIFTEEN

C HRISTIE'S HEART PULSED IN time with the heavy thuds of fading boots. She needed to find Charlie and Phillip and get off the island. Silence filled her ears for several minutes before she bolted from the room. Soldiers raced around the hallways. She dodged between shadows and doorways, pressing herself into the wall to hide from harried eyes.

She needed to get back to the eastern beach, but that's exactly where Barnes would expect her to go. It was possible she had already lost the flying machine and her only way off the island, but there was no better option.

The orange of flames filtered in through the glass of the compound's front doors. Two young men guarded the exit. She knew their type: wide-eyed, fearful, and eager to prove themselves. They would put up a scrappy fight.

Christie fingered her aigrette. She had reloaded her poisoned quill in the greenhouse before she had left with Charlie and Phillip for Oceana. She could poison both of these soldiers if need be, but that would require a sprint across an open hallway and close, out-numbered combat. Her two lock picks were useless. The cold metal of her thickest feather met her tips. She grasped it. Placed correctly, it could be just the thing.

She twisted the bumpy tube off the bottom of the quill and held the ropy vanes of the feather between two fingers. With one swift scratch, she struck the feather against the sandpapered tubing. It took three blows for the wick tips of the feather to ignite. The tipped ends smoked gently with the flames.

She snuck a look around the corner again. The guards took turns glancing down each side of the hallway. That left her about a second when their eyes met in the middle to implement her plan. She waited for three passes to make sure she got the timing right. Then she touched the burning feather tips to the end of the tube. The powder inside the casing ignited, and she tossed it across the floor and under the door on the opposite side of the hallway.

One, two, three.

She glanced down the hallway.

Four, five.

Any time now.

Six, seven, eight, and then—

Smoke streamed out from under the doorway. She leaned back and pressed herself against the wall, clicking the feather vanes back onto what was left of the quill in her aigrette.

"Fire! The fire has spread!" The guards pressed forward and into the room.

Smoke billowed out, and Christie used the cover to dart through the front doors. The muggy night air made it easy to travel unnoticed. All hands and eyes were busy keeping the explosion controlled. She made her way north over craggy hills. Her boots soon met shifting sand. Now she just had to make her way toward the east side of the island to find out what happened to her ride.

Christie stuck close to the rocky dunes and tried her best to step on the grassy overlays that encroached on the moonlit beach. Sand eked its way into the crevices of her boots, itching her legs and sticking between her toes. Rough granules chaffed her skin, scraping her leg with filth. She would need a bath. To get clean. To get off the sand that was trying to scratch its way in. If it got in . . . she would never be clean. She never would be anyway.

The setting fog muffled voices up ahead. Christie crouched and drew closer, dodging behind a particularly weather-beaten boulder. She peered over the side. Several soldiers scoured the rocks up ahead. Her flying machine was nowhere in sight. She ducked back down.

What to do? If she lingered too long, the search party would find her. She could try and steal something from the hanger to get off the island, but Barnes would probably be expecting that too. She tugged at the cuffs of her gloves. The humid air made them stick to her skin, and (*fire and damnation*!) there was sand inside them chafing her fingers. She swiped out what little she could reach and watched the granules fall to the earth.

Could this day get any worse?

She shook her head and took another glance over the side.

A muscled face and furrowed brows met her eyes on the other side of the rock. Her heart seized, sucking the wind out of a scream.

She was in for it now.

Commander Austen's brushy brows merged so tightly, they looked like a fuzzy asp on his forehead. "What in the world were you thinking?" His voice was a whisper but he may as well have bellowed.

"What do you mean? I came here with a secret. I shared the secret, and I didn't even get paid. Why am I in the wrong here?"

"Enough," he cut her short. "Did you do that?" He pointed above the hills and to the dark swirls choking out the stars.

"No." She sounded more indignant than she meant to. Though it was technically the truth. *She* did not light the fire.

Austen growled. "I'm serious, Christie. Did you do this?"

Christie set her eyes on his. "I did not."

He shook his head. "You know you're slated for execution the second you're found, don't you?"

His words sunk into her bones, and she swallowed. "Then let's hope I don't get caught. Besides," she said and forced a grin, "I'd be a pretty ruddy spy if at least a few people didn't have it out for me."

"I'm serious, Rushing. This isn't a lone person with a grudge. This is all of Oceana and its men, airships, firepower, everything. If they find you, there's nothing I can do to help."

"Then help me now." She touched her hand to his in a fleeting gesture of hope. "Please."

He looked over his shoulder before sliding behind the rock with her. He opened his mouth to speak, then stopped and pinched the furrow between his brows. "Did you mean what you said?"

"When? Just now? Because I said it twi—"

"No." His fingers pinched harder. "About there being a traitor?"

"Oh." Christie paused to weigh her options.

He would probably let her go if she could convince him she was in the right. But it would also be putting him in the crosshairs of a conspiracy she could not wrap her head around. Barnes knew Austen had already heard her accusations in the command center. It would be better if he knew why he was being hunted if it came to that.

"Yes. I mean it. And it's Barnes. I stayed behind and heard him talking about it."

Austen put his face in his hands. "You spied on the captain. Are you steaming mad?"

"He's guilty. And I'm a spy. What do you care, now that you know he's dirty?"

"It doesn't work like that," Austen said. His hands dropped to his sides and tensed and released a few times. "You need to leave."

Relief flooded her. He had come through for her. He was someone she could trust. Christie shot him a smile. "Thanks. Now, where's my airship?"

Austen looked up at her, his eyes slits under a thick layer of brows. "We don't have it. The beach was empty when we arrived." His eyes burst wide. "You're not working alone."

She took a step back from his reach. If Austen didn't have the machine, Charlie and Phillip must have reached it in time. A tightness in her chest loosened, then wound back up. Did they leave without her? Did they chicken out? Think she was a lost cause?

A soldier yelped from above, "There she is! Behind the rocks with the commander!"

Austen grabbed her coat and threw her to the ground, hurling her onto her back. His heavy boot pressed into her chest. "Sorry, but it's pointless for both of us to go down for this."

Christie winced from the weight. A rock speared her back, and the sounds of footsteps tussled through the sand toward her. How would she get out of this one? The screaming increased. Her heart pulsed against the sole of his boot. But the footsteps retreated instead of surrounding her.

What was going on?

A whirring buzz rocketed past, drowning out the screams. Red wings caught the moonlight, the underbelly as crimson as a robin's, as the flying machine blocked the clouds overhead.

Christie grabbed Austen's boot from off her chest and twisted hard. He toppled to the side too easily, and she scrambled up the rocky crag to get to higher ground. The summit of the hill. So close. She only needed to climb to the top.

Her coat tightened across her shoulders and pulled her backward. A guard dragged her down the sandy side. She scrambled to get off her stomach, leaning with all her weight back up the hill. The soldier yanked harder. She toppled back down. Her knees sank into sand. All her progress lost. She kneeled only a meter from the bottom.

Using the last of the downward momentum was her only chance to break free. The flying machine—no, the *Robin*—roared overhead once more.

Faint yells from Phillip carried over the din of steam engines and soldiers. "Slide! Slide!"

She gained her footing once more and leaned forward, stretching her coat taut. She turned her head and waited. The soldier's grip slackened to allow for another hard tug, and that was her moment.

She flipped onto her backside and skidded down the slope. Her steel heel made contact with his shin, and she felt something crack. He toppled backward clutching his leg as two more soldiers gained ground across the beach. She turned and dragged herself through the shifting earth back up the hillside. This time she made the summit. The *Robin*, was at an apex, turning around with the moon as a backdrop. They would be coming in from the west.

She ran along the top of the ridge toward the east. She only had a dozen yards before the sand gave way to a rocky cliff. If she timed it right, she could jump onto the wings of the *Robin*. If she miscalculated, she would have rocks for a face.

She pelted forward and pounced over stones and through scraggy brush. The *Robin* caught up and droned beside, then past her. She wasn't going fast enough. Her boots were not meant for sand racing. She lifted her knees higher, made her strides longer, and leaned forward into the salty breeze that parched her mouth. The end of the sandy backbone loomed in sight. A large boulder jutted into the air. The perfect springboard. Charlie arced the *Robin* out and made a turn so it would pass right under the edge.

It was now or never.

Christie thrust her leg forward and bent her knee to leap off the ledge. Her boot hit the boulder, but its hold gave way. The gritty dusting on top of the rock slipped her foot backward. Her shins scraped against the sharp edge, and she plummeted off the side and into the soggy air.

SIXTEEN

— • —

C HRISTIE GRASPED FOR A hold as she fell over the side of the ridge, but the ledge was behind her. Her fingers reached for stars and filtered through their light. She clutched the back of her neck as the sandy beach hurtled closer. The tannish brown turned a bright red. Her side hit the wings of the *Robin* with a thud. The blow knocked the wind from her lungs. She struggled to draw breath. The plane dipped, and she rolled off the wing and past Phillip's outstretched hand.

She reached for him but found the metal frame of the *Robin* instead. Releasing her ribs, she gasped for air and dug her fingers into anything they could find. It was no use. Her gloves were too slick. Clinging to a machine for dear life would never have made her mother's list of glove-approved activities.

Phillip stood on his seat, reaching down the back of the machine. Even with his lanky frame, he was nowhere near close enough to help. Her foot found purchase. She pressed her knees into the metal and slipped a fingertip of her glove between her teeth. She bit hard, pulled the glove free, and repeated with her other hand. Her legs shook with the effort of hanging on and slipped off the side. The rest of her followed, air encompassing her torso and whipping in every direction. In a last attempt at survival, her fingers found the canvas of the *Robin*'s tail. She seized the taut fabric and forced it around her fingers.

A set of choppy clangs barrelled down the side of the *Robin*, leaving bullet holes in their wake. If she didn't fall, she'd be carved up instead.

Despite the wind rushing past her, her lungs struggled to hold more than a teaspoon of air.

Phillip turned and appeared to be arguing with Charlie. Couldn't they get along for five seconds before she fell to her death? Phillip ducked as another round of bullets smattered the side. The nearest piece of lead lodged itself a nose's length away, chipping flecks of red paint in her direction. Christie cringed and pulled herself into a little ball. But she was too weak, and her lungs too empty. Her feet unfurled like a flag of surrender.

The clanging stopped.

Phillip popped back into view, motioning at her with his arms. He pointed to himself, then her, then made a big arch. It meant nothing. She shook her head. He gave her a thumbs up. They were going to implement their cockamamie plan whether she understood it or not. A bullet tore through the fabric she was holding, creating a rip that unspooled more with each thrum of her heart. Whatever they were doing, it had better happen quickly.

As if Charlie could hear her thoughts, the *Robin* shifted upward in a sharp ascent. The red fabric continued to lengthen, and she ripped farther and farther away. How was this helping?

She mustered what air clung to her lungs and yelled, "Phillip! Charlie!" But the wind whipped and snapped, stealing her words away.

They reached a full upward trajectory and silently, eerily floated for a breath.

Her stomach shot into her heart, crushing them both with a nauseating lurch.

Charlie took the *Robin* into a nosedive, and the world rushed toward her, slinging her stomach the other way. Her wind-blown feet whipped toward the front of the *Robin*, and she gasped. Sea-drenched air assaulted her face. She smashed her eyes shut to keep away the sting. The force slipped the cloth from her hands, and she toppled across the machine. She flew head-over-heels toward the propeller, grabbing what she could along the way. Her hands met fabric. She seized upon it, drawing herself in.

The *rat-a-tat* of gunfire pelted them once more.

"Get down," Charlie yelped.

Christie obeyed, digging her head into the scratchy cloth clenched within her fists. The gunfire quieted. The shouting men on the shore grew distant. Charlie righted the *Robin*, and their course evened out with a small limp, the tattered tail of the machine tousling in the wind behind them.

At last, Christie could breathe.

She inhaled humid air. The pine and tobacco of cologne teased her nose, like a barn full of sweet-smelling hay. A smooth button rubbed against her face. A shirt. She was holding Phillip's shirt. Which meant she was holding Phillip. Her fingers tightened with embarrassment, but she didn't pull away. The flaps of his suit coat created a barrier from the world, and the warmth of his body protected her cheeks from the salty wind. For a moment she wished to stay. If she could just linger a while longer in the safe . . . .

But that would not do. The warmth of others was just another thing that could be ripped away from her. Like her parents had been. Like   Charlie

. . . .

What were her priorities after all? Gaining control of her life. Finally. Permanently. And for that she needed solitude, to avoid people who could manipulate her emotions. But how would she do that now? Now that Barnes, the commander of Oceana, was out to get her? All those years of currying favor gone to waste. Could she even get an island now? Maybe if Barnes was ousted, but not if she were dead.

And then there was Thorton. Surely, he knew she was double-crossing him. That meant no paycheck for the deadly work she had just completed. It also meant another bullseye on her back. So what was the point? She buried her head further into Phillip's firm chest before realizing it. Her fingers froze around the fabric.

What was she doing? Clutching a man like a bolt around a screw? Getting close to him would only bring her trouble. Her island may be out of reach, but solitude was not. Pull it together. Move on.

She extracted herself from the haven and into a whirling torrent of air. She tilted her chin up only slightly so as not to reveal her radiating cheeks. Phillip stared straight ahead, his pallor rosier than on the first flight. She snuck a peek sideways to where Charlie flew stony-faced, both hands firmly clenched around the steering mechanism.

"What are you so mad about?" she asked Charlie. After a successful escape, he should be gloating.

The scratch of fabric chaffed on her exposed fingertips. She was still holding Phillip's shirt. And she was missing her gloves. She dropped her hands and searched her pockets. Empty. The pair must have blown away in the chaos. She took a deep breath. She was fine up here, away from it all. She sidled in between the two boys and placed her hands firmly on her knees. They both remained stoic, a furnace on one side and a chilly breeze on the other.

She cleared her throat. "Quite a bang-up job you two did back there. That was a bally big explosion."

Silence.

She glanced between the two. Not good. She knew what both of them were like when unhappy. Unpleasant was an understatement. After all, Charlie had once tried to shoot her. And Phillip—she grimaced at the warning he gave her.

Why was she worried about them right now? She had bigger concerns.

She still could not fathom why Thorton had her steal a shipping schedule for Oceana, to then have Oceana give it back to him, only to return it to them again. It was nonsense. And what was happening on the twenty-third? She couldn't find out without the shipping schedule, but there was little chance of getting that back. Charlie would not be happy when he found out who had the documents now.

Charlie.

Charlie knew what was on the schedule. She just had to get him to share.

It was a small hope, a sliver of direction, but it was enough. She had her next goal. Bleed Charlie for information. Now that was something she could do.

The majority of the flight home passed listening to the puffing churns of the engine and smelling the fish-scented spray of the sea. Charlie pouted to her left while she planned her next move, and Phillip . . . who knew? Probably trying to keep the contents of his stomach from flying away with the wind. They dipped toward the ocean only once on the ride back to refuel the steam engine's water stores through a funnel below the front wheels. She held Philip's arm to run her hands through the waves, and his muscles tensed at her touch. She pulled back up and did not try again.

They neared the familiar bleak cliffs of the Ravensworth estate, and the cave yawned open. Ana must have closed it upon their departure and watched for their return. What else had the Baron built her to do? Luckily, the water churned too silty this time of year to support traditional trade and travel. No ships graced the harbor, no cargo the docks. No one was around to see their secret.

Charlie zoomed them through the gaping cave mouth and stuck the landing on the narrow wooden slats. The *Robin* bounced rhythmically to a stop. Ana restrung the *Robin* and hoisted it back into its holster. Charlie sunk onto a barrel on the deck of the *Ol' Bird*.

Christie followed suit. Her first instinct was to sit two barrels down—close enough to talk, but far enough to pretend she could not hear—but that would not do. Not if she needed him to open up. She trailed her fingers along the farthest barrel and slid over to the one Charlie sat on. She slapped his knee, and he scooched over enough for her to slide up next to him. His warmth trickled over and down her spine. She breathed through her nose. It was going to take effort to keep things light, to swallow her memories and sugar her voice.

"Thanks for flying the *Robin*, today."

"The *Robin*?"

"You like the name? I came up with it on the beach while I was having my ribs crushed."

She grinned at him with the tease of her sixteen-year-old self. And for a moment, she imagined she was that version of herself. The one who wasted countless afternoons laying beside Charlie in the hay of the barn, talking about everything and nothing and the nothingness of everything. It seemed so long ago.

Now, darkness blurred the edges of the memories, casting them in shadow. Her smile fell.

"You showed a lump of dash fire out there. I was impressed."

Charlie arched a brow. "What do you want?"

She bit off a curse. Why did he have to know her so well? She played it off. "I know I've been a bit of a saucebox toward you lately, but I really appreciated your help." She gently knocked her knees into his and let a timid smile make a home on her lips.

One arched brow turned into two before furrowing back down. "Where's Phillip? Out tending to other damsels in distress?"

Christie swung her knees against his hard this time. "I have never been, and will never be, a damsel in distress, thank you. And he went to go check on his father."

"Could have fooled me." He bumped her back. "Distress seems to be your constant shadow." A hint of his classic smirk crinkled his eyes. She wished it was the whole thing. She didn't know what to make of the new, guarded Charlie.

Besides, what could she say to that? She dipped her head, and a mass of curls fell into her face. Her right hand darted to her hair.

Her aigrette!

She ran all ten fingers through her tangled mane. It was gone. Her heart squeezed the last bit of sanity from its worn beats. It was silly, ridiculous even, the attachment she had to it. But the barrette was more than her toolkit. Wearing it felt like carrying around a piece of her mother. It was weakness, and several times she had tried to throw it into the Thames. Or the Atlantic. Or anywhere she would never have to see it again. But she could not do it. And now that it was finally gone, her soul was nothing more than a shell.

"You okay?" Charlie asked, tilting his head.

"Yes, I just . . ." She couldn't finish the words. Maybe she could go back and find it. Scour the beaches. Steamarine the ocean floor.

Charlie's hand on her knee melted her thoughts. She pulled her eyes from her worries to look at him.

Waves of sandy hair stuck up in every direction, and a flood of images from their childhood shone through her feeling of loss. Swimming in their knickers. Picnics in flower-strewn fields of pink and gold and robin-egg blue. Star-gazing on the roof of her parents' manor, hands clasped and hearts as one.

"You look awful." She forced a smile and tried to quiet her fidgeting hands. "Though I think the mustache is growing on me. I see you ignored my advice about shaving it."

Charlie's smirk appeared, this time in full array. "I knew you'd come around once you saw how well it fit my devilish charm."

"Naturally." She knocked his knees again.

"Naturally."

They sat in silence for a moment, their legs still touching. Being with Charlie again, like this . . . It helped ease the pain of losing her mother a second time. She could feel the remains of her old self stirring beneath the layers of hate she had piled on top. Removing a brick here. A nail there. But how could things go back to the way they were? She let her hair fall between them.

Did she want them to?

"So, are you going to tell me what you need," Charlie spoke first, "or keep this charade going longer? I don't know how much more I can take." The corners of his grin twitched, but his eyes lost their sparkle.

Something stirred inside her that she thought was long dead. A desire to trust. To tell Charlie everything she had learned so he could help her piece together the puzzle. But could she trust him?

Once again, Charlie's touch pulled her from her thoughts, only this time his hand covered her own.

"I'm so sorry," he said, "about the Baron. I did what I could after, or I tried."

"It's okay," she said, wishing he would stop. The warmth that flooded her heart started to cool. "We don't need to talk about it."

A second hand joined his first one and wrapped around her own. "Yes, we do. You were right. I should have done something from the start. We were so young. I was so young. I shouldn't have let him take you."

The bricks of her rage fell back into place, cold and rigid. "Like you said at the ball, what could you have done? Who are you to me? And I to you?"

He stuttered.

She waited, her hand a tight ball beneath his.

" . . . I should have married you myself."

The ball burst, and she pulled her hand free. "I did not want to marry anyone!"

His hands hovered helplessly in the air, blown apart by her outburst. His words came out in a whisper, "What would you have me do?"

"I don't know." She turned away.

What *did* she want him to do? The lie she had just told, that her rage created, hung between them. She would have married him in the tick of a pocket watch back then. But what did knowing that do now, besides salt her wounds? "I don't know."

Tension filled the void between them. Part of her knew asking him to give up his life—to marry young against his parents' wishes and face their disinheritance—was not a fair thing to ask. But life was never fair, and for once, she wanted someone else to pay the price.

Charlie straightened up, his eyes no longer on her, but on the ship. "Well, if you didn't want to marry me anyway, then there really is nothing I could have done more than what I did. I shall no longer trouble myself with it."

"Trouble yourself?" Christie nearly burst her stay-lace. "Since when did you and your gigglemug ever trouble yourself with anything?"

Charlie stood up and strode a few paces away before turning. "I've been tormented since that day. I lost most of my soul in agony over how to make it up to you, and the rest when I tried." His face softened. "And I would take you now if you would have me."

"And yet, you were not the one who lost your freedom."

"I lost everything," he said. And his words no longer burned. They ached. "I lost . . . you. And I have missed you every day since. Why do you think I—"

"Oh stop." She could not bear to hear the words. "Stop this at once. You did not want me then. And I do not want you now."

Her words sliced the tension and replaced it with ice. Charlie looked to his shoes. To the railing. To the *Robin*. Anywhere but her. And she did not blame him. How could she? She had waited for nearly eight years, formulating and contriving what she would say to him. How to make him hurt for what he had done. But now that she had?

She felt empty.

And petty.

And heartless.

A spilled piece of luggage abandoned in a train station.

Her fingers fumbled for her aigrette and met nothing but a tangled mess. She gripped her roots and pulled. Pain stretched across her scalp and ate away the knife in her heart. She wanted to scream into the black, but she was worried it would hear and come and eat her too.

Charlie stood a moment longer. Opened and closed his mouth as if he were about to speak. Then walked off the deck, down the bridge, and into the pitchy dark of the tunnels.

Christie stretched out her hand, a silent beacon to call him back. But it was no use. After everything they'd been through, after years of telling herself she never wanted to see him again, her inner darkness missed his light.

But after what she said to him, would he ever come back?

Seventeen

P HILLIP STEPPED LIGHTLY THROUGH the tunnel, a bounce in his step as he made his way back to where Christie sat. She leaned over the railing waiting for who knew what, a limp husk of misery. Her mission, while a success, failed to profit her at all. Her oldest friendship was a rat's nest because she could not let things go. And worst of all, her resolution to be independent of others had crashed and burned. Instead of planning, she was sulking, and she hated herself for it.

Phillip took two stairs at a time up to the bridge. The length of the wooden slats ran parallel to the *Ol' Bird*, and he stopped just below where she hung her arms off the railing.

"What's the matter with you?" he asked, craning his neck up. Silky strands of his hair parted on his forehead and swooped gently behind his ears.

Christie's chin rested on her hands. She did not care to move them. "I could ask the same of you." The words were smooshed between her sealed jaw. "You're quite dapper."

Phillip tucked his hands into his pockets, his tall frame leaning back like a tree grown against the wind. "My father's in good health today. The best I've seen him in a while. We actually talked like we used to."

Christie nodded, her chin rubbing against the veins in her hands which popped and crackled with the weight. "He does seem to enjoy talking about his pirating days."

"What are you talking about?" The light in Phillip's eyes sharpened.

She didn't care. "I just assumed you were talking pirates with him, what with your newfound identity and sense of adventure. When I chatted him up about the *Ol' Bird*, he seemed quite interested."

"I absolutely did not talk about any of this," he gestured his arms out wide, "with my father. I'm trying to help him rest, not rile him up."

"Your loss," she muttered.

What did it matter anyway? Her sense of direction had vanished. What was her goal? She had pulled exactly nothing out of Charlie. Her island was out of reach. Burying her past had only managed to drop her into a tunnel of lies and mystery. Very literally. And all she had gleaned from her recent adventures were secrets that made no sense. She could not even go back to Phillip's father and ask about the schedule. She had lost her chance by being too curious about these stupid caves.

"I answered your question," Phillip said. "Now you answer mine. Why are you wasting away the day pouting? You really are a terrible spy."

His words would normally fan a flame of indignation within her chest, but there was not even a faint flicker inside to begin with. He was right.

"Yes. I am a terrible spy. The whole reason I snuck in to see your father was to find out why his name was on Thorton and Blackwell's shipping schedule, and I couldn't even do that. And then I was with the man who made the schedule himself, and all I managed to do was lose my temper."

Phillip's head dropped back down, and he walked back across the bridge. Great. Her whining had scared him off too. But she was wrong, he made his way to the corner and pulled himself over the landing and onto the deck.

He stepped over some rope and a bucket to perch next to her on the railing.

"What is this shipping schedule you keep talking about?"

Christie stared down at the bridge. Another mistake she could once again attribute to Charlie. How had she let her guard down enough to slip up about the schedule? She had been about to tell Charlie everything earlier, before .. she did not want to think about what had happened. Her chin bounced on top of her hands. What did she have to lose now? She might as well tell Phillip—and Charlie, if he ever came back—the truth. Then, at least, she could enjoy their mutually assured destruction.

She reached into her corset for the torn corner of the schedule, and Phillip's eyes darted to the ceiling.

"It's the safest place for it." She found herself defending her actions. Heat crawled up her neck and spread to her cheeks. "Grow up."

"Don't mind if I do." Charlie's head appeared by their feet. "I'll watch you any time, just say the word." He flashed his teeth, but not in his usual lop-sided grin. And not at her.

Christie kicked a pile of rope off the edge at him. He had come back. The unfamiliar warmth she had felt earlier kindled within her again. But she was still mad that he had left in the first place. Though which time? Probably both. And why was he so cavalier? It was just as she had supposed. He never cared about anything for too long. And yet, she yearned for him to look at her with more than a sneer and for him to say something to her that wasn't cloaked in the suggestive humor he used with all the other ladies.

"What are you scrounging around for anyway?" His glance brushed past her and onto Phillip.

Phillip's placid expression tweaked with something else. Something that pinched the corners of his lips with a hint of sour. "Christina says she has a shipping schedule from your company with my father's name on it. Care to explain?"

Charlie's jaw slacked into a smirk. "We do business all the time."

"*We* do business. *Not* you and my father."

"And my—" Christie's throat caught. "The Baron's name is on there too. But he's dead." The words chilled her lips as they passed.

Christie extracted the corner of the shipping schedule she carried with her and unfolded it at an angle so both of them could see. Her hands clammed with sweat, leaving pudgy marks on the edges. Showing them the schedule felt like opening a hole into the well of her soul. What if all her secrets spilled out? What would they think if they knew what had happened to the Baron? What she had done?

She raced to crumple the paper and tuck it back into hiding, but Charlie grabbed it from her hands.

He twisted and turned the paper, as if reading it from a different direction would help decipher the only two lines on the parchment. A tease, as always. And not the tender-hearted Charlie she had crushed just hours ago. Maybe that Charlie was gone forever, at least from her?

She reached over the railing to snatch it away, but he pulled it back.

"No need to fret, my dear." He winked in her direction, though he still would not look her in the eyes. "I see now where the confusion lies."

He reached inside his breast pocket and pulled out an identical, whole schedule, unfurling it with great panache.

"Look at these other lines. They state the first and last name of the recipient, no titles. Whenever a title is used in place of a given name, it signifies a code or secret locale, if you will. My father set up the system long ago to make it as difficult as possible for someone to compromise the schedule. Say, by stealing it and selling it to the highest bidder." He shot a tight-lipped half-grin at her, and the betrayal in his eyes seized her heart with a grip far worse than the Baron's.

Christie trained her eyes on the schedule to avoid his gaze. Now that he had finally looked at her, she wished he had not. She shifted focus to her indignation. "You had a second copy of the schedule with you the whole time and didn't say?"

Charlie shrugged. "I don't recollect it being any of your business. And you refused to tell me it mattered until you were upset about it. Sounds like you have a problem opening up to people and asking for help."

Christie scowled. He could not be insinuating that the reason he had never come for her was because she had failed to ask? She ground her teeth so hard, they could start a fire.

So what if he were? What could she do about it now? Start another row? The last one still sat bitter on her tongue. And it didn't matter anyway; she was after solitude. She needed to stop worrying about Charlie and focus on the mess of circumstances the schedule left her in now.

Had she really abandoned Oceana and come back to her nightmare all for a flam? All to find out that Baron's name on the shipping schedule was just a code for something else? She waited for relief to wash away her rage, but her temper just burned hotter.

Why was she still here? She should cut her losses and fly the coop while the fox was away. But where would she go? Oceana and Thorton were hunting her down as sure as she stood on an airship's hull in an underground cave. She continued to grind her teeth until it hurt. Staying with Charlie and Phillip was her safest bet until she decided where to head next.

Phillip took the schedule Charlie offered him. "So what do these code names mean then?"

Charlie shrugged. "I have not yet earned that sacred trust," his voice mocked in a frilly tone.

"But you wrote the schedule," Christie said before snatching it back from Phillip.

Charlie nodded. "I did." He pulled his hand below his chin so his bird ring glinted in the dim lights of the cave. "But my father still writes the mini-schedule for all high-profile or top-secret clients. I then integrate their assigned code names into the master list, giving them priority slots and the best ships."

Phillip's brow creased. "Well, someone on the ships has to know what those code names mean for the shipment to be delivered."

"The captains of our three finest vessels know. And my father. That's it."

Christie rubbed her thumb along the coarse paper. "What about Thorton?"

"Hm?" Charlie inclined his head her way, though he kept his eyes on Phillip. "I don't believe so. They set up the business that way on purpose, to prevent corruption and delineate duties. My father handles all the shipping, Thorton the finances."

Christie folded the corner back up and tapped it against her knee. Maybe there was a chance yet to salvage this secret. She had a nose for this sort of thing. Unfortunately, the next step would be one she'd have to fight for.

She twisted to face Phillip. "We have to talk to your father."

"Absolutely not." Phillip's calm demeanor tensed. "How many times do I have to tell you? Leave him be."

"It's the only way."

Phillip tossed the hair from his eyes. "I don't see you hunting down his father." He shoved his finger at Charlie.

"My father's not her type. Too . . . stodgy, I'd say. Not crazy enough either. Oh yeah, and there's the whole him not being titled issue. I remember you insisting on that criteria for future husbands in your youth." He turned his burrowing eyes onto her. "Don't you?"

Christie's wince morphed into a glare. He was going to drudge that up now? Like it would have made a difference. "Mr. Blackwell isn't going to just hand over trade secrets because we ask him nicely. Your father, on the other hand, seems willing to talk."

"Well, maybe if Charles could handle his affairs in a competent manner, his father would hand him his trust willingly."

Charlie jumped and grabbed the edge of the banister, climbing up the wooden ledge. He pulled himself to full height in front of Phillip. "Do not speak about what you do not know."

Charlie's temper was wasting time. Christie kicked his shoe off the railing. He dipped with the loss of balance and swung himself over the banister to her other side, landing with a thud. He cursed, still clenching the railing. She was getting nowhere with Phillip. Mr. Blackwell would be a harder sell. Maybe even a forced sell. But trying him would be better than fighting with Phillip all night.

"I'm sorry, Charlie." She turned to him. "But I think Phillip is right."

Charlie stiffened. "You know my father. I've done everything—"

"Not about that. I meant about him having the information we need. He's our next stop, whether we like it or not. I know he can be a bully, but . . ." Christie forced her eyes up to the oceans within his. "We can do this. I believe in you."

And in another flash of warmth and past, of barns and fields and starry skies, she did.

EIGHTEEN

Frfrom up in her vantage point, Christie could see Charlie hesitate before knocking on the door of his father's home. She crouched behind a roof gargoyle on the nearby library. The twists of fog swirling the air dampened the colors of the night and tasted like day-old water. In this case, it was a good thing the Blackwells held no title. A stakeout of a country villa would have required her to hide in a ditch or climb a tree.

A tendril of hair brushed her face, pulling a wisp of memory to the forefront. She *had* told Charlie she would only marry a noble. She had never meant it, just used it as a hand to play when he was acting obnoxious. Though it seemed he had taken her words to heart. That couldn't have been the reason he left her with the Baron, could it? She tucked the hair behind her ear. Why think about that now? Her mind was as moth-chewed as her old dresses.

The crunch of dirt broke the silent night behind her. She snapped her head around. Searched. Moon-stretched shadows and empty roof. A faint scurry of something that wished to stay hidden. What were the odds something shared the roof with her? An owl? A rat? Heaven forbid. She had once done a job in Alsace Lorraine that required far too much time in the sewers, keeping the beady-eyed beasts at bay.

Still, a man would be far worse. She scanned the night's strongholds, sweeping her gaze back and forth. Better not to risk it. But did she have time to move to a new vantage point?

The muffled creak of a door across the street pushed its way through the fog. It would seem not. She crouched sideways, one ear on the rooftop and her eyes on Charlie's house. Charlie's father appeared, slapping him on the back and dragging him inside.

She pulled her coat tight around her neck. Charlie had insisted he go alone to face his father, but she refused to let such a crucial step in their plan go unsupervised. Especially considering how Charlie's father had always been a terribly brash and quick-tempered man who loved power more than people.

She pulled the binoculars out of her satchel and aimed their lenses at the window into the parlor. Wooden ducks sat on the mantel, framed by towering pictures of people she didn't know. She often felt like she did know them though, considering how many times she had sat in that very room waiting for Charlie to finish his studies. The pinched-nosed lady with a frumpy bum who she called Agnus. Or Giacomo, the spindly man with a kinked rat tail for a mustache. Had wasting her hours reading Verlaine in that parlor been improper? Maybe. Boring? Absolutely. But worth it? She was not so sure anymore.

She flicked her binoculars to the other window. No sign of either of the Blackwells. Of course not. That would have been too easy. Blackwell Senior must be receiving Charlie in his office upstairs which only served to make her job harder.

She eyed the street below before climbing down the rutted sides of the library columns. She landed in the street puddles with a splash. A startled-horse-whinny later, she was across the street and sizing up the outside of the house. Not much had changed, though the trellis that had once run up the front was missing. She'd have to make her way up in the back. Dodging into the dark alleyway between homes, she spied her target: a cast-iron downspout that ran from the gutters to the ground. Metal brackets pinning it to the stone face had always allowed her footing to the second floor.

With a double check down the alley, Christie cinched her gloves and grabbed hold of the pipe. She walked her feet up the wall and wedged her boot into a hole between the piping and a bracket. Her head hung to the side of the office window, and she eased herself up so she could listen.

Charlie and Mr. Blackwell were definitely having a row. A bad sign, however expected. And with every pitch and raise of voice, the outcome solidified. It would take a miracle for Charlie to leave with the documents they needed.

Christie leaned a few centimeters closer to peek inside, careful not to sully her coat. A low creaking stretched the night air. She froze before taking a furtive glance behind her. The metal bracket had pulled away from the stone on one side, leaving the downspout unsecured. One wrong move and she'd encounter a violent meeting with the ground.

What were her options? Attempt to climb back down? With the pipe coming off the wall, there was a good chance her descent would wake the neighbors. Or worse, draw attention from the Blackwells. But if she waited out the argument to sneak inside after, the gutter might not hold. She weighed her options, arms shaking from the effort to remain perfectly still. The odds favored waiting. Despite their volatile tempers, the Blackwells ran hot and burned out quickly. She should not have to wait too long.

Water leaked out the joints of the water spout, slicking her hands with chilly droplets. Every minute or so she shook her hand free to keep her hold. At last, the furor died down to gruff whispers, then silence. The light in the office flickered off. It was time to act.

Christie held her right foot in place and reached for the window ledge. When her hands met stone, she grasped for the lip. Her fingers dug into the pocked face of the brick while she brought her left foot over and scrounged for a toe hold. A small corner jutted out just above her boot. It was all she needed. She shifted her weight over to her left leg and hoisted her elbows over the ledge. Her right foot found a hold against another brick and she freed one hand to shimmy the window open.

With a quick hoist and a clumsy tumble, she made it inside the office. She rolled under a nearby cherrywood desk, staying low to the ground. Had they heard? She held her breath and listened to the tick-tock of the clock, to the distant rattle of wheels on cobblestone through the open window. And to the voices still growling down the hallway. Growling, but not at her. She was safe for now. But she had come in too early; they were not yet downstairs.

She headed for the door, placing one foot carefully in front of the other. Unless things had changed, the floorboards in this room still creaked. She could not risk being caught. Blackwell Senior would try to beat her with a fire poker, and Charlie, insulted she had followed him, would likely stand by and watch, forever blaming her for not trusting him to do the job on his own. Sanctimonious Charlie was the worst.

She tipped her head toward the crack in the door. Charlie and Mr. Blackwell stood at the end of the hallway, Charlie a step lower on the stairs.

"I have done everything you've ever asked of me," Charlie said. "Always. Even—Even when it came at great personal cost."

Mr. Blackwell harrumphed. "Is this about that Rushing girl again? I did you a favor. With dead parents, she had no influence or connections to offer the company. I don't know why you keep risking your neck for her. As far as I can tell, her husband has been dead for a year, and she has yet to come knocking on your door."

Christie's hand tightened on the doorknob. Why were they talking about her?

"It's not always about the company," Charlie seethed. "There are more important things."

"Which is precisely why you don't have the secret codes. You are far more committed to that old flame and your various schemes to save her than anything of true worth."

With one eye on the lit hallway, Christie exhaled, silent and slow. When had Charlie ever risked his neck for her?

Charlie's hand flexed open and closed, open and closed. As a youth, those twitching fists always led straight to a fight. But fisticuffs were the last thing her plan needed right now, even if Mr. Blackwell deserved a good decking. Christie prepared herself to spring into action when the violence erupted, though she was not yet sure if she'd jump into the fray or out the window.

The tension between the two burned brighter than the flickering lights in the hallway as they hashed out an argument they'd clearly had before. Then Charlie's eyes shadowed and his face fell. His hand went limp and he turned.

"Goodbye, father." He plodded down the stairs.

Mr. Blackwell followed a moment after.

No fight.

Christie's tense muscles relaxed only slightly. She bit her lip, the pain of indecision seeping into her skin. This awful house had always felt caged and depressing, and she wanted nothing more than to get out. But Charlie's hands had been empty of documents when he left, and his sorrow lingered on the stairwell, tingeing her escape with guilt. Maybe he really had changed? Tried to make amends? And if he could, so could she. But just this once. It would give her a reason to say hello to Mr. Blackwell. They still needed his information, and Charlie had certainly failed to get it.

The thump of footsteps coming up the stairs sent Christina further behind the office door. Her hand shot first for her aigrette, and pain seared her heart. She dipped instead to the Good Baron. She would be just fine without her brass feathers. And her mother. No need to play coy with Mr. Blackwell. He would respond better to her gleaming bulldogs anyway. She waited in the shadows, breathing through her mouth despite the dusty air and musty pine scent of day-old cologne.

Blackwell's portly frame pushed the door open. She kicked it shut behind him. He twirled around just in time for the Good Baron to make a home under his chin.

Christie said nothing. There was no need to. The hardening fear in his squinty eyes told her he knew.

"Little Lady Rushing. Or is it Ravensworth now?" He choked the 'R's out around the barrel catching his throat.

She shoved the gun harder against the folds of his chin.

"What do you want?" He winced.

"You know what I want."

His tiny eyes narrowed further. "You're here about the Baron?"

Her left hand twitched toward Rudy. Logically, there was no need for emergency measures, but hearing *his* name, in this place . . . .

"He did you a favor, you know. He did all of us one."

Christie released the Good Baron and slashed the metal hilt against Mr. Blackwell's cheek. He stumbled back, landing in a heap in the corner below the window. The start of a red welt bloomed, encroaching on the eye above.

"The Baron only took."

Mr. Blackwell gently prodded his wound. "Not the Baron, you vazey ratbag. Charles."

Charlie? Christie leveled the Good Baron again at Mr. Blackwell. What was he talking about? What did Charlie have to do with the Baron?

Mr. Blackwell pulled himself up, his pudgy hands pressing into the cherry wood of the desk he used for balance. "You and Charles would have made quite the pair. What with his temper and your quick draw. You wouldn't have lasted a week before killing each other."

He was making fun of her now. And where was her voice? She wanted to rage. To yell and throw things. But about what? With her head swimming in new, incomplete information, Christie struggled to refocus. What was her goal? Not to let this jollocks goad her, that was for sure. She was here to do what Charlie could not: obtain the code information for the shipping schedule.

With new energy, she poured fire into her gaze. "You will give Charlie what he asked for."

"Not a chance."

She lowered the aim of the Good Baron from his head to the crotch of his pants. The smug half of Mr. Blackwell's face fell.

"Now."

Mr. Blackwell eyed her warily before pulling a key from his trousers and unlocking the desk. He snatched up a dark brown folder, extending it toward her.

"Did I say give it to me?"

His grimace darkened. "Charlie has already left."

"Then figure it out."

The anger in his eyes lingered on her a moment longer before he tugged open another drawer and pulled out a carrier bag. He slipped the paper inside, his gaze never leaving her face.

"Edward!" He bellowed. "I've a message for Charles."

"What are you doing?" She cast a nervous glance toward the door.

His tight smile widened. "Calling my errand boy, of course. Do you want Charlie to get the papers or not?"

Christie hesitated. "You try anything, and Edward will be sending Charlie your head along with those papers."

His smile vanished.

She stepped back into the shadow of the door as the harried errand boy appeared. If his sallow and pocked skin failed to show the wear of his hard master, the fact that he was still on call this late certainly did.

Mr. Blackwell looked past the boy to where she stood in the shadows. She slid the barrel of her gun out so it glinted in the light. He handed the boy the satchel and tugged nervously on his sleeves. "Charles just left. Fetch this to him, no dawdling."

"Which way did he—"

"How would I know, you blasted boy? Do your job."

The young man's curly head bobbed in an awkward bow as he scurried out of the room.

"Satisfied?" Mr. Blackwell smeared.

"Very." Christie held the Good Baron on his ruddy face as she shifted her way out the door. Once in the hallway, she turned to run.

"You Ravensworths are all steaming mad," he called to her back.

His words roughed her ears as she holstered the Baron and fled down the stairs. She grabbed the railing at the bottom to make a sharp turn.

She was not a Ravensworth. And she was not mad.

Still, her mind suffered under the weight of Mr. Blackwell's other words. What had Charlie to do with the Baron?

Nineteen

CHRISTIE TRAVELED AT A dogged, haphazard pace to make sure she arrived back at Ravensworth manor before Charlie. By the time she rounded the familiar cliffside, the morning sun burned its way through the ocean. Maybe the messenger had caught him while he was still out, giving her more time. Who knew? But when she hopped down the grave to find the cave empty, her sweat-streaked run felt worth it. She stood on the edge of the large cavern that held the *Ol' Bird*, unwilling to go on. It had been over twenty-four hours since she had been alone. In the dark.

Weariness dragged on her mind, and the shadows loomed larger than normal. The whirring spurts of Ana's steam could be heard clanging around the cave's recesses. Sweat chilled her skin, and the cool air of the cave crept up her neck.

A thud.

A ruffle.

A brush of light in the belly of the bird. She grasped the handle of the Good Baron but did not draw. Was someone else in the cave with her? Was something? Maybe someone *had* been watching her outside the Blackwell home.

She crept forward, her strides long and lean. Past the rope switches, across the bridge. Up, and up, and over until she stood on the *Ol' Bird*'s deck. A floorboard creaked where her steel toe pressed. Not a muscle moved until she was sure no one—no thing had heard her.

Water dripped in from somewhere above, and the steady drip, plip, drop served only to unnerve her. She had heard sounds like this before. Somewhere dark before.

Had she been in the caves before?

Her hands hovered in front of her, palms turned toward the sky. Except, down here, there was no sky. And she remembered. The poppy blood. The poppies. The blood. Her own. Hands shredded with blisters and wear. From work. From practice after practice. Starved and beaten, for what? To train. To prepare for the day death came for her so she could slit its throat. To lunge and dodge and cut and bleed. Over and over and over and over.

Until it was over.

Something scraped below her in the hull. She tensed like a child caught red-handed.

Red hands.

She needed to move on. Get out. Be free. But something lurked beneath her. She forced herself forward, step by step, centimeter by centimeter, nerve by ever-tensed nerve. The stairwell down below lay heavy before her. One step. Two steps. Then three, five, seven, nine. There were nine steps.

She crouched below the balustrade, peering into the ebony room. Boxes stood in the forefront. And past that? A wisp of ghostly light trailed from one side to the other. Its pale glow briefly illuminated the boxes, rope, and crates it passed before relinquishing them back into the coal-black of the shadows.

The eerie glow reached the far end. She dashed forward. Ducked behind the crates. But she was distracted. Her knee brushed the splintery wood with a bump.

The light stopped moving. Snuffed out.

She was alone in the dark. Again. Except she was not alone.

Her touch on the Good Baron turned into a grip. Her left hand brought Rudy up. She popped her eyes over the edge, surveilling the room.

Waiting.

Seeing nothing.

The room was too dark.

Her mind was.

Everything always in the dark.

A tight hand grasped her shoulder from behind.

She screamed and whirled around, putting her guns between herself and the unseen figure. Pale skin caught slivers of light that braved the inky shadows through the floorboards above.

"Put the gun down." A whisper in the black.

Her finger slid onto the trigger. Her heart churned fear into blood, pushing it through her trembling limbs. Could this be the Baron's ghost? She aimed to kill. But kill what?

A white hand jutted out and grabbed the barrel of her gun in her left hand, shoving it to the side.

"Would you just put it down?" Phillip's face morphed into shadow-filled clarity.

The tremors in her arms turned into the shakes. Too much adrenaline.

She yanked Rudy away from his grasp and shoved the Good Baron into Phillip's shirt. "What gives? I could have shot you."

"I see that." Phillip's mouth made ghostly shapes in the faint light. "Your gun might as well be a cannon. I don't know why you lug that thing around."

Christie holstered her firearms. Her fingers tingled. "I lug it around so I can shoot strange sounds in the dark."

"It wouldn't be dark if we turned on the lights. Then this kerfuffle never would have taken place. I think I spotted some sconces along the walls, I just don't know how to get the power going. And don't bother trying to cross the middle of the room. There's some sort of barrier in the way."

Christie ignored the sweat dripping down the creases of her corset. The realization that she could have shot Phillip enveloped her mind. How could she be so careless? And with Phillip? What was she so afraid of? The Baron was dead. Rotted. Deceased for evermore.

And yet . . .

And yet, being back here, the Baron's power over her seemed to be stronger than ever. Why? A murky thought descended. About tea. About poppies. About guilt.

"Aha," Phillip declared from across the room. A click broke the dark, and lights along the walls flickered on. "See? Much better."

Christie did see, though no amount of light could explain what was going on in the center of the room. She scooted forward for a closer inspection. Corrugated metal up to her waist pinned in a gaping hole lined in rubber. Inside lay an entire hull's worth of—

"Sand?" Phillip bent over the metal and ran his fingers through the salty specks. "The pipes under the ship . . . They suck up sand. But why?"

"Oceana." Christie said and scooped up the tan earth. "Your dad, the Baron, Mr. Blackwell, they were procuring and shipping sand to Oceana for islands."

"But that's treason," Phillip said, tossing the sand back into the bin.

"It didn't use to be. Only after the treaty. Your dad said something had happened, something that spooked everyone. That's when they stopped. But I guess they never delivered their last shipment."

"Fascinating," Charlie's head popped over her shoulder from behind.

She flinched, the rush of the Baron's hold on her still coursing through her veins.

"I knew my dad was a scoundrel, but a traitor?" Charlie whistled. "That beats it all."

Christie pinched his nose and used it to pull him to the side. "Get what you needed from your dad?" She scanned his face for signs of bad news. Had the courier reached him in time?

His cheeks stretched to make room for the grin he slapped on. "Exactly what we need."

She exhaled too far, and her corset pinched into her ribs. "Well, let's see it."

Phillip walked around the bin of sand separating them and towered over her. Charlie untied the canvas of a courier bag and slid out the brown folder. Inside lay a stack of papers the width of a plank.

Charlie leafed through it briefly. "Divide and conquer?"

She nodded, grabbing the top third. Phillip and Charlie halved the rest. She sifted and sorted, running her finger down each page looking for clues. Names, dates, and places that meant nothing to her filled the pages. She flipped, and flipped, then caught herself. She backtracked to the page she had just been on. The Earl of Portsmouth sat in the middle of a column of names. In the corresponding list on the adjacent page sat the destination: London. That couldn't be right. There was nothing secretive or elusive about that. She studied the other columns. Under cargo: cotton. She sighed. The benefactor: Lord Edward Cavendish, Duke of Devenshire. A decrepit old man known for nothing. A balmy bit of wrinkles. And not helpful at all. Her finger trailed further down the page.

Was that?

Her nail dug into the paper, underlining the entry near the bottom of the page. Her lungs shrunk, leaving a space in her corset. She inhaled several times, breathing in nothing.

Her nail pressed further in, tearing the page. She found her voice. "Charlie, look." Her finger trembled on the paper.

Lord Rushing, Earl of Avendel sat in the middle of a column of names. How dare they? How dare they use her family name?

Charlie and Phillip appeared over each of her shoulders. Charlie tugged one of her curls, releasing it with a spring.

"I'm sorry. I forgot his name was in here. It's nothing personal, Christina," he whispered. "All the names chosen for secret codes are people who are either dead, like the Baron . . ."

Christie tensed at the name and turned her glower on Charlie.

He shuffled and tugged at his collar. ". . . Or are no longer active in society, like Lord Sheffield."

It was Phillip's turn to go rigid, though he almost always was anyway. "Very clever of you. Using the ill or deceased to further your secret works, knowing they wouldn't be making any shipments to confuse things."

Charlie grunted. "I didn't do this. Any more than you started an illegal smuggling ring."

Phillip's jawline squared, the jut of his chin two sharp corners.

She brought her hands together to crumple up the document. Stopped. Grimaced. It was just paper. Ink. The forgotten name of her childhood. Of her heritage. Yet she could not desecrate it. Her family may have left her, but the weak part of her had forgiven them, knew it was not their fault, and hated herself instead. And now, with her aigrette gone, all she had left of them was their name—her name—as a ruse on a cipher.

But what did she care? She wanted to be free of society, right? To break the chains of aristocracy that had doomed her in the first place? Then why could she not crumple the paper? Why did the rumbumptious mockery of a proclaimed bloodline have such a hold? It was ink. Her blood: ink. The red now black. And yet she did care. If she had nothing but bad memories left, what was she? Who was she?

A Rushing.

And that was all.

And if she lost that? Her very name? Neither Charlie, nor Phillip, nor anyone else would want anything to do with her. Not that she wanted them to want that.

Unless she did?

She pulled the paper taut with a crisp tug and analyzed the black words, honing in on the data to quench the emotional tap that was spewing nonsense inside her. In the corresponding list on the adjacent page sat none other than the name Barnes. And next to that, two sets of longitudinal and latitudinal degrees. Just like the ones Mr. Thorton had hired her to alter. But different.

"Charlie, wasn't there a map in the packet?"

"Yes," he said, raising a brow. "How did you know?"

Christie flashed her eyes wide. She slipped up again. Crikey, she was the worst spy ever. "I saw the corner. Just get it out. I need to see where these coordinates fall."

Charlie furrowed his brows and studied her face for a few seconds. "Fine."

He grabbed the map and handed it to her. She flapped it open and traced her hands along the degree lines. The coordinates landed on the outer perimeter of Oceana's territory, each at their closest points to Americana and Britannia.

A shadow darkened the map in the shape of Charlie's head, a giant sea creature emerging from the papery depths to take Greenland.

"That's right on Oceana's patrol route." He reached his arm across her and traced a crescent shape on the west and another on the east side of Oceana. "Here. They patrol in the shape of an egg, a stream of warships on either side, up and down. We always have to make sure our ships pass through at a set time so the patrol can establish a checkpoint. It's a headache."

Christie bit the inside of her cheek, mulling the smooth skin between her teeth. How did these locations correlate to the arms deal she had overheard Thorton talking about?

"I know that look," Charlie said, staring right at her.

"What look?"

His arms folded across his chest. "You know something that you're not telling us."

"I have a thousand things I know that I'm not telling you."

"I mean about this. Come on, spill it. Or Phillip here will have to get rough."

Phillip's posture stiffened next to her, but he didn't interject. Apparently, they both suspected her. She had almost told them earlier. Had already shared bits and pieces. Maybe it was time? This whole mess did seem bigger than she could handle herself. Besides, with the mess they had helped her create, her island dimmed further and further into unrequited hope.

Phillip's hand slid onto her shoulder, and she was grateful her coat hid her goosebumps. She never expected his shows of . . . what? Comradery? Assurance? Either way, and though she'd never admit it, she was glad she had not shot him.

His voice was steady as a ship in port. "You can trust us. We are in this together. If there's treason in our pasts, it's better to know now and come out ahead of it."

She looked to Phillip's storm-grey eyes and nodded, a ghost of a smile shading her lips.

"Quite pragmatic of you, ol' boy." Charlie plopped his hand on her other shoulder. "What he said."

She tugged on the edges of the papers. If nothing else, talking with them about this puzzle would keep the Baron off her mind.

TWENTY

T HE LIGHT FROM THE sconces flickered over the schedule as Christie looked on with Charlie and Phillip. Christie leaned against the metal frame of the sand bin. If she was not careful, she would sift away in the grains.

"These coordinates here." She pointed to the corresponding lines. "They're what I was doing in Oceana."

"For your benefactor?" Charlie asked. Every second his face eased closer to hers.

"For . . ." she pulled away so she could look at Charlie. This news would not go over well. "For Mr. Thorton. He paid me to change the path of two of their warships to coordinates that overlapped into Americana and Britannia. He also . . ." She looked to her boots then back up. "Was behind me stealing the shipping schedule in the first place."

She closed her eyes and braced herself for his rant.

Silence.

Maybe the betrayal was too much for him? She risked opening one eye to a squint.

Charlie studied the papers in her hand, unmoved by her revelation.

"Did you hear us, Charles?" Phillip asked. "Your insider is Thorton."

"Hm?" Charlie intoned, not even looking up. He was just playing with them now. "I knew that already. But thanks."

Phillip put his long fingers over what Charlie was reading. "You accused me of being a double-crossing pirate when all along you knew I was innocent?"

Charlie picked Phillip's hand up like a wet rag and tossed it to the side. "That's mostly accurate. Though you are a pirate. Or, at the very least, your father was."

"Let's stay focused," Christie said, ignoring the smirky twitch of Charlie's lips. "This set of coordinates falls right on the line of Oceana territory."

"On islands?" Phillip asked.

"Not that I could see."

Phillip's chestnut hair tickled her cheek as he bent his lean frame over to peruse the map. "And the ones Thorton had you change in Oceana?"

"As far as the map reads, just ocean."

"So we are on a wild goose chase." He snapped back up.

"People don't hire me to steal things if nothing is going on," Christie said. "We have the pieces, we just need to put them together."

Charlie flapped his pile of papers in the air and leaned against a stack of crates. "Why did Thorton go to all the effort of sending airships to open water? Oceana is allowed to patrol their warships through both their own and other country's waters during peacetime."

"What if it doesn't look peaceful?" Christie's mind churned. "I overheard a meeting between Thorton and a black market dealer."

"Yes," Phillip interjected. "But you said you didn't know what goods they were discussing."

"I lied," Christie said, her eyes darting to Phillip before slipping to the beveled edge of the metal rim holding in the sand. Little tan and white grains stuck in the crevices. "He was talking with an arms dealer. It sounded like a shipment of weapons is being delivered on the twenty-third."

Phillip's blank mask grew stony. "Well, that would have been nice to know sooner. Like when you accepted payment for the job."

"I didn't know if I could trust you." Christie shuffled her papers uneasily.

"Have I ever given you a reason not to?" Phillip's stormy eyes peered at her.

"No, but—"

"And has Charles?"

Her tongue pushed against the back of her teeth.

"And yet you trust him." He shook his head and ran his hand through his hair. "Unbelievable."

"I didn't say that." The pinch in her chest tightened with his look of betrayal.

A smug look played in the light on Charlie's face. "Let's get back on track, you two. You said the twenty-third, right?"

She nodded, still sulking from Phillip's attack. She was a spy, what did he expect? And his comment about Charlie gnawed at her. Did she trust him? How could Phillip tell? And if she was starting to, why hadn't she learned her lesson from the last time he broke her trust? Her heart? And why did Phillip care so much anyway?

Charlie pushed on. "Did you manage to overhear information about a specific month for this delivery? Or time? Or anything else?"

She shook her head and fought the urge to tuck her thumbs into her corset.

"Today's the twenty-first," Phillip said.

"Two days," she said, urgency kicking up her heart rate. "If it's this month, that's only two days to stop whatever is happening."

"Do we even want to stop what's happening?" Charlie asked, shuffling the papers back into his satchel. "I mean, this sounds way above my pay grade."

"You own the company," Christie replied flatly.

"Correction. My dad owns the company. I'm just a glorified errand boy."

"Scared?" Phillip's voice surprised her. His usual blend of cordiality and patience was tinged with a hint of spice. "Or do you care only about yourself?"

Charlie stepped towards Phillip. Even pulled to his full height, he was a head shorter than Phillip. "We don't even know what's happening. For all we can tell, Thorton just wants to trade some goods under the protection of an unsuspecting Oceana so pirates don't attack."

She should step in and stop their quibbling, but something Charlie said stopped her. "I think you're right."

"What?" They both turned to her.

Phillip's crossed arms broke free. "You can't be serious?"

"No, listen. What if Thorton does want Oceana to be present when the illegal weapons are transferred."

Charlie shook his head. "If Oceana knew what was happening, they would confiscate the entire lot, so that doesn't make sense."

"You're missing the point," Christie said. "Thorton and the captain of Oceana's navy both know what's on the schedule."

"How?" Charlie squinted at her.

"Because both Oceana and Thorton paid me to steal it."

"You cheating little doe," Charlie said, but his voice dripped with the breathy air of pride.

"Besides." Christie pointed at the line in the scheduler. "Captain Barnes' name is listed as the person who scheduled these deliveries."

Phillip's bony finger tapped his elbow. "So they're in this together. Thorton went through Oceana to steal the document from his own company to cover his tracks."

Charlie's head bobbed in agreement. "He started pestering me and my father about the schedule and the secret cipher. Asking where it was kept. When it was written. How far we schedule out. That's when I suspected it was him. He never cared one farthing about it before then. And I was doing a fine job keeping the schedule from him until a little vixen came to call."

Christie's cheeks warmed at the nickname he used for her back in their apple-stealing days. "Am I a vixen or a doe? They seem quite at odds with each other."

"When it comes to you, they're both right on point." He stared at her intently.

She dropped her eyes and blushed. She itched to feel her corset as much as she wanted to find a way out of this particular line of conversation. "So they're conspiring together to steal weapons? But then why do we have multiple sets of coordinates? The ones in Oceana's territory, and the ones in Britannia's and Americana's."

Charlie frowned. "And why did Thorton pay you to change Oceana's coordinates? If Oceana is in on the scheme, they could have changed it themselves."

That was the question Christie struggled with. She leaned against the metal rim of the container, drifting her fingers in and out of the cool sand. "I guess that depends on if there is more than one traitor in Oceana. Or if Thorton's planning to double-cross the entire country."

The bridge above Phillip's sharp nose took on a crease. "Oceana picks up the black market weapons, then unsuspectingly travels into territorial waters."

Christie nodded.

"Then, if they're boarded by international troops for inspection by a foreign power, they'll look red-handed and be accused of trying to start a war." Phillip's crease smoothed. "We're talking global repercussions."

"Because they have weapons on a warship? That makes no sense," Christie said.

"These won't be just any weapons." Charlie said. "Undeclared guns and rounds. The treaty mandates Oceana keep a running total of all their weapons and where they are. When Americana or Britannia discover a small army's worth of undeclared weapons, there'll be a real fuss. Sanctions, declarations of betrayal, and inevitably war."

"But why would Thorton want that?" Christie mused aloud.

"I don't know," Charlie said. "There's also no way to guarantee Oceana's ships would be boarded. There's a one in five chance a cargo airship is stopped for inspection, but the odds are even lower for foreign war vessels. There would have to be a reason to stop it, but the coordinates just lead to open water."

The three sat in silence, Charlie thwacking the satchel against his thigh. Christie dusted her hands off and reached for her aigrette. Her fingers stopped, rigid. She had lost it. How could she forget? She might as well have lost an arm and a gaping piece of her heart. She took a musty breath to clear her thoughts and pulled her hair down on either side of her face so she could think.

What would be a sufficient reason for such a high-profile inspection? It would have to be enough to risk an international egging if their hunch was wrong. As far as she could tell, a hostage situation was out of the question. There were wars and rumors of wars, but then why all the effort to arrange the weapon transfer if there was already a plausible cause? A prisoner transfer? It would have to be a high-profile prisoner. Like a war criminal or a traitor.

Christie's head snapped up. "Phillip, your dad said something about quitting the smuggling business because of treason."

"My father is not a traitor."

"But what if that means he knows something? What if they all did? Your father said they found out something so awful that they all abandoned their secret work, and the Baron went mad with paranoia. I think the missing piece in our puzzle lies with your father."

Phillip's pale skin darkened. "How many times do I have to tell you? We are not involving my father any more in the matter."

"Why not?" Charlie jumped in. "We involved mine."

"So why not talk to him?" Phillip quipped back. "It went so well last time, yeah? Got your daddy's approval and the paperwork to prove it. Go call him a traitor."

Charlie's fist open and closed, open and closed, and Christie took a step back. She should do something, but what? Charlie's was a fire that could only burn itself out. And Phillip was being entirely unhelpful. Maybe they would put each other out. She tugged at her glove. Her mother would be abhorred.

Charlie's glare shifted to something triumphant. "At least my father could take it. Yours looks like he'd keel over with the breeze if you weren't force-feeding him to keep him alive. Miserable sot. Let that shell of a man die already, or are you too worried you'll fail at running the estate without your daddy holding your hand?"

Phillip's pale skin blotched red. He swung his fist hard against Charlie's jaw. Charlie stumbled back before rebounding like a cornered fox. His fist collided with Phillip's left cheekbone with a *smack*. Phillip hooked the back of Charlie's neck into a hold, and Charlie pushed forward so they fell into a struggling heap.

Christie glowered as they wrestled. Or maybe instead of burning each other out, they'd kill one another.

"Enough," she cried.

Charlie landed a punch in Phillip's gut with a grunt. They rolled toward the center of the ship and haggardly jumped to their feet.

"Stop fighting."

Charlie took a wide swing, and Phillip popped him in the nose. Charlie jumped at him. They took turns pulling and pushing, swinging and dodging.

They were a bunch of diddling blokes. *Idiots*. She had had enough. Christie stepped forward, shoving them both so they tumbled into the vat of sifting sand. Charlie gasped, granules pouring from every crevice in his cravat. Phillip's wide feet and long legs sank deeper with every step until he, at last, pulled himself from the sinking hole his pride had placed him in. He spilled out of the container, sand pooling around his shoes. He looked at her, his eyes wide.

"Ready to behave?" she asked.

He *harrumphed* and strode out of the room, his stately figure undermined by trailing bits of beach.

"Tough sale," she said, turning to Charlie.

He slipped once in his effort to scale the metal sides. When he found his feet on solid ground, he brushed the tan grains of sand from his coat and out of his cuffed pants. "Indeed. Now, if you'll excuse me, I have an ego to nurse."

"Charlie," she called after him.

He brushed her off with a wave of his hand and stormed out of the room.

Alone. Again. She wrung her hands together. This couldn't be her fault. They were acting like children. And yet, it was always people leaving her, not the other way around. Did that make her weak? Them strong? What about her made people want to leave? And why did she care?

She didn't.

And she would prove it. Next time, she would walk out on them first, leave them alone. And then she'd be the strong one.

But first, she would stick it to Phillip and follow through with a plan. *Her* plan.

She looked at the trail of sand marking Charlie's wounded retreat. But she couldn't follow. It was Phillip who needed persuasion, and she would rather suffer the wrath of the Baron again than fail. Phillip would talk, even if she had to play nice to get him there.

Twenty-One

C HRISTIE WOVE HER WAY out of the *Ol' Bird* and through the dimly lit caves in search of Phillip. A scattered pile of sand dusted the clay floor. She quickened her pace and rounded a sharp corner. Phillip sat on a crate at the end, his face cast with orangey light from a bulb overhead. His bricky nose offered little insight, and what she could decipher did not bode well for the conversation ahead.

But she had to try.

Phillip's father was the key, and Phillip needed to play his part. She and Charlie had already sacrificed. It was his turn. And though he often acted hard, he did not respond kindly when others acted the same way towards him. That much she had learned.

"Walk with me?" she asked, keeping her words light.

Silent, he relented, taking one step for her every two.

"I've yet to explore these caves. I don't even know where the second entrance is. I couldn't bear wandering the darkness alone." She cringed with the admission.

But if Phillip refused to engage with necessity, maybe he would respond to vulnerability. It was a stinging pill to swallow, but she *was* responding to necessity. It's what kept her alive.

The tightness in his arms loosened with her words as he strolled beside her. Maybe he had forgiven her for earlier. "So there's more than just impulsive decision-making going on in your head after all."

She stifled the hackles of indignation. He had no idea. But it was better he think her incapable of sustained subterfuge. It made her hand stronger and kept closeness at bay. "I don't have time to plan ahead, my thoughts are too busy burying the past." She reached up and rubbed her arm to keep away the chill. The soft pad of her glove offered a sliver of comfort there under the earth. "That's why I hate this place. Too much dark. Too much . . . Baron." They reached a dead end and turned around, the exit nowhere in sight.

"It certainly lacks a touch of home," Phillip said. "But you can tell care was put into it."

Christie snorted. "The Baron didn't care about anything."

Phillip turned with her down another dimly lit hallway. "A man who cares for nothing would not go mad with paranoia."

Christie felt her muscles tighten even as Phillip relaxed. "Fine. The Baron only cared about himself, happy?"

He ran his hands along the walls, zig-zagging in search of hidden marks. "Perhaps."

She should control her temper, but Phillip's intrusive statements ensnared her common sense. She was not used to playing nice. And some strange, back-stabbing part of her wanted Phillip on her side. Wanted his understanding, and worse, his approval. She pushed that desire from her and back into the dark.

They reached an end to the hall and opened the door that marked it. Phillip's attention found its way to a strange box next to the entryway of the unfinished room. She had not actually expected them to look for the entrance to the caves. Had he really found it?

A lever with a metal ring around it lay encased behind a caged panel. There was only one light in the room, a flickering old thing that sat by the door. Shadows yawned and stretched on the rough floor, and something cloaked in terrifying blackness hid in the back corner.

"This could be our way out," Phillip said, poking his fingers through the metal wires. "But how do we get it open?"

Christie tugged her attention away from the corner and took a closer look around the edges of the box. In the middle of the wiring on the right side, a tiny pinhole punctured the metal. She stood on her tiptoes to check the top and other side for similar markings. The bottom last. It was the only one.

"What about this?" She rubbed the pad of her finger over the hole, then moved so Phillip could inspect it.

"Could be, but we will need a key. Or pin, or—"

"This?" Christie reached for the smallest feather in her aigrette. Her fingers met with the cold air drifting from the corner. "Drat it all."

She leaned her shoulder against the earthy wall. What was she without her aigrette? Who was she without her mother? A mess, probably. Things happened so quickly after her parents' passing that Christie never had the time to consider that. She had spent all her time planning and running. Angry and vengeful.

Who would she be when it all stopped?

Despite being in the middle of the complex, the clay in the soil still held the musty dampness of too much rain. There were hints of something else too, something her guilt recognized. Something like desperation and poppies.

Christie sniffed hard to clear her nose and poured her attention into how to open the lock.

Phillip bent forward, his back a level plane as he eyed the pinhole. His straight lips curved downward at the ends, softening his face and making his sharp nose look like a bird beak. She held up her ring for comparison. Definitely similar. The pinholed box behind the ring blended into the forefront, the tip of the brass bird's beak touching the out-of-focus hole.

"Wait. Let me try," she said, sidling past Phillip.

She took the ring off from her gloved finger and exhaled. With steady hands, she slipped the bird's beak into the hole, careful that the dip at the end of the brass stayed above the catch. Once fully inside, she tipped the ring up so the dip clicked into place. The cage popped free, and she moved the wires aside to pull the metal ring.

A rattling churned the earth around them, and a wooden panel lifted open above their heads. Phillip reached up, the earthy ceiling only a couple of centimeters above. A ladder lay rolled up in the rim that separated the house above them from the caves. He untied the binding and the ladder clattered down.

"Spies first," Phillip said, gesturing her toward the unknown above them.

"No." Who knew what traps the Baron might have laid, what tortures might be in store?

"No? Then how about assassins?"

She swallowed, her throat dry despite the damp cavern air. He couldn't know about what had happened between her and the Baron. But why say it? And why now? Maybe he did suspect. There were rumors after all.

"Or potential assassins, at least," Phillip continued. "I saw you trying to kill Charlie with your eyes back in the hull. It's a shame you didn't succeed."

He didn't know. A brief moment of relief washed over her then vanished as a horrible weight settled on her shoulders. How could she climb that ladder with the burden of her past? But a chill from the depths of the corner spurred her up rung by rung. Her head hit metal and wood. She rubbed her scalp. The panel covering the exit had bumped into a rolling chair when she had opened it. The only place in the house with one of those was . . . .

"What do you see? Is it our entrance?" Phillip asked from below.

She swallowed hard and stuck her arm through the crack she had managed to open in the hatch and pushed the chair out of the way. She had never been on this side of his desk before. How could she? He was always there. She pulled herself up, her elbows creaking from the slow effort, and slipped onto the plush rug.

The Baron had concealed the entrance to the cave by hiding the latch under the chapel design of the Persian rug under his desk. The edges of the center church were cut along with the wood below to form the latch in and out. And his chair always sat on top. She shook the curls from her face. She had never suspected, never had a clue.

"Christina?" Phillip called from below.

She had forgotten to answer him. But what to do now? The dust swirled along with dread, and she needed a moment to collect herself. The dark of the cave's corner filled the void and stretched up toward her. She yanked her feet up. Climbing to a standing position, she knocked the trap door shut again. A clinking sounded as the locking mechanism fell back into place.

"Christina?" Phillip's faint voice muddled through the wood. "Are you okay? What's happening?"

Ana's scarlet eyes appeared between the French doors of the library, the anamaton seemingly trained to come with the cave's closure. Her heart rattled within her chest. She opened her mouth to respond to Phillip, but nothing came out. Too little sleep and too much excitement twisted her mind.

She pulled her gaze from the anamaton's blood-red glow, searching for something concrete. Something to ground her in reality. A cast iron paperweight. A pen. A bottle of ink.

Her hand rubbed her chest, and her eyes shifted to the black stain that marred the carpet as much as it did her soul. The cold dark of the corner below called to her, and memories broke the dams of repression, flooding her mind.

He was in one of his moods again. She tried to straighten her back, but it stung from the day before. He picked up the bottle of ink on his desk and threw it at her. She didn't move. He had taught her long ago that flinching would invoke a greater punishment. Instead, the bottle hit her chest. Ink splattered her face and oozed down her dark green dress.

"You failed. Again." His voice etched the words into her soul.

She clamped her mouth shut, her teeth bars that kept her screams from escaping.

"Nothing to say?" His voice dripped with venom. "Fine. You can train instead of eat. Maybe that will teach you the lesson you should have learned this morning. How not to die."

Christina's shoulders remained tensed, waiting for another blow, whether physical or verbal.

The Baron pushed back his chair and stood next to her, he facing the door and she the curtained window. Her breaths came out hard, and she struggled to keep her chest from heaving. She sealed her eyes shut and waited.

His hand touched her cheek, but instead of a sting, it was soft, gentle. She tried not to pull away though her skin crawled.

"I know you want kindness, but that would mean your death." His caress turned into a painful pinch. "And despite what you think, I'm not here to kill you. The hunt is on and we will survive, you and I. We may wish for death by the end, but by then we will have won. Now, time for more training."

Training always started the same way, her getting knocked out. Christie tensed for the blow, and this time it came.

A thud jarred her feet from below, shaking away pain's grasp.

A muffled Phillip called out, "I tried my ring but it won't budge. You have to get off of the door."

She slapped her cheeks to chase away the chills and stepped aside, lifting the carpet flap. A tiny hole punctured a metal plate just like the one underground. She inserted her ring, and chittering filled the wood.

Phillip climbed his way up. "I was worried something had happened to you when you didn't respond. Are you okay?"

Christie tipped her head up and down once.

"Good," he said. His eyes lingered on her, and warmth returned to her drained cheeks. He offered a reassuring smile before scanning the room. "I didn't know the Baron was so well-read. Maybe somewhere in these books is an answer to our question."

"Maybe," Christie said absent-mindedly. He was wrong. The only thing in these books were the shattered pieces of a madman. "Or we could just ask your father." She chomped her teeth through the last word. Too late. So much for being coy.

Phillip grabbed the thickest book from off the shelf, his coldness returning, and smacked it onto the Baron's desk. "Get to work."

Christie, Phillip, and Charlie spent the rest of the day and into the evening taking turns napping and rifling through the books in the library. Christie drew the last sleeping shift and left the two men reluctantly. They were like gasoline and fire, and she worried she would wake to an inferno she could not put out. But she had been up all last night journeying home from the base in Oceana and had yet to stop and rest with new discoveries and pieces of information tempting her waking hours.

Christie trudged up the stairs to her room and brushed the dust off her bed. Slipping under the barely used covers, she closed her eyes. The darkness in the corner met her, and she flashed them open again. She calmed her rapid breathing by counting over and over. With a final deep breath, she shut her eyes once more. Again the blackness met her, but this time it held. And a nervous sleep took her.

A clammy hand on her forehead woke her. She bolted up, sweat streaking her pillow where she had lain. She had been dreaming something terrible, but the picture of what it had been faded into bleary edges. Phillip sat next to her, his hand still recoiling from where she must have startled it.

"You were screaming," he said. His stormy eyes washed over her. Through her. And she shuddered at what they would find.

"I'm just worried," she said hoarsely. Thirst scratched at her throat despite the moisture in the air. How long had she been screaming? For her throat to ache? For Phillip to hear her?

Phillip placed his hand on her knee, the sheet shielding her from his warmth. "Is it the house?"

How could she answer a question like that? In this room where the evening light filtered through the thin curtains of her window?

"What happened here? To you? To the Baron?" His gaze continued to burrow through her protective layer. The church pickaxe of his nose softened.

Her first reaction was to shut him out. To cloister up and hide the source of her rage. Yet something in his demeanor invited confidence, and that nagging desire to gain his approval nipped at her heart.

But how could she tell him? How could she tell anyone? Especially Charlie?

She could not.

And that was why she had sought her island in the first place. Maybe Oceana was out of the question, but she could still keep herself from letting others in, from finding out her secret and hating her for it.

She forced words through her arid throat. "What time is it?"

"Half past eleven."

"Did either of you find anything?"

Phillip pulled his hand back and shook his head.

"You know what this means, right?"

"That Charlie talks to his father."

Christie sat up too fast, hitting her scalp on the headboard. "No, Phillip." She searched for words to explain why. Words that didn't mention how she had threatened Blackwell Senior. "I know your father is ill, but he did not seem upset by our pirate conversation. He seemed excited, interested. I think he likes the adventurous part of his past and wants someone to talk to about it. Besides, if he passes—"

Phillip blanched. A warmth she had not realized had his features sank into the shadows, and a coldness blew between them.

She was pushing him too far. Eventually, he would snap and something would break between them. Something that could not be fixed. But she had to find the answer.

She persisted, "If you lose the chance to talk to him, won't it gnaw at you, never knowing what really happened?"

An apparition of emotion fluttered across his stony features.

A moment passed. Then two.

"Fine." He stood up and straightened his suit coat. "I will talk to my father. But I'm no fool. I know there's something in this for you; I just can't see it yet."

He gave his tie a final jerk before walking out of the room. The blankets felt too hot, and Christie kicked them off in a storm of feet. She had gotten exactly what she had wanted. So why had Phillip's fallen face made her feel so crummy?

She slid out of the sheets and hurried to lace her boots. Despite Phillip's facade of even-handed candor, she did not trust him to tell the whole truth if he discovered his father really had committed treason.

She hated to admit it, but Phillip had been right. There was something in it for her. She needed to know everything, to learn the secrets of this puzzle so she could find the right buyer for the right price. Her island may be out of the question, but that just meant she needed money to stay alive. To escape—as soon as the bounties on her head were dissolved—from Charlie and Phillip and the strange hold they had over her. Especially since she had had the opportunity to learn the answer from Lord Sheffield before, but had failed to ask the right questions. She needed to make it right. To put things back in her own hands.

If there was one thing her past had taught her, it was that she did not need saving.

Twenty-Two

P HILLIP STOPPED OUTSIDE HIS father's door and rounded on her, pointing a finger at her chest.

"You are not to say a word," Phillip hissed under his breath.

Christie nodded and pretended to tie her lips shut. At least they were inside and out of the rain. Phillip had made them pause on his driveway, scanning the treeline for a full ten minutes before coming in, certain he saw someone hiding where the field met sparse forest. He acted more paranoid than the Baron ever had when it came to his father.

Even worse was the fact that Phillip had made her trade in her pants for a dress, and she wasn't about to waltz around the countryside in her tattered ball gown—if it could even be called a gown at this point. That left the itchy, green wool piece with the stain down the front. Her own darkened version of The Scarlet Letter. Now she was not only encumbered and unable to easily access her guns, but hideous.

Phillip took hold of the doorknob to his father's room and guided it open so as not to make a sound. His father wheezed in a ball of sheets atop the bed. The room stood unchanged from when she had visited last except for a lit stick of orange blossom incense. Loose tendrils of smoke snaked their way through the air.

"Father?" Phillip bowed before approaching the bed. "Are you awake?"

"Yes, yes." The breath between his words slowed his speech to a slog. "Alfred said you were coming."

"I am sorry to disturb you. Maybe we can come back later. After you get another nap."

Christie stepped out from behind Phillip. No way was he going to put this off until later. Had he forgotten the deadline? They only had a day and a bit left.

"It's nice to see you again, Lord Sheffield." Christie bobbed her head.

The Earl flicked his gaze to her face. "Ah." Another belabored breath. "Ravensworth. Back again so soon?" His wrinkles stretched with the bones of a smile.

"I'm afraid so," she said. Phillip had a death glare just for her, but she tucked up her hem and sat on the edge of the earl's bed anyway. "Phillip has something very important to ask you. Don't you, Phillip?"

Phillip's face shifted from stony to murderous, his eyes narrowed and his nose pinched. "No." His teeth stayed clenched.

"Yes, you do. Don't be shy."

The earl's eyes slithered between the two of them and his eyebrows lifted. "Phillip, are you wishing to marry?"

The light red of Phillip's face burned into cherry. "Father, how could you think such a thing? I've promised to devote my time to only you until—until you are well."

His father breathed out a laugh that devolved into coughs, his whole frame shaking with the effort. When the tremors passed, he looked to Phillip. "I wish you would. A bright young lady is just what you need to help you stop worrying so much."

Christie looked between the two, waiting for Phillip's protest.

Instead, he turned to her with straight lips and solemn eyes. "Christina, I—I know this isn't the right time, but my father has a point."

"I'm sorry?" Christina asked, standing up from the bed.

"I love my father, but my future matters too. And it would make him—me—it would make we, I mean us, indescribably happy if you would agree."

Needles shot from her heart and up the back of her neck. "What, exactly, would make him, you, we, us so happy?"

"A life together," he said gently. "Safety. Comfort. For me. For the both of us. Let me give that to you."

"I'm not a charity case," she spat the words. Why did everyone think she needed saving? She was surviving just fine on her own. "And I'm certainly not going to—to—to marry someone who's doing it just to make their father happy."

"I'm not offering charity. I'm offering—" His voice caught. "A new life. A home with me. Free of spy work and explosions and selling secrets."

And all at once her insides broke. Burst. Melted. How could he be saying this to her right now? When she could finally see her goal in sight? When she was almost free? All she had wanted since her parents had died was a home. A place to feel safe. And here it was, on a silver platter with Phillip. But she could not give up all she had worked for, lay low, and rejoin the gentry. She could not depend on others again. A home like that would be just as much a prison as her last one, bound by expectations and guilt. She could not be the refined person he wanted her to be.

"I'm sorry, Phillip." She choked the words out. "I will always have secrets. Your life is with your father, and mine is elsewhere. My future does not involve you, or anyone else."

"You can't be serious?" Phillip sputtered.

Christie kept her eyes trained on Lord Sheffield. "Don't we have work to do?"

Phillip's mouth pinched into ugliness. "So you're just going to ignore me? To pretend I didn't make an offer of marriage?"

"You said it yourself; it's not a good time."

"Is this about Charlie? Is that why? You want to be with that off-the-cuff coward?"

Christie snapped her head towards Phillip. "I didn't say anything about Charlie. I don't want to be with you because a life bound in marriage has never done me any good. As far as I'm concerned, I never want there to be a someone else." She wasn't sure if it was the conversation or the heavy scent of burnt oranges, but her head was spinning.

Lord Sheffield cleared phlegm from his throat. "I'm sorry I caused you two discord. I won't press the matter." He patted the bedspread between them. "If it is not your future, what have you come to inquire about, Phillip?"

Phillip's thin lips pressed into each other, and his arrow-straight back twitched under his coat. "Nothing."

The silence in the room grew. Christie could swear she heard the smoke wafting. Enough was enough.

She leaned close to the earl so he could hear her clearly. "We want to know about the sand. And the reason you stopped smuggling. And why there's still a shipment in the bottom of the *Ol' Bird*."

Lord Sheffield's breath rattled, but no more than normal. "Right to the point. I like that." His eyes slid to Phillip. "I know this all must be rather shocking to you."

Phillip took his father's hand, shooting a glare her way. "We don't have to talk about this if you don't want to. Your health is the most important thing. You don't have to cater to Lady Ravensworth; she offers nothing in return."

Sheffield patted the hand Phillip had placed on top of his. "We must. It is long overdue." He coughed twice, pulling his hand up to his mouth to cover the spittle that dripped from the sides. "As I told Lady Ravensworth, we shipped sand for Oceana until the treaty. Regulations tightened and inspections increased, so we quit the sand business. Picked up imported goods, exotic animals, things like that. Then Thorton tells Blackwell that Oceana was looking to shore up some of its weaker islands. Nothing illegal in that. And all the commercial ships had been stripped of their sand-gathering equipment. We could charge whatever we wanted." A coughing fit stopped his progress, and his eyes lost their focus.

Christie looked to Phillip. "He's slipping. This is what happened last time. What do we do now?"

"Patience," Phillip whispered, his gaze not leaving his father's face. Tension lay in worry lines that traced his forehead.

Christie tried to settle her nerves and wait, but Phillip's devotion was a pin in her heart. When was the last time someone looked at her like that? If she had accepted his offer, would he look at her that way too? She pressed her nails into her palm. After all the pain she had suffered, why did part of her want him or anyone else to hurt? She pushed herself off the bed and over to the window. A shadow caught the corner of her eye down in the bushes. A cat?

"Phillip?" The rustle of Lord Sheffield's voice stirred from the bed.

Christie scanned the foliage once more before reluctantly turning. She had been off her spy game ever since Charlie and Phillip had showed up, but something irked her.

"Father," Phillip said. "Why is there still sand in the hull of the *Ol' Bird*?"

"Because we were too scared to deliver it."

Christie abandoned the window for the edge of the bed. "Why?"

"Ravensworth?" He studied her face. "Why? Because it was too dangerous. Thorton was mistaken. The sand wasn't for fixing old islands. The coordinates we were given led to empty ocean. We were being paid to build new ones."

Phillip leaned back in the wicker chair he sat in, his hand leaving his father's to rub his temples. "So it was treason."

"We didn't finish it, Phillip. Our black contacts slipped us a note that speculation was stirring in the House of Lords. We took the last shipment of sand back with us to avoid treason charges, to be safe."

Phillip hunched over, placing his elbows on his knees. It was the first time she had seen him anything but rigid. "Which is why the sand's still in the hull."

Christie tapped the rough fabric of her dress. "So Thorton's plan won't work. No islands, no reason for an inspection."

Lord Sheffield gasped, wheezing in horrible, raspy breaths. "The islands were built."

"How?" Christie's words came out as bark. But she would not apologize. They were so close to the answer.

"When we stopped, Oceana sent spies, assassins, thugs to try and force our hand. Thrice, Baron Ravensworth walked the line of death. He survived through pure grit, I imagine. I suspect my poor health is also the result of several poison attempts damaging my liver. We were in more danger than ever before. We called off our smuggling business for good, stowed away the *Ol' Bird*, reported it sunk in a storm, and circulated the news around to our contacts. The islands were meant to be two sentinel posts to act as

Oceanic embassies, central to some cockamamie plan they have. And each just needed one more load of sand to crest above the waves when we quit. If Oceana went to that much trouble to try and make us finish, you can bet they spent just as much getting someone else to do it for them."

"But you said you were the last ship outfitted for the task."

Lord Sheffield's throat rattled like an engine out of steam. "You underestimate the power of money, of what people are willing to do to get it.

Money was the one thing—besides salty water—Oceana was flush with, what with all the aristocrats and new-blood Americans buying up their private stays. It was also the one thing she needed and the reason she traded in powerful secrets.

Phillip grabbed a rag from a bowl by the bed and cooled his father's forehead. "We should take a break."

"No." Christie tensed her jaw in defiance.

Phillip's hand froze mid-dab, and he glared at her. They locked in a silent struggle. But she would not back down. She had to get the answers. Her life swirled in uncertainty, and she needed this to work. Lord Sheffield was right. If money could build those islands, money could fix her problems, and she finally had the chance to get enough to make a difference. If she could figure out the secret of what was going on, she could sell it. To Britannia or Americana. Or wield it as blackmail against Thorton or Oceana in exchange for an island. And Phillip was not going to get in the way now.

"Where were the islands you were sent to build?"

"Christina, he's had enough." Phillip stood up and blocked her way to his father.

She met his challenge, tilting her chin up. If she pushed Lord Sheffield, and something were to happen to him, Phillip would never forgive her. But if she gave up this opportunity of freedom, and another failed to come along, she would never forgive herself. And that was a burden she knew too well. She had to take the chance.

She ducked under his arm and crawled up the bed so she was centimeters from Lord Sheffield's face. "Where are the islands?"

Phillip grabbed her shoulders, but she shrugged herself free. She took hold of the silk lapel of Lord Sheffield's pajamas and squeezed the smooth fabric between her fingers, drawing him close. "Where are the islands, you daft man?"

"Christina!" Phillip grasped her arm and pulled. She fell back onto the scarlet bedspread.

Lord Sheffield gasped in gargled breaths. His skin grew pale and sweaty with every exerted breath. "Who are you, my dear?"

"No! Not again." She was tired of waiting for answers. She was tired of Phillip. She was tired of playing these games. She jumped back up and grasped the old man's collar, shaking him so his head lolled from one side to the other. "Sheffield, you slimy son of a steambagger, where are the shipping documents!"

"Christina!" Phillip ripped her off the bed and thrust her onto the floor.

Her head banged against the plush rug, and she struggled to see past Phillip to his father, to hear his answer.

Lord Sheffield fell back upon his pillows as spittle dribbled down his cheek. He pointed a shaking hand to the desk by the window. She rolled away from Phillip and yanked open the drawer. Nothing but a few pens and letters sat inside. She scooped the contents out and threw them on the floor. She roughed her hands around the inside, checking for a latch. A small gap in the back answered her searching fingers. She pulled the wood up and slid it out. At the bottom of the drawer sat a small leather satchel with several documents and a map tufting out. Finally.

"Got it," she said and tucked the papers into the left pocket of her coat. "Let's go."

Phillip stood next to his father's bed, his face a quarrelsome mix of ashen and anger. "You have crossed a line, Christina Ravensworth."

"It's Rushing, not Ravensworth. And we have a job to do, or did you forget?" Her defiance felt weak, like the last glowing coal in a dying fire.

"My father is not a job. He is a human being. Who is sick."

She had gone too far. Her brows sank along with her heart. "What exactly are you accusing me of?"

"Right now?" Phillip's voice carried threatening tones. "Being a monster."

"A monster? Is it monstrous to survive?"

"Is that what this is about? Survival?"

"Life is survival."

Phillip threw the rag at her feet. "Life is about family and relationships."

"Maybe for you." She crossed her arms and slid her thumbs to where her corset should be. "Some of us didn't have the luxury of growing up with living parents. Friends. All of this." She nodded her head around the room.

"You could." His face and words fell. "Let me give them to you."

"Not this again!" Christie threw her hands up between them. "I will never love you or anyone else. Got it?"

Phillip's smooth face crumpled into ugliness. "Then you are worse than the Baron."

Christie swallowed the bullet of his accusation. There was no way. She was nothing like the Baron. She was nothing like *him*.

Pain tore through her shoulder. Her heart burst. The accusation was too much. But then red. Blood. But not poppies this time.

She had been shot.

A man in black stood in the doorway, his gun still smoking.

Twenty-Three

CHRISTIE SANK TO THE floor, warmth oozing from the hole below her clavicle as chaos unfolded in the room. Phillip's father lay curled on his side, coughing. Phillip ran for the door. The assassin met his attack, and the two entangled.

Christie assessed the carnage seeping through her shirt.

Liveable.

The bullet went through her coat's front right pocket. With a grimace, she reached her fingers like tweezers down into the pocket and pulled out the small leather satchel with the documents inside. A singed hole tore through the corner. *Blood and pistons.* What if her information was ruined? She yanked her coat to a section without a gaping hole and pressed it over her wound, trying to keep the red off her hands. She had to keep it off her hands.

Across the room, Phillip still grappled with the dark assailant, but not well. He was going to get himself killed. And she was lucky she had not been. The smart move would be to jump out the window. Surely she had just enough strength to climb down the vine-covered trellis that covered the brick on this side of the house? But if she left, Phillip, and likely his father, would die.

It was a heavy price. But one she had to bear. She was so close to escaping this life and the shadows of her past.

She moved the papers to the bottom right pocket. They would be even more useless blood-soaked and illegible. Pushing off the ground with her right hand, she found her feet and opened the window. The brawl thudded against the wall, and Christie turned. The assassin landed a blow in Phillip's stomach. He doubled over.

With a yell, Phillip charged the man and grabbed for his gun. But her would-be-killer was too quick. And Phillip's death would be too, if she didn't act. She glanced longingly at the window and fought through pain to grab the Good Baron and Rudy from their thigh holsters under her dress. The assassin kicked Phillip and lifted his gun. She was too late.

Bang.

Bang.

Bang.

Phillip's knees hit the ground, and his hands splayed out on the rug. Their attacker sloughed against the wall. Heavy with a limp, he slowly rounded the corner to trudge out of sight. Red stains smeared the wall where his back had rested. She had fired three shots, and all had missed the assassin's heart. Of course. Even under the threat of death, she could not land a mortal shot.

She had only ever killed one man.

Phillip's pale face turned to look at her, sweat beading on the tip of his nose and the arch of his brows.

She opened her mouth to say something. But what?

A harsh wheeze rattled from the bed, and Phillip jumped up. Mid-dash toward his father, he stopped.

"Christina, are you—is your wound—" He reached toward her while his father rasped on the bed behind.

"I'm fine," she said, pushing his hand away.

"But you're bleeding . . ." He reached again, his storm-grey eyes beset upon by a furrowed brow.

"I said I'm fine," she snapped. "Go tend to your father. He's what you really care about."

Christie angled her chin and pushed her way out of the door. She took to the hall to chase down the man she had just shot. The man who had tried to kill her. Crimson drops led down the stairs like breadcrumbs of death. To death. Alfred lay curled in a ball at the foot of the stairs. Dead? She paused only to nip at him with the toe of her boot. His hands tightened over his head. Alive. He'd be fine, the coward.

The front door swayed with the breeze. She struggled to lift the dirty hem of her dress and pocket Rudy. If she had to shoot long distance, she would need both hands to steady the Good Baron. Especially with her left arm weak and bleeding. She stepped onto the porch with two long strides.

The assassin sprinted clumsily across the green lawn. Christie swallowed hard and wiped the red of her hands on her dress, more dark stains on the wool and her soul. She rubbed and rubbed, the black silhouette of the assassin growing smaller in the distance. Her hands trembled as they flipped over and over. And over and over. There was so much red. So much blood. But the man was getting away. She pulled her shaking hand back on track. This was no time to fall prey to the past. Balancing the barrel of her gun on her forearm, she took aim. His back was in her crosshairs. A final shot would lay him low. Her finger twitched on the trigger.

Bang.

She smashed the butt of her gun against the door frame.

She couldn't do it.

All the talk of monsters, the shadows at the manor, her guilt. What had she become? Surely not the Baron? He would have shot the man, then stepped on his throat until he confessed who he was working for. She had chosen not to do that. So she was not the same.

But each step in her reasoning spooned out a piece of her soul. The logic of her defense, the need to be right, her harassment of a dying man. The nightmares, not of what she had done, but of who that made her.

She was just like the Baron.

After an excruciatingly slow and painful walk home and an agonizing trip upstairs to put on her corset, Christie shuffled into the library. She would have preferred the passageway through the grave, but with her shoulder still weeping, the library entrance would be easier. She kicked the carpet away and sat for a moment in the rolling chair to catch some air. Every breath sent jolts of pain across her chest and back. The iron scent of blood made her woozy.

She tried not to think about the sticky mess she would have to clean off her corset. And coat. And hair. She would never be clean. Both her hands were steeped in blood. Her own, this time. She was the poppies. She was the perpetrator. She was the victim. And she would never be clean.

The ink bottle on the corner of the desk mocked her. Were her insides as dark as that?

Apparently.

She leaned over and thwacked the glass onto the floor. The lid popped off and the inky black seeped into the carpet. Not a new stain, just darkening the one that was already there.

The effort aggravated her wound and red trickled anew. She needed something better than leather to stop the bleeding, to hide it from her sight. After a moment of painful hesitation, she ripped open the top drawer. Then the next, and the next, until all five drawers revealed their contents. She grabbed a handkerchief from the center one. Folding it thrice, she braced herself and mashed it into her wound.

Christie breathed through her teeth, refusing to concede to the pain. She ran her free hand toward the backs of the drawers. Where was the brandy the Baron drank? She needed something to clean her wound, and it was better than nothing. Her hands met a thick notebook.

The Baron's scheduler.

She thumped it on the desk, turning to the inky pages to drown out the pain, to bury it and the poppy red that marked its place on her soul. If there was one thing she had learned from the Baron, it was how to ignore pain, how to put it off to deal with later. Though if things went her way, later would never come.

The book landed open on a page from a few weeks before the day she had joined this life of darkness. She flipped ahead, driven to find out if any of his meetings had foretold her doom. Nothing unusual. A lawyer. A pub. A tailor. A strange mix of both caring and not caring about what society thought. Then, blotted in hastily the morning of their wedding: Charles Blackwell.

A scarlet drop blighted the bottom of the page. The kerchief had seeped through. She smeared her soul's paint across the page with her thumb, rubbing the color into Charlie's name over and over and over. Had he tried to save her and failed? Or had he come to mock her pain?

She clawed at the page, ripping it from the binding and crumpling it up in her left hand. Her weary fingers squeezed the dry paper. She was done thinking about the day her life ended. Isn't that how she had started down this path in the first place? She grimaced and shoved the wrinkled paper into her right pocket.

She should go down now.

But morbid curiosity pushed her back to the scheduler. To her obsession. She *was* obsessed. Just like him. She was no better. Maybe worse. After all, she had never seen the Baron kill a man.

She turned the book page by page to get to the end. Training. Dinners. Meetings with no names. Then his final week. His final day. Inked in the final time slot, just after lunch in town.

Tea.

"You are not suited for a desk." Charlie startled her from just inside the French doors. "Though much less intimidating. I'm more worried about getting my knickers switched with a willow branch than being shot."

Christie slammed the scheduler shut, and the thud echoed the pounding in her heart. Why had Charlie come?

With a twinge of pain, she unholstered the Good Baron and chunked it onto the desk. "How about now?"

"Better." He grinned. "You know, I was going to give up on you. But playing the chase is much more fun."

"Then why don't you chase me down something for this?" She flapped open her coat.

Charlie's slack jaw tightened up. "You got yourself shot?"

"What do you think?"

"Stay put," he said and dashed out of the room.

She groaned and shook her head. What did he expect her to do? Take a leisurely stroll through the garden?

He rushed back into the room, his arms full of towels. "I sent Ana for water and something to sanitize your wounds."

"Are you sure she won't try to drain my blood instead?" Christie tried to smother her pain with sarcasm. But the bite of her tongue was not hard enough, and she still had to blink the sparkling dots from her eyes.

"Har har." Charlie stepped behind her and grabbed the collar of her coat. "Ready ol' girl?"

Christie braced her knees on the inside panels of the desk. "Just do it."

Agony twisted through her nerves, up into her brain, and everywhere else. But the coat came off. She looked away from the poppy red as Charlie chucked it to the side.

Ana clunked into the room with hot water, a crystal decanter of the brandy Christie had searched for, a small bag of doctoring supplies the Baron had used on her before, and mothy-smelling tea. It set the platter on the desk and took up residence in the corner of the room.

"Now the fun part," Charlie said, digging out a pair of silver scissors from the bag.

The light from the windows glinted off the blades. She shuddered and turned her head away. This would not be like all those other times the Baron had stitched up the wounds he himself had inflicted. Charlie was not the Baron.

She was.

He slid his fingers into the handles and snip-snapped them twice in the air before placing the bottom of the scissors under the shoulder of her sleeve. The cold metal sent shivers down her back and offered a small reprieve to the heat building in her chest. He set to work opening and closing the blades along the top seam. The *thwick* of cutting fabric marched along, perpendicular to her neck.

"Final snip. You ready?"

Christie nodded. "Just peel the fabric off the wound slowly."

He made the final cut, and the back corner of her shirt fell away. Charlie held up the front. A mocking grin tugged at his lips, and Christie blushed. At least she had her corset on to cover herself somewhat. But what could be done? She'd rather bleed to death than go to a hospital. The closest one was kilometers away and full of people who would ask questions she had no intention of answering. And Phillip was too busy tending to his father.

Snideness engulfed her thoughts. Why did she care what Phillip did? And why would he be any better than Charlie? He would not.

Charlie teased the fabric off her clavicle. The stick of dry blood tugged at her skin.

"This is not how I pictured undressing you for the first time," he said.

His playful smirk fell as he pulled the shirt from her wound. The mottled hue of her skin showed purple and black, and bits of white fabric tufted out of the ragged hole.

Christie stared at the dark stain on the floor as Charlie poured the burning brandy over her wound. A cleansing pang emanated from her mouth in an abrupt exhale, and the sharp smell of alcohol watered in her eyes.

He offered her the decanter, but she refused. With a potential international war on the horizon and an assassin out to kill her, she needed all her senses about her. Especially since coming home had made them rusty. Weak.

Maybe the Baron had been right all along. She was not fit to survive. Not if she kept failing.

The fabric finally released its hold on her skin in a rush of both pain and relief. Charlie pulled out a set of tweezers. He eyed the wound from several different angles. His hand stretched forward slowly, then pulled back.

"Just do it," she said. "I can take it." Anything was better than leaving the hole open to bleed red. Through the bite of pain, she had managed to keep her desire to scrub at bay, but the drip of her soul could not be stifled by willpower alone. She needed Charlie's help this time.

The sharp ends of the tweezers dug into her flesh, and a cry barrelled its way through her clenched jaw. Charlie yanked his hand back, dropping the tweezers on the floor.

"You said you could handle it."

Christie's teeth ground against each other. "I can. Just talk to me about something."

Charlie picked the tweezers back up and pulled a set of matches from his pocket. He scratched one into life, a tiny flame eating away the dark tip of the wood, turning death into light.

"Did you get what you needed from Lord Sheffield?" he asked. His steady hand pulled the metal back and forth over the flame. After a few passes, he shook the light out.

"Barely. It's in my pocket." She twisted her torso like the barrel of a gun in the final seconds of a close-quarters fight. Her boot hooked under her coat lying on the floor, and she dragged it back to where she could reach it. Before she could snag it, Charlie pinched it up.

"Why don't you ever ask for help? You're bleeding all over the desk and yet insist on bending over to stain the rug, too." He handed her the tweezers and dug around in the coat pockets. Out came the map and documents from Sheffield's desk. And out came the crumpled bit of scheduler.

"Eh? What's this?"

"Trash." Christie kept her gaze steady, but the muscles in her hands clenched into a fist. What excuse could he possibly have for coming to visit the Baron on her wedding day and leaving without her?

He plopped the stack of papers on the desk and uncrumpled the scheduler. His eyes scanned the page. His mouth twisted at the ends. And he threw it in the wastebasket on the side of the desk.

Without a word, he plucked the tweezers from her hand and set to work. The mini knives bit her skin, but her worry over Charlie was worse. So much worse.

For once, she didn't know what he was thinking. And for the first time in a long while, she cared to.

Twenty-Four

T HE SUN ROSE THROUGH navy waters, the horizon a bland mix of pink and purple. Christie cast her gaze down the side of the ship, entranced by the churning gears speckling the side. When activated, they swirled in the pattern of flying gulls. The frontmost and largest gear carried wings that dipped and lifted in time with the steam puffs churning from the ship above, and brass-tipped wings shimmered in the growing light. The *Ol' Bird*. It was the perfect name.

Christie writhed under the bandages that wrapped her shoulder like a secondary corset. Charlie had tied them so snugly, she could barely move her left arm. All in silence. She scowled at his newfound ability to mask his emotions and shifted her focus to preparation. Poor Rudy would be out of commission for a while with her arm the way it was, which would be a problem since they were on their way to attack a smuggling vessel full of weapons.

Phillip had returned late the day before, his face ashen and his manners terse. With neither man talking to her about anything but business, planning went quickly. They would head to the coordinates they had gleaned from Mr. Blackwell's documentation. Once they stole the stolen goods being stolen again by Oceana's government, they would make their way to the coordinates found in Lord Sheffield's papers. The same coordinates Thorton had had her change in Oceana. The coordinates masked by her family name. All one and the same.

They had chosen the location in Britannian waters and were headed towards the potential center of a war. Though, all in all, her day could be going worse. She could be reliving the day before.

Getting shot.

Realizing she was the embodiment of her own worst nightmare.

Crushing the feelings of a friend who had tried to help. Or two friends who had tried to help.

But today was a new day, and more than anything she yearned to shoot something. To get back in the field. To be useful and independent again.

Footsteps stole through the breeze behind her. "Be on the lookout," Phillip's voice clipped. "After Charlie's joyride emptying out the cargo hold this morning, we are running late. It's possible we have already missed the exchange, and the ships with their deadly verdicts are heading off into the sunrise."

Christie nodded as strands of hair danced across her face. She kept reaching up to adjust her aigrette, failing, and wanting to punch something instead. The hum of the motor and the spraying snaps of steam billowing out behind them made it hard to hear Phillip. But his main point came across: if things failed to go right, they would pay with their lives. And that was true more than he knew. More than Charlie could know. She had the *Robin* stocked on the ship for a reason: her escape with a trunk full of secrets.

She had nothing concrete yet, just documents with coordinates, and her own incriminating job she'd done for Thorton, but in the collie shangles ahead, she planned to find some evidence and flee. It was her last ticket out of society and the mess of emotions and betrayals that came with it. Her last chance to leave before she would miss more than her aigrette every day.

Phillip stood statuesque behind her. Charlie steered in the captain's box on the upper deck. She should say something. Apologize for the way she had treated his father. Explain herself, if she even could. But what was there to say that she wouldn't obliterate by leaving? Still, the very tug of humanity she was trying to escape pulled at her.

She turned.

"No need to say it." Phillip stared straight ahead.

"What?"

"You were about to make a fool of yourself by expressing shells of emotion. Don't bother."

The desire to make amends smoldered into ash. "How do you know I wasn't turning to demand an apology out of you?"

The trace of Phillip's lips slipped downward. "I suppose I do owe you one, for offering you something you so completely loathe." He twisted his face into a grimace. "A life free of worry, of loneliness, of well, whatever shady things you do. I'm sorry I wasted your time."

Christie chewed on the inside of her cheek. His bitter tone and wounded eyes burned like alcohol on a wound. She was sick of his podsnappery, of his pretending to care. He barely knew her. No, he in no way knew her. If he had, he wouldn't have offered his condescending charity.

"You offered a life bound to the dictates of society," she muttered. "To you. No thank you. And by the way, the Good Baron and Rudy don't usually work for free. So you're welcome for me saving your life."

"You've always been selfish."

The wind slapped his words against her cheeks. "I was just trying to do a job. It's not like I did any lasting damage. Your father is fine."

"My father is dead!"

Her hair whipped and the breeze howled and the steam of the *Ol' Bird* chugged faster than her slowing heart.

"Phillip, I'm—I'm so sorry. I didn't know."

"You didn't know you killed him? Or you didn't know how selfish you are? How could he survive what happened yesterday?"

Her sympathy grew pointy edges. "It's not like *I* shot your father."

Phillip barked out a laugh. "That gun-wielding maniac was there because Thorton wants you dead. How is that not your fault?"

"Me? You're a loony. The assassin was most likely a hire from Oceana because *you* blew up their ammunition stores."

Phillip's hair slipped, shading his eyes as he shook his head. "That was Charles' idea."

"Oh yeah?" Christie smirked and loathed herself for it. "Then who lit the match?"

The planking below Christie's feet shifted right, knocking her into the railing. The air rushed from her lungs, and she struggled to breathe, to make sense of what Phillip had said. She was not responsible for that death. She could not be. It was not her hands holding the gun. Covered in blood. The red of poppies. It was her blood spilled on the rug, not his.

The ship shifted again, and she slunk to her knees. Oxygen filled her lungs, and she looked to the captain's box where Charlie waved frantically and pointed to the horizon.

"They're here." Phillip directed her attention to two dark blips bobbing where the sun met the sea.

The trade had started. But where was the third ship to catch them in the act? Christie plucked her binoculars out from her belt. The nearer vessel released steady two-off puffs of steam in the pattern of a Blackwell and Co. trading vessel. The other, an uninterrupted stream of an unaffiliated airship. She scanned the horizon.

There. Due west. A heavily armored airship reflected polished steel and needed no steam to identify it, though its heavy belches of thick plumes added to its bellicose stature.

She signaled to Charlie, and their airship dipped down in descent. The *Ol' Bird* would be harder to maneuver in the water if the attack moved eastward, but it would also allow all three of them to ride the *Robin* to the trade and refuel their water stores. Charlie had made it feistily clear he would not be left behind to babysit.

"Come on, Phillip." She ruffled off the poison of his earlier words. "Time to get our boots dirty."

Phillip turned against the breeze. "Oh, you're not coming with us."

Christie stopped mid-step. "Oh, yes I am."

"No." He shrugged. "At least, not in the *Robin*. Charlie and I had a chat. You're going in the depths where you belong."

Christie swallowed. Did he mean?

"You're going in the *Fish*."

Christie sat on the lip of the steamarine in the release room. There was enough space to fit two watercraft with a walkway down the middle to the control panel. A large, rubber-lined hatch would open below the *Fish*, plummeting her into the murky depths of the ocean's dark. Christie hit her fist on the metal, and cold zinged to the tips of her fingers.

Those ack ruffians, relegating her to this dreary beast. And without consulting her first. If this was because Phillip thought she was a—that she had—She turned her head and spat.

"I don't recollect the *Fish* doing anything to offend you." Charlie appeared in the doorway to the release room.

Christie's spine prickled. "No, you did. Come to gloat?"

Charlie stroked his chin. "Is there something to gloat over?"

"How about shoving me into this metal coffin and sending me out to sea like some waterlogged sailor?"

She waited for Charlie's snide retort about how she was a fish out of water and bubbling mad.

Instead, he walked over and leaned his elbows against the steamarine. His sandy hair sifted back and the ocean stared up at her. "I figured you wouldn't be too happy. You seemed quite free in the air. But the *Fish* is the easier machine to run. The trading vessels have already landed in the water and completed the trade. Oceana's making its descent now. We can steal more cargo with you in the *Fish* helping out. That way, we can use the *Robin* to distract them from the air while you go in the backdoor."

Christie blinked through his logic. Just because it made sense didn't mean she had to be happy about it.

"You've proven to be much better at all this spy stuff than me and Phillip. We'd make a bungling mess if we tried to sneak through."

His flattery tipped her into his emotional tide, and she fought to swim back to reality. "I thought you were mad at me."

Charlie's lips puckered into his thinking face. "Not mad. Hurt."

The weight of Phillip's conversation already hung like a noose around her neck, and here Charlie was helping her bind the cords of another. She struggled to stay afloat in the darkness.

"Because I crumpled up your name?" It was a dumb thing to say. But her blood pounded harder and harder in her ears. She couldn't think straight.

"Because you called my attempt to come for you trash."

Christie dropped her gaze into the pitchy hole of the *Fish*. Had he really come for her?

"I'm sorry," she whispered the words for the second time that day.

"It's okay. I understand." Charlie's lips smoothed into a flat line. "My attempt *was* trash. I came for you and left without you. The whole 'the thought counts' idea is rubbish."

She teetered on the edge of pain and morbid curiosity. The words escaped her mouth unbidden. "What happened?"

He leaned his forehead against the *Fish*. "I wasn't strong enough. He threatened—I don't know—everything, everyone. My dad, the business, my future aspirations. None of it mattered. Until he threatened you."

Charlie's sandy hair dusted his eyes and hid them from her. What would she see in them right now? What would he see in hers?

"He said if I made things hard for him, he would make you suffer." Charlie let out an uncomfortable laugh. "But he did that anyway."

"He did."

But just because she had lived in darkness, did not mean he had to. She bore enough guilt and hatred from the life she had left to cover both of them.

Christie nudged his head with her foot so he would look up at her. "It's not your fault. You could not have known he was a monster." And in that moment, the burden of her anger toward him lifted. He did not know. So why had she blamed him all these years?

"But I should have when he said those words. I wanted to give you the world, Christina." He took hold of her boot and laid his head on the laces. "You deserve the world."

Christie's chest twisted and bloomed. Her mother used to say the same thing to her. And the ebb and flow of her emotional dam, bursting forth for the first time since she could remember, was too much. She shivered. "Who are you and what've you done with the real Charlie?" She grasped for a way to lighten the mood. "And why are you being so nice to me?"

"Why are you being so hard on yourself?" The cresting waves of his ocean eyes became endless pools with the dip of his brows.

Christie wanted to break through the waves of his gaze. Even darkness inside the *Fish* seemed safer than what she might slip up and say next. Should she tell him what she had done before she'd left? So he would not come after her? So she could spare him a life bound to a—

"I've got something for you." Charlie stood straight and slapped one of the *Fish*'s copper eyes. "After all, you mean the world to me. And we can't know what will happen next." He slid his hand into his pocket. "I've missed past opportunities to do this, and I think it's time."

His eyes held hers as he knelt on the ground.

Christie sat stock-still. Should she slide inside the steamarine and lock herself in? He could not be serious. Heat drained from her cheeks and pooled in her chest.

"Christina Rushing," he said in a solemn voice, "you dropped this." He tugged his hand free, and brass caught the light.

"My aigrette!" Christie slid down the side and landed in a heap.

She snatched the feathers from his hand and squeezed the tines into her skin. How had he found this? Who cared? She flung her arms around Charlie. He caught her tight and slipped his arms around her waist. With an intoxicating inhale, she breathed him in and savored the juniper and cedar, the nutmeg and spice. He smelled the same as he had when they were kids. Back when they were whole.

"I know how much it means to you," his voice vibrated deep within his chest. "I found it in the *Robin* when I loaded her up." He stroked her head, each finger slipping through her tendrils to her scalp.

She closed her eyes as his fingertips sent tingles down her neck. So what if they had broken apart? Charlie had just restored a piece of her soul and stitched a bond between them. Maybe she could stay? Abandon her plans to leave and make this work?

Charlie's arms stayed snug around her. She leaned into his chest, soaking up the first ray of warmth she could remember since her parents died.

Died. Death. Cold. Cold-blooded. He could never want her after he learned the truth.

Her arms collapsed to her side, and she tucked her head down as she pulled away. Charlie caught her arm, plucking the aigrette from her hand. He tilted her chin back and pulled the hair from her face.

Christie bit back a memory, and another toppled over in its place. "You used to fix my aigrette all the time as kids. Remember?"

"Mmm. It wasn't so deadly back then. One wrong move and I'm afraid I'd poison myself."

Poison. She swallowed hard. If he only knew. And yet, a smile ghosted across her lips. "I promise I won't kick you this time if you do."

Charlie grinned. "I'd like that very much." He finished with her hair and kissed her forehead. "All done."

Phillip burst through the door and into the release room. "What are you two doing? Oceana has already started boarding Blackwell's ship. If we don't hurry, the cargo will be in the sky, and we won't stand a chance."

Charlie rolled his arms into a bow and topped it off with a wink. "Duty calls." He marched out of the room.

Christie reached for the cool metal of the *Fish* as she watched Charlie go. His warmth lingered on her skin. In her heart. Blanketing her mind. Maybe he would still want her. The only way she could know was by staying to find out. Or asking him to leave with her. Either way, that all depended on her surviving the skirmish ahead. And she had every intention of doing just that so she could come back home.

TWENTY-FIVE

THE LIGHT OF THE sun filtered through the salty water, giving Christie little direction. But a little direction was all she needed. The giant keel of Oceana's warship parted the water like a heat bubble. She propelled the *Fish* as fast as it would go to get out of the murky foam. Alone again, and in the dark, the corner under the Baron's desk reached its tendril-like grasp for her. She needed to break away from the fathoms of sea crashing in on her. Back to the surface. Back to the light.

It would have been better to steal the cargo on Blackwell and Co.'s trading ship, but they were behind because... she had gotten distracted. A smile teased the corner of her lips, alleviating some of the dark.

The whirl of bubbling water churned behind her, and she directed her steam plume east so the *Fish* shot west. She dipped under the warship's keel and popped up on the opposite side. Charlie and Phillip should be drawing attention to the skies back the way she had come. She eased the *Fish* up and extended her scope. The misty spray of lapping water made it hard to discern anything. She scanned the deck and bow. One guard stood by the entrance to the inflation chambers for the balloon. She honed in on the man. Tall, burly, with a red commander's stripe down the front of his coat.

She pulled her eyes away and rubbed them before taking another look. Maybe her job would be easier than she'd supposed. She located the ladder up this side of the ship and took aim.

Christie propelled the *Fish* over to the metal plating of the hull. She shifted the *Fish* upwards, cresting over the frothy waves. With a pull of the longest lever, which Charlie had instructed her to use, the mechanics in the engine clinked and clanged. An arm extended out the side. With a jarring hum, the magnet on the end charged and connected the steamarine to the warship's iron frame like a pilot fish. Time to suck off their parasitic cargo and take it for herself.

Christie unsealed the rubber on the hatch and emerged into wet air. She slid her feet over each rung of the ladder so the metal bars caught the dip between her heel and the ball of her foot and heaved herself up. Her shoulder burned and ached, complaining with every exertion of muscle.

When she had reached the top, she puffed and rested her head on the final metal bar. The slippery rungs teased her hand's grasp. She hooked her left arm under with a groan. With her free hand, she flipped the lapel of her coat. Her wound had seeped through Charlie's bandages, all his work covered in her trauma. In her red. Her hands crushed the leather as darkness clouded the edges of her vision. She flapped her coat back over. No time to think about that now.

Her left elbow still hooked, Christina pulled out her binoculars and peeked over the side. The deck stood empty. She shifted the lenses up to the guard post. Empty too. That couldn't be good.

Her view darkened into the grey-blue of military pants as a soldier walked by, and she slipped back. Her elbow caught her fall, and the skin around her wound tore. She bit back a cry as her binoculars tumbled from her grasp, splooshing in the waves below. She gasped and struggled to find her footing. Her right hand grabbed the ladder, and she pulled herself close to the ship.

When the tumbling sky steadied in her sights, she assessed her situation: caught with a wounded shoulder on the ladder of a giant ship that could take flight at any moment. The situation was all over red. A bungling disaster. Pain seeped out of the bullet hole and weeped into her nerves. She fought white sparks from her vision and let the cool metal of the ship sooth the heat burning from her shoulder.

Oceana's ship buzzed to life, its belly groaning and creaking. They must be preparing to lift off again. If she didn't hurry, her chance would be lost. After another moment of listening, she popped her head over the side. The soldier was gone. She steeled herself against the agony and hefted herself over the side. The ledge to the deck was steeper than she had anticipated, and she tumbled onto the metal sheeting. She jumped back onto her feet and hurried toward the closest door in a crouched run. She pulled herself straight into the doorway, listening.

Shouts rang out from the other side of the ship. Charlie must be making a pass, low along the deck on the other side. She imagined soldiers jumping out of the way and Charlie laughing. She risked a peek upward. The *Robin* crested over the top of the ship and followed the spires up to the captain's box. It arched over the top, between the box and the bottom of the navy helium balloon, swollen with hot air, much like Charlie. As the *Robin* dropped into the curve on the downside, Phillip fell from the passenger seat.

She cried out before clamping her mouth shut. She stepped from her doorway. There was no way Phillip could survive a fall from this height. But he didn't fall all the way to the deck. He caught the edge of the captain's box, his long frame dangling like a string on the tail end of a kite. She held her breath. Phillip grappled his way back over the side. He made it. She exhaled. He had completely bypassed the guards and now had control of the ship.

"That was clever. Genius even."

"I know," Christie shook her head. "That is, if it was intentional. Which I have a mind to doubt."

Christie froze.

Austen's hulking frame marched into view. His bald head caught the light of the sun, and his glare channeled it into fire.

"You didn't notice me behind you, did you?" he asked. Was he amused or angry?

She stiffened. "I noticed you, why else would I chat with you in such a cavalier manner."

Austen's lips stayed flat. "Because you're careless and distracted. How did you become our best spy again?"

Christie's indignation burned hot before petering out. People kept questioning her skills. It's not like any of them were professional spies.

What gave them the qualifications to judge her? Her mouth twisted. Though to be fair, she had done a wretched job as of late.

"It's good to see you again, Commander. I'd love to stay and shoot the breeze, but I have things to do." She grabbed the doorknob and pulled, dashing inside just as Austen reached for her.

She pelted down the stairs, following the curves and twists of the landings. It was no use. She did not know where she was going, and door after locked door, her route led her to a cage: a small room as deep as the stairs would go, the door barred in front of her.

Austen stomped down the stairs behind her. "Please don't run from me, Rushing. Don't make this harder for both of us."

Christie turned and pushed her back against the door. "Make what harder? I haven't done anything."

Austen's face puckered. "We both know you left off the 'yet'. If you come quietly, everything will go better for you."

Sweat trickled from her hairline and down her neck. "Austen, you deserve better than working for a two-timing captain. He's the one double-crossing Oceana's best interests."

Austen's forehead wrinkles stacked on top of each other, each massive ripple a ledge for sweat to drip off. "What are you talking about?"

"The weapons you just confiscated, they're going to be used for war."

"Most weapons are, Rushing." His forehead made way for a cocked brow. "We confiscate black market goods all the time, and yes, sometimes we reallocate them to our own resources. There's no double-crossing in that."

"No. They're a foil," Christie said. "Thorton paid me to change Oceana's logs. You're headed to Britannia waters with a cargo hold full of weapons. Weapons they will see as intent to start a war. He and Barnes are working together. Barnes must have wanted to cover his tracks, that's why they had me come in and change the coordinates for your next destination."

The words were enough logic to help her argument, but something in them still refused to make sense. If Barnes knew why she was there, why hadn't he left her alone in the command room? Or had he done that by rushing out and not looking back?

Austen crossed his arms and bore his stare into hers.

She swallowed and held his gaze.

"Are you sure?"

She nodded.

"No," his frown deepened and his hand shot out.

She flinched.

But his hand landed on the doorknob beside her waist. She eased to the side, and he unlocked the door.

"Come, we are going to clear this whole mess up right now."

Christie's eyes wandered to the stairs. Could she survive a meeting with Barnes on his own ship in the middle of the ocean? Should she make a run for it and just leave the cargo behind? She didn't need it for her future anymore. Maybe she and Charlie could find a place to hide away from the upcoming war.

No.

She blinked the thought away and followed Austen. If Charlie was going to accept her despite—she exhaled—her past, then she needed to be able to show him she was trying to be better. She needed to see this through.

Austen led her through a dimly lit room with a wiry cage for the floor. Through the next door lay what she had come for. The hull opened up like the inside of a giant egg, the walls glowing luminescent with metal coiling and tubes, veins to give life to what grew inside. And in the center: crates and crates of weapons. Barnes and his soldiers were inspecting the haul.

Christie kept pace behind Austen, hiding in his broad shadow as he marched into the room. He stopped in an oval of mustard light, his shadow casting tall along the mesh flooring. She peeked around his bulging arm.

Barnes turned at the interruption and waved for his men to stop their digging. "What is the meaning of this? Commander Austen, why are you not at your post?"

"Sorry for the interruption, sir." Austen saluted. "There has been a complication. One of the men on the flying contraption has landed on the boat."

Barnes' face purpled, and his teeth chomped together. "Then why are you down here? Go fix it."

Austen shifted from foot to foot, and Christie ducked her head back behind him. "Yessir, of course sir. But—" Austen hesitated. "I thought you should know you have a visitor spreading rumors that—" His shoulders tightened. "That you're betraying the welfare of Oceana for personal gain."

Cries of outrage from Barnes' men erupted on all sides. Why had she rushed down here so quickly? She should have known Barnes would be reveling in his haul. She had walked right into a rat's nest.

"How dare you?" Barnes' challenge bounded off the metal in the room. "Show my accuser and stand aside so I can rip out their gutless spine."

Austen remained, and Christie's chest flooded with relief. Too soon. Her shield stepped left, and she stood barren under the oval lamp.

Barnes' nostrils flared in accent to his widening eyes. "You." The words shot spit across the grating despite his clenched teeth. "Arrest her at once."

Several men weaved through the crates toward her. Should she grab the Good Baron? Or would that make things worse?

Austen stepped forward. "Sir, I cannot in good conscience let you take her until you assure me her allegations are false. To allow you to be in sole command of your own accuser goes against the laws of Oceana."

One of the men moving to surround her hesitated. Murmurs ebbed and flowed around the crates. Maybe she would have a chance after all.

"Get out of my way." Barnes lowered his voice.

"So you deny it?" Christie stepped out from behind Austen once more. If she were going to get out of there alive, she had to level Barnes. And that meant she had to stop hiding behind her muscle-clad shield.

Barnes sneered. "What exactly am I supposed to be denying? You have yet to make any concrete accusation." He waved at his men. "Arrest her before I hold you in contempt."

Some men shuffled forward, guns drawn. Others, yet, hung back.

Austen's deep voice interrupted the uncertainty. "Address her claims once and for all so we can secure our ship. There may be an intruder on board, but if there's a snake at the head of Oceana's helm, we can never be safe."

Christie took strength from Austen's words. He believed her. And he was defending her. For the second time that day, she wanted to build a friendship. To trust in someone as they trusted in her. Her decision to stay grew from a flicker into a blaze. She had made the right choice. She could create a new home, a new life, with people who would not hurt her.

She leveled her eyes on Barnes. "You arranged for the weapons deal between the black market ship and Thorton and Blackwell, Co., didn't you?" Her voice rang clear and repeated itself in softening echoes throughout the steel-clad hull.

"False." He said before jabbing his finger in her direction. "Now arrest her."

Again feet hustled forward, closer and closer. And in the crowd of soldiers, one limped with a familiar gate, his shoulder bandaged just like hers. So Barnes had hired the assassin after all. Her blood boiled. She thrust her hand in her coat, and through the pain in her shoulder, wrenched out Charlie's shipping schedule.

"Stay back." She challenged the soldiers. "I have proof." They paused and looked between her, Austen, and Barnes. "On Thorton and Blackwell's shipping documents, under the code name of Lord Rushing, Earl of Avendel." Her family's name stuck to her tongue like cotton gauze. She pushed through. "You are listed as the payer of the aforementioned treasonous expedition."

She thrust the documents at Austen who held them up for the soldiers. Doubt swelled into cries of outrage.

Barnes' red face sallowed. "Forgeries. All of them. She's a low-life. A spy. A wench for hire! Arrest her."

"Lies." She balled her hands into fists. He would pay for calling her a wench. She had not yet even reached the climax of her accusations: international war. "There's more. Barnes arranged—"

"Enough." Austen held his hand out. "We have more than enough to arrest him for now. Our ship is still under attack. And presumably by one of your men." He looked down at her.

"Who, Phillip? You have nothing to worry about. We're just here to make sure that the weapons—"

"I will not be reassured by your words."

Her face stung. What had happened to trusting her?

"Commander Austen, there are steps that we need to take immediately. You must stop this ship from heading to its next destination."

"No." The muscles in his face turned to rock. "We must arrest Captain Barnes for his crimes." He turned his attention from her to the soldiers in the room. "I was second-in-command of this ship and the army of Oceana. I am now first. Arrest him." He pointed at Barnes.

Barnes cried out, kicking at the men who ventured too close. "How dare you mutiny. This is treason!"

A soldier grabbed his arm, but he whipped it free and grabbed his gun. He leveled it. Not at the soldier.

The black barrel stared directly at her.

She crossed her hands in front of her chest.

Bang.

She waited for the pain. The searing of ligaments and the agony of muscle being split in twain. Instead, the grating below her feet tremored with the weight of a fallen comrade.

Austen had taken her bullet. Blood oozed between his fingers as he cupped his shoulder. A matching wound to her own. She should not have been so hard on him for doing his duty. Only a friend would risk death for another.

She rushed to Austen's side as men swarmed Barnes and wrestled him to the ground.

"Austen, your shoulder. Are you okay?"

"I'll be fine." His baritone had a touch of hardness. "Stand back and let me be."

Christie made room, and Austen hefted himself back onto his feet. "Take him to the brig," he repeated his first order as captain. "And if he wags his silver tongue, cut it off."

Three soldiers dragged a kicking and screaming Barnes from the room.

Austen faced the rest of the men. "Grab the cargo. Haul it up deck. I don't know who I can trust after our ex-captain's betrayal. I want the crates where I can see them at all times. And get this ship into the air. No more delays. We have priorities to maintain." Austen turned his back and headed toward the door.

On deck? In the air? That was worse. So much worse. There would barely need to be an inspection at all. She needed to get Austen to turn the ships around before it was too late. She shoved her way through busy soldiers and tugged on Austen's sleeve.

"What is it?" he asked. His brows morphed once again into lumpy hills. He pushed her to the side of the door so the soldiers could pass through with their crates.

"As I said before—" She paused as more soldiers bumped by. "You need to skip the next set of coordinates. It's a trap."

"A trap?"

"Yes." She nodded, ducking her head sideways between passing men. "For war. There's an elaborate scheme Barnes set up involving the cargo and new islands."

Austen's eyebrows shot up. "You know of new islands?"

She threw a hand in the air as the last two soldiers and their crate passed through. "Yes. That's what I've been trying to say this whole time. Things are so much worse than they seem."

"That is clearly the case." His thick fingers thrummed his chin. "There is much to do and little time." He stepped through the doorway.

Christie followed, but his hand reached out to stop her.

"Commander?"

"It's captain now. And I'm sorry. You are still a spy on a vessel that is under attack by your command. You must stay in here until I can sort everything out."

"No way. I just saved Oceana from war! I caught a dirty captain. You should be thanking me." She pushed her way through the door, but Austen caught her coat and yanked her back with a tug.

"I cannot allow it. Now, stay here, or I'll put you in the brig with Barnes."

"I can take him." Her spit was as thick as her bravado as it seeped down her throat.

Austen left and shut the door behind him. The oval lights flickered with a buzz and winked out.

She was left in the dark, once again.

TWENTY-SIX

W HILE TIME TICKED EVER-ONWARD, the dark ate its passing and engulfed Christie in forever.

Forever alone.

Forever in black.

Dark was the absence of light, but it was also the absence of hope, and the corner back at the Baron's manor had found its way there, into the hard-metal casing of an empty hull.

She should explore, search for a way out. But how could she with the inky depths lurking in wait to take her soul? She fought to take back the light, the peace of her newfound healing, but the weight of ebony and shadow pulled at the frayed edges of her subconscious.

The door wrenched open and Christie jumped from where she sat, pulling back onto her knees. A pair of soldiers shoved elbows and knees into the room before slamming the door shut once more.

An "ooph" emanated from somewhere next to her, and she caught a whiff of barn-housed hay.

"Phillip?"

He grunted in reply.

"What happened? I saw you take the captain's box."

"Clearly, I was outnumbered in this foolish plan."

Christie let silence sit between them.

She shifted off her knees to keep them from going numb. "So what do we do now?"

"Isn't that your job to figure out? You're the spy after all. You're used to treasonous nonsense like this."

She frowned into the black. "Well you're the one who's all about plans, right? So plan something."

Feet shuffled toward the door. Dim light filtering through the door's creases outlined Phillip's lanky silhouette. He leaned his head against the metal before feeling his way closer to her. She reached for him and found the starchy folds of his pants. He kneeled in front of her. The lines of his face left dark hollows over his eyes, like a fleshless skull. She could feel his breath on her cheek.

"I do have a plan. It's already in play. We just need to survive it."

That didn't sound good. "What do you mean 'survive it'? What did you do?"

He leaned closer, so the moisture of his breath dampened her ear. "I set a timer for the hull's release. All the weapons will be sucked out."

"And us with it!" She pulled her head away. "We need to stop this. Austen will let us out in due time. He owes us. We will be fine."

Phillip's hand jutted into the dark and grabbed the collar under her mass of curls. He pulled her back close to him. "Your Austen kicked me down the stairs before throwing me in here. I don't know what kind of man he used to be, but his new position has made him cruel."

Christie's hand clawed at Phillip's grasp. She slipped out a feather and raked the tines against his skin. He gasped and let go. "You know, I'm beginning to think you've gone through a change yourself. Or maybe you've always been cruel, and I didn't know it. I don't blame Austen for kicking you down the stairs, I want to do that myself right now."

Phillip's voice hissed. "You can judge me all you want, but Austen is as dirty as all the rest; I can feel it. And I will make everyone involved in this scheme pay for the death of my father."

Christie sat stock-still.

Revenge.

That's what he was after. That's why he'd agreed to come on this trip even after his father had passed away. He was no longer out to clear the charges of treason from his family name, but to assuage the pain of his grief with rolling heads. He'd made it clear, earlier, that he held her accountable in part for his father's passing. Did that mean he would make her pay as well? And what of Charlie? Thorton? The assassin on the ship? Who did he truly blame, and when would he stop?

She grasped her quill and eased herself a few centimeters away from Phillip. "You need to tell the guard so they can stop the hull's release. We will either be sucked out into the freezing ocean or plummet into it from hundreds of feet in the air. Either way, we're toast."

"We will survive. You and I. We may be miserable by the end, but at least we will live."

Christie's heart thumped in slow-motion, each thundering beat a wave of ink lapping at her soul. Those words. Just like the Baron's. The words of heartless ambition, devoid of anything but hate. The dark had found Phillip too. And she was once again trapped with a soulless monster. But maybe this time, there was still hope.

The metal around them shuddered. The shell of the egg was cracking.

"Get ready to swim," the darkness spoke in Phillip's voice.

"Phillip, you have to stop this. There is no cargo in the hull. All the weapons are up on deck."

"Too late."

The floor beneath their feet burst open. The ocean gaped ten meters below them. The airship had started its ascent. Christie crouched down and grasped for the floor's grating with one hand, tucking her feather back with the other. Sharp metal bit her fingers as the smell of salt and seaweed raced around her. Phillip clung to the grating as well, climbing down. She followed suit. Maybe if she could get to the outside of the ship, she could grapple her way to the *Fish*. She needed to hurry. Too much higher and the *Fish* would not survive the impact of hitting the water either.

Her shoulder gnawed, and white sparks flashed their way into her vision. Her left hand weakened and numbed. She could not hold on much longer.

Christie reached the bottom of the hangar doors and looped around to the other side. Her right hand found a hold, but her left faltered. She swung it up again, and again, its strength gave out.

The doors reached their apex, jarring her grasp. Her bones rattled. Her fingers slipped.

Christie tumbled through the air, flipping once, twice, too many times, until she lost which way was up. Waves smashed into her back. Bubbling water consumed her breath. She sank deeper and deeper. Her arms lost their pull, her legs their kick. A whirling plume shot down next to her, shaking the airless sleep from her mind. She thrashed out in the last of her hope.

Pulling, tugging, reaching.

Then air. Salty, moistened air exploded in her chest with a strained breath. She spluttered and coughed the dark of the ocean from her lungs. Phillip burst from the water next to her, the mop of his hair obscuring the hate she had seen earlier in his eyes. Would he drown her here now?

Christie paddled, hacking the water from her lungs. Oceana's airship shrank in the sky. It was nearing sunset. A whole day of work, and war still loomed on the horizon. Would Austen heed the warning?

A puttering zoom crashed her thoughts. She spit water from her mouth and looked behind her. Charlie and the *Robin* were circling overhead. Then a rope appeared, tossed over the side and tangling in the wind like a little girl's hair ribbon come loose. The end trailed through the water and zipped by. She grasped at it and missed.

The rope serpentined its way back through the water, and she reached out once more. Contact. A jolt tremored through her body and burst out of her wound. Water plowed into her on all sides, pushing her down. The waves won. She tumbled back into the depths, kicking again for the surface. For the light. There was no way she could hold onto that rope, not in her current state. She would be left here to drown.

The rope circled around behind her, and she trod water. Was there a way to loop it around just her good arm? No. It was moving too quickly and the threads would bite her skin. Maybe Charlie would give up and throw something down for her to float on until the *Ol' Bird* could slosh its way over.

A heavy weight crushed her from behind, scooping her out of the water. Phillip had one arm entangled in the rope and the other wrapped around her waist. Water sprayed out around them, and she clung to the woven threads with her good arm as they lifted from the ocean. Phillip tucked her within his grasp, and for the second time, she wondered if he would take the chance to end her. To get high enough so he could drop her back down and exact his righteous revenge from above. She clutched the rope tighter, she would not go so easily.

But the stretch to the *Ol' Bird* passed quickly, and still alive, she and Phillip clattered onto the rough deck.

Charlie looped the *Robin* around and struck its wheels upon the deck just past where they lay. He bumped and braked to a stop and jumped over the red door to get out.

"What happened?" he asked, his boots clopping across the deck toward them.

He scooped her up in his arms, and her chest burned with exhaustion. She gasped as he tugged on her shoulder to inspect her.

"Sorry, Ol' girl." He let go and offered Phillip a hand.

Phillip pushed it away and stood up by himself. "What happened is nothing. Christina failed to keep the cargo secure so it could be jettisoned into the ocean."

Christie framed Phillip in her bent brows. "No, instead *we* were jettisoned. How was I to know to keep the cargo in the hold if no one told me the new plan in advance? Besides, I could have fixed this if you hadn't made it look like I was running away. I told you, now that Austen is captain—"

"Do you just hop from traitor to traitor?" Phillip asked. "Thorton, Barnes, now this Austen character. When will you learn to trust the people around you instead of your shadowy contacts?"

Christie jabbed her finger at him. "Trust you? You're insane."

Charlie stepped between them before Christie could let fly more than her finger. "Let's just take a breath here. If the cargo is still on Oceana's ship, then we still have a job to do."

"Why do you even care?" Phillip's voice matched his icy demeanor. He folded his arms across his chest. His pointed nose lifted aft as if the briny smell of the ocean was too much. "What's your interest in all this? Your father didn't commit treason, and his vessel just sailed clear."

"I'm here for Christina." Charlie stood tall and stared at him.

"Then you're a blind fool. You know you're chasing the wind, right? Here today, gone tomorrow, and with everything dear to you in tow. When the time comes, only I will be here to say I told you so."

The waves rocked Christie back and forth, churning her stomach. How did Phillip know she had originally planned to leave?

But she had changed. She had decided to stay.

The corner of the manor's caves shadowed her, even in the sun.

If she was just like the Baron, maybe Charlie *should* leave her. Escape before she ruined his life, like the Baron ruined hers.

She broke away from them and marched toward the captain's box as quickly as she could. She scaled stairs and climbed ladders. A panoramic view of the navy ocean, topped by the silvery bottom of the balloon above, met her inside the steering box, and she set to work getting the *Ol' Bird* into the air. Charlie had taught her the basics of ascent. And flight. And how to trust again.

But what if Phillip was right? What if she was too flawed to stay and be of good use to anyone? After all, neither of them knew how much of a monster she actually was.

The ship whirled air and sea and steam as the balloon heated and rose, jostling the ship. She took her frustration out on the control panel with a smash of her fist. A curse echoed from the hallway. Charlie had come. He always did. But he would not if he knew.

He pushed his way into the captain's box. "Everything okay in here?"

She nodded.

"Do you know what's gotten into Phillip? I think he's spent too much time in the caves with your creepy butler." Charlie's grinning face appeared to her right.

"His father died."

Charlie's smile dissolved. "Why didn't he tell me? He doesn't have to be here right now. I'm sure he has more than enough on his mind."

"He wants to be here." Christie focused on the controls. She notched up the accelerator and tapped the pressure gauge for the balloon. Those were the only two things she really knew how to do, but it kept her mind off of Charlie. And herself.

Charlie swooped onto the control panel, and the ship responded to his touch. Their acceleration increased, and their direction changed eastward.

With the ship in order, he leaned back onto the windowed wall and tucked his hands into his pockets. "Why would he want to be here, stopping a war some wicked crackpot concocted? I'm pretty certain the only reason you and I are here is because we have a death wish."

Christie's finger froze on the gauge. She smudged it off slowly and rubbed the tip on her coat. "He has one too. Just not for himself."

Charlie tucked his lips inward and made a *smirching* noise. "So he's gone to the dark. It was only a matter of time. What with me and you and already there. So who's on his list? He's always looked at me with a cynical eye."

"Not you." Christie's thumbs slid up to tuck themselves into her corset. "At least, I don't think. And you're one of the few people in this mess who hasn't gone dark." She lifted the corners of her lips into what she hoped was a smile.

"Christina," he said and reached for her.

She brushed him off. "There's Thorton. Barnes, though he's imprisoned now. The assassin, though I don't think Phillip knows he's hiding on Oceana's ship. Maybe Austen, though I don't know what he's done to make the list. He's the only reason I'm alive. Oh, and me, though Phillip seems to be drawing that out."

Charlie pulled his hands from his pockets and rotated his bird ring. "Well, we can't have that now, can we? Not after you've just started coming back to me. I'll keep an eye on him. We need to keep him from doing anything stupid. Phillip's a man who can't bear the burden of death. He'll go straight up bonkers, and we don't need another Baron on our hands."

Another Baron.

Her eyes fell to her boots. Did he mean her? Her veins chilled. There was no way he could know.

But he should.

She had to tell him.

Christie nodded. "Charlie, there's something I have to tell you."

The sun reached its farthest rung on the horizon, filling the box with orangey light. The brass bird flashed with brilliant whites and golds, and only Charlie's silhouette remained. Christie's words disappeared with the shadows, caught up in the sun's glow. A minute passed in the radiance, and Christie soaked up the warmth. It may well be the last time she felt it.

With a final, bobbing burst, the luminescence faded, and the shade of life crept back in. And on the horizon with it, Oceana's warship and the dusting of an island in the waters.

Twenty-Seven

CHARLIE LEANED FORWARD AND double-checked the trajectory of the *Ol' Bird*, pulling levers and adjusting the steam release.

"Looks like we're in for some more action."

Christie felt the moment slipping away. She needed to tell him about the Baron—about what she had done—before it passed. She would not have the strength to do it later.

"Charlie, before we go on. I—I've done something."

"Oh?" Charlie asked, but his attention hovered on the window. He squinted.

"If you could just . . . look at me? It's . . . " Christie's thumbs slipped deeper into her corset. "It's quite terrible, and I need to know you're listening."

Charlie's gaze continued to look beyond her before readjusting to meet her face. "I don't think this is the right time."

Christie's thumbs hooked up beneath her stays, her knuckles digging into her ribs. "It will never be the right time. That's the problem. I need to tell you whether it's a good time or not."

"Christina..." Charlie's scrutiny again slipped to the window.

"No, Charlie." She sprung her hands from the corset and grabbed his shoulders. "I have to tell you."

He swooped his arms around her and pulled her in, pressing his cheek against her hair.

She breathed him in and found her courage. "I killed the—"

An explosion ripped through the air, consuming the Baron's name with its rumble. The *Ol' Bird* shuddered, knocking Christie into Charlie. They fell to the floor, Charlie on top, and her wound burning from his weight. He jumped up, pulling her with him. Creases lined his brows, but a hint of a smirk rested on his lips.

"You alright?"

She nodded, brushing wild curls from her face.

"I told you it was a bad time." He winked and let go of her hands to clatter over the control panel.

Christie pushed open the closest window and scanned the deck for Phillip. He was leaning over the railing on the east side. She called to him through the wind. His face shot in her direction. Another blast rattled the airship, and Phillip tumbled, grabbing the railing as his feet went up and over the side. He clung to the metal, both arms wrapped around a railing support like a bolt around a screw.

"Phillip!"

She yanked open the door.

"Christina," Charlie's voice barked over the ruckus of fire, splintering ship, and angry engines.

Her hair whipped over her shoulders as she craned her neck to see him.

"I don't care."

Her world froze despite the chaos. His words rang crystal clear.

"I don't care what you did. What you've done. I've—" His usually upturned lips pressed into a shut door. "I don't care."

His voice rushed around her and pushed her out of the door. Could he mean it? Without knowing what she had done?

She slid down the sides of the ladders and jumped multiple steps before making the main deck. Her boots thudded on wood, masking the thundering in her chest. Or did he know? Had he heard her despite the explosion? Had he known all along?

Phillip's arms slipped a titch as she dashed closer. She grabbed his elbows and tugged, but her left arm was too weak. She would need leverage. The wind blustered by, and the *Ol' Bird* listed to the right, Phillip's legs along with it. Her knees hit the railing, and she crouched down. Phillip's white knuckles hovered just above her right shoulder.

Christie reached back and slipped her hand into his. She tensed her leg muscles and thrust herself upward, pulling his arm forward and over her shoulder at the same time. The engines groaned, tugging the *Ol' Bird* upright. Christie tumbled onto the deck, pulling Phillip behind her. Her shins hit the deck, and she winced.

Phillip shifted to a crouch. "Took you long enough." But his voice had released some of its darkness.

"We've got to go." She bent past the pain and was on her feet again, running toward the *Robin*.

Only one ship hovered against the horizon: Austen's. Which meant Britannia hadn't shown up and started firing. The trail of steam coming from Oceana's warship puttered heavy and thick; the ship wasn't moving. The mass of hulking metal and welded seams held its ground and fired another shot. A high-pitched whistling screamed as the projectile streamed across the expanse toward them. Christie braced herself against the railing as the *Ol' Bird* took the hit with a groaning shudder. Swirling black burst from the far side, smelling of sulfur and rotting eggs, of acridity and fire.

These were not warning shots. Austen was shooting to kill.

But why?

Fear streaked through her. Why was Austen firing at her? He was smart enough to recognize that the only other ship above the water had to be hers. Why wasn't he focusing his efforts on preventing the war she had warned him about? Did he still not trust her because she was a spy? Or was this all a show for his men? Whatever the reason, if they did not stop, the *Ol' Bird* would be downed for sure, and everyone on it. She had to get to Austen and convince him to stop.

She reached the *Robin* and slid into the pilot's seat. Phillip climbed in on the passenger side, jostling her with his elbows.

Charlie popped up at her side.

"No way you're flying this complicated thing. This is no *Fish*."

"I'll be fine," she said and started the little engine with a yank on a pull cord. "Trust me." The flying machine puttered and shook before sorting out the steam within. A little funnel puffed out wispy steam.

"Did you hear that?" Charlie grabbed her hand. "The steam's almost out. You barely have enough to make it over to that ship. And even then, if things go wrong—" He pulled her hand to his chest. "You won't have enough to make it back."

Her fingertips thrummed with his hammering heart. "Worried about me?" She tried to look as coy as he usually did.

"Always," he said and kissed her hand.

"Then let's hope this goes right. You bring the *Ol' Bird* around and see if you can figure out how to make those pipes on the bottom work. Maybe we can suck up the islands before Britannia arrives."

Charlie's grip on her hand tightened. "I can't let you go. Not without me."

"Everything we're trying to do will be for naught if you don't stay and fix the islands." She pulled her hand free and started the *Robin* forward.

Charlie moved alongside, his feet quickening from a walk to a jog. "I'm not losing you again. You can't shake me. Not this time."

Christie pressed her fluttering fingers into the steel of the steering mechanism. Oh, how she wanted to linger. But it could not be. "You must stay, Charlie. You cannot come."

"Last time I didn't come with you was when all our troubles started. With the Baron and all this."

The wind whipped through her hair, tangling it into impossible snarls. So true, his words. And entirely unhelpful. Her stomach lurched as the wheels bumped and the wings caught the lift of the breeze.

"Stay," she yelled over the snap of gusting air. "You're safer here."

The wings tightened as they lifted off and zoomed over the railing of the *Ol' Bird*. She shouldn't look back. What good would it do besides fill her with worry? But she had always been weak around Charlie. She pulled the hair out of her eyes and glanced back at the deck. No one.

No one?

She did a double take. A jarring thud shook the *Robin*. The balance of the cockpit now skewed to the back.

Phillip peered over the side, his knuckles white on the frame. "He jumped, that ruddy idiot."

"What?" Christie threw herself half over the side to see.

Sure as the red in Ana's eyes, Charlie clung to the metal bar between the wheels. That crazy, half-baked scoundrel. Part of the reason she left him behind was to keep him safe, and now he was pulling these insane antics. His feet kicked about wildly, then flew up as the flying machine took a nosedive toward choppy water.

"You're as dim-witted as he is," Phillip gasped. He grabbed the steering and righted the *Robin*. "Between the two of you, it's a miracle we're not fish food yet."

Christie swatted his hands off the wheel and took hold once more. "We need to ground before he falls."

"Is it a need?" Phillip stared placidly ahead. The late sun amplified the greenish hue of his skin.

"Charlie," she called over the side. The wind whipped the words away as soon as they left her lips. "Charlie, stay still and hold on. We'll get you to safety."

The shell of the *Robin* shuddered with more than the air current. What was Charlie up to?

She leaned over until the red metal dug into her ribs and she could barely keep hold of the steering. Charlie appeared just below the wing. He grappled his way up and over, tucking a foot here and there, and thrusting himself over the gaps in the taut fabric.

"What part of stay blooming still are you not getting today?"

He shot her a smirk and kept climbing.

Why did she even waste her words? Of course, Charlie wouldn't listen. He was headstrong and foolish, and someone she could not lose again. Her heart seized every time his hand slipped. Her knuckles whitened with every jostle from the wind. But, at last, he made it to her. His knees clamped around the metal joist of the wing, and he leaned over so his smug face was entirely too close. She could not hide behind her hair now. He dipped his nose so it touched her own, and she soaked in his eyes. The *Robin* tilted sharply. Christie pulled her hot cheeks away from Charlie. He certainly would be the death of her.

"Hey, you fools." Phillip's dry chastisement cut through the wind. "Keep your unsavory gimmicks until we're on the ground. Your display, while nauseating, is not enough to stop an international war. Which is what we're here to do, lest you forget."

The sting of both the wind and Phillip's words brushed her cheeks. He was right. She was forgetting herself. Forgetting their purpose as they sailed so close to Austen's ships she could count the railings. She straightened her shoulders and focused on the airship ahead. Charlie, on the other hand, did nothing of the sort. He nestled in closer, resting his head by her neck. His warmth was a thrill against the cold of Phillip next to her. She did not pull away.

"Christina," Charlie's voice hummed for her ear alone. "About what we were saying on the ship."

"No." She stopped him. She had almost lost him over the sea, she could not bear to lose him over words too. "You were right. It's not a good time."

"Christie." His hand reached out, and his eyes pleaded. But for what?

Those eyes. Those oceans, washing her heart in waves of guilt. If she failed to tell him now, she may never get the chance. "Charlie, I—"

"I killed the Baron." His words ghosted past her ears as a shot rang out from down below.

The wings of the *Robin* caught aflame, and they plummeted toward the deck of Oceana's warship.

Twenty-Eight

A BLACK, BURNING VEIL of smoke enveloped Christie, burning her lungs as much as Charlie's admission burned in her mind. What had his whisper meant? How could he have killed the Baron when it was she who had poured the poppies in his tea?

But the *Robin* tumbled from the sky more rapidly than her thoughts, and those concerns would have to wait.

She could not see the deck of Austen's ship, could not brace for it, but she knew it was there. They barrelled mercilessly toward the hard wooden planks. She pulled up on the steering mechanism with all her might. Phillip joined her, his lanky arms reaching out of a dark, acrid cloud.

It was no use.

Charlie leaned across her, pulling stops and flipping toggles.

"Release the mini-balloon," he barked over the wind.

Christie shook her head. "We'll fall even faster."

"Yeah, but in a straight line. Without the power of the engine, the mini-balloon is knocking us about in the wind. Our only chance is to cut it."

Christie scrambled to turn around, banging her elbows and hips on the jarring metal frame. She leaned over the back. Reached for the screws and thick lines tethering the balloon to the main frame. No knife. She scanned the flying machine for something sharp.

Charlie's arm slid protectively around her. That soft-hearted cumberground. He'd get them both killed if he didn't hang on for his own safety.

Then Phillip looped his hands around Charlie's belt, knuckles tight and white, though he refused to look at them.

The churning engine coughed a splutter of steam, clearing the smoke in time for them to see their doom. Metal wrenched in shrieking gasps. Fire exploded in stinging, burning, blinding bursts. Charlie was thrown from her. The *Robin* ground to a halt, tipping Christie over the front. Fire scalded her wrist, singeing the glove on her hand and catching it aflame. Head over heels, she landed on her side. Her fingers were seared with each lick of fire. Her very protection now burned her skin. To expose her flesh, herself, with the promise of gunfire and blood ahead, how could she? Her skin blistered in agony. No choice.

She ripped off her smoldering glove, let the whipping air and cold sun soothe her boiling flesh as she rolled like a barrel across the deck. Agony twisted out of her shoulder. Wood splintered against her cheek.

And the light.

Fading. In and out. In and out. White sun. Black. Grey smoke. Black. The crisp blue of a soldier's uniform.

And red.

Everywhere.

She had to get up.

She pushed through the biting heat in her shoulder. Climbed to her knees. Phillip lay to her right, his body loose, like a ragdoll. He couldn't be dead. Could he? She reached trembling fingers over and touched his neck. A pulse. Heaven be. He was either unconscious or playing dead. A bullet ate wood with a crack to her left. Christie recoiled, fighting her impulse to run. She could not abandon him here. Not like this. Not after everything terrible she had done to him and everything kind he had done to her. She needed to learn the word sorry, to stop making excuses. But that, too, would have to wait.

"Phillip," she hissed through her teeth, scanning the debris on the deck for enemies and safety, for a sliver of hope.

His limp body remained still, useless as a stripped screw. She couldn't be headed to hell if she was already there, right? So what was there to lose? More bullets skiffed across the deck as she grabbed his shirt and yanked him toward the fire. Backward, one foot behind the other. Her shoulder screamed, and her burnt hand stabbed at her nerves. Was there anywhere safe on this godforsaken ship anyway? And where was Charlie? She'd never get them both to safety in time, not at this rate.

A breeze blew refuse from the flames across the deck. Her chest shuddered. Soldiers, half a dozen or so, surrounded her in a half-circle, the *Robin* to her back. She dropped Phillip's shirt and released the Good Baron from its holster with her good hand. Pulled out Rudy despite the blistering in her left. Locked her elbows. Took a breath.

This was not going to end well. And after all that she had been through. After the Baron. Spying. Phillip and his father. Losing and finding Charlie. And all for what? What had she left? A handful of bullets. And the curses that sat on her tongue.

The soldiers lifted their guns.

"Bedswerving zounderkites," she spat, hoisting her guns shoulder height and leveling them at the two nearest soldiers.

Could she kill them if necessary? Would they haunt her dreams like the Baron after she'd killed him?

Pistol clicks clacked the air, their barrels pointed directly at her.

"You fustilarian rakefires. Do your worst."

Shots shattered the air. She flinched and fired back, waiting for pain, but the men scattered. She touched her shoulder, her chest.

Bullet-free.

But how? She whipped around. A smug face poked up behind one of the flaming wings. A pistol gleamed in the sun. Charlie. She smiled. He always came back. She looped one shoulder under Phillip's arm, and Charlie dashed out to grab the other. Blood trickled down Charlie's right cheek and ear, and black patches marred his clothes, flaking here and there as they dragged Phillip behind the burning *Robin*.

"You're a dolt," he said with a twitch of his lips.

"And what would you have done when faced with a firing squad?"

"I certainly would have used better curse words. Who taught you to swear anyway?"

Bullets cracked the metal next to them. Shards flicked past her nose. She peered over the smoking wing. Two soldiers lay face down, Charlie's impeccable aim their cause of death. Four more men ghosted about the deck, hiding and dodging and popping off an occasional shot that sent her heart racing.

"How many bullets left in that toy you call a gun?" she asked.

"It is a bit trite, isn't it?" He held up the silver specimen for inspection. "I could use an upgrade. Let me have one of yours." He reached for Rudy, and she recoiled.

She leaned back too far, exposing herself to the deck, and another bullet flayed the deck to her right. She scrunched herself into a ball to reduce her exposure.

"Just give me your gun." Charlie held out an open palm. "I only have a shot or two left in mine, and we both know I'm the better shot."

She scowled and relinquished, holding on so he had to yank the handle from her grip. "Its name is Rudy, by the way."

"Ah, baby Rudy." He gave the gun a caress as another bullet whistled past his cheek, stirring his hair. He didn't flinch. "Serve me well."

He nudged his head to the right, and Christie got in position behind the hot metal of the *Robin*. She crouched so she could jump up or lean sideways to take a shot. He did the same but on the left. She grabbed a bright red scrap of the *Robin* that wasn't on fire. Charlie eyed her and gave a nod. She hurled it over their cover, and Charlie popped his head out the side.

Three shots rang out.

Charlie pulled his head back in. "Two on my side, two on yours. Though one of yours didn't fire. He's either running low on ammo or a steadier hand with more training."

Christie nodded and did the math. "I have two bullets left in the Good Baron. There should be three in Rudy."

"Then we have plenty when you add the rounds in The Silver Beast."

"That's a terrible name."

"Ah. Back to the drawing board then. In the meantime, toss up another distraction and cover me from your side. If I'm lucky, I can take them all out." He gave his pistol a twirl.

"Show off," she muttered, but made ready the next projectile.

In truth, she was glad Charlie was there to protect her. To shoot the men she didn't have the stomach to kill and with enough skill that they didn't have to die at all.

"Make sure you cover your side so they don't hit Phillip. He's still breathing. We need to get him out alive."

"I can't help it if a stray bullet—"

"Don't even think about it."

Charlie pouted. "As you wish."

"And Charlie." She dropped her glare. Soaked in his ocean eyes. "Don't get shot. We have things to talk about." She made her voice light, but her chest tightened with the words. With weakness.

The Baron had always chided her for letting emotions take over, but he was dead now. And why? Because of what she had done, because she had poisoned him. Or had she? What of Charlie's admission before they were shot down? Blackwell Senior's words floated to the forefront. What had Charlie to do with the Baron?

Charlie gave the nod, and she lobbed a piece of wood tied with bright fabric over the top. She leaned to the side and scanned the deck. A soldier appeared to the left. She took aim. Charlie's gun barked sulfur and powder, and the soldier fell. A movement to the right. She leveled the Good Baron at his chest. Moved it up to his shoulder and fired. The man moaned before slinking to the deck. Two left. Two left. But where were they?

A shadow behind the haze. A flash of blue. Somewhere to the center-right. Charlie must have seen it too. He leveled his gun and fired. A ricochet.

"The Devil take it," Charlie cursed. "There's more smoke on this ruddy deck than in hell."

She squinted. The sharp smell of the burning engine scratched her throat. The gritty air burned her eyes. And again she saw it. A pass of blue. But its movements were off. Unnatural. Back and forth, like a pendulum.

"Charlie, wait."

He shot. Another bullet wasted.

"I think it's a decoy." The coat swung again through the smoke. This time, a black hole marked the fabric's chest. "Our backs!"

She flipped around too late. A muscled man with a bandaged chest and shoulder made a final thrust through the debris and grabbed Charlie by his neck. The assassin from the chateau. So Barnes *had* sent him. Too bad Phillip and his bloodlust lay unconscious. Charlie kicked and thrashed, raking Rudy along the man's arm. Christie aimed. *Engine knock and a bloody explosion.* She wasn't good enough to make this shot. Another soldier appeared. She shifted her aim.

"Ah ah," the assassin said in a growly voice. "Unless you want me to snap this chicken's neck, I suggest you put your gun down. You've already caused me quite a bit of trouble."

Charlie coughed out a string of gutturals. Was he trying to tell her something or just bent on using his dying breath to curse?

The man shook Charlie quiet.

"Drop it, girl."

She looked at Charlie's purpling face. To the scrawny gunmen to her left. To the ape of a man hurting Charlie. Then squared her jaw. "Take me to Austen. He will clear this all up."

The assassin laughed and snarled something terrible with his teeth. "Austen's the one what sent me."

"No. Not if he knew it was me. This is a misunderstanding."

The light from the fire burning up the *Robin* flickered on his teeth. Charlie's squirming had died down to a twitch. "Austen's always been the one paying my bills, and you, Christina Rushing, have always been my target."

She dropped the Good Baron on the planks of the deck. It clattered to a stop a few meters away.

It was not possible.

Austen would never send an assassin to kill her. He was her friend.

"You lie." Her voice trembled, but she pushed through. "And you're making a mistake. This ship is headed toward Britannia. Toward starting a war nobody wants. We came to warn Austen. To stop this ship."

The thick soldier's sneer remained, but his grasp on Charlie loosened. Purple drained from his face.

"What's she talking about, Commander?" The scrawny soldier asked. "What war?"

He opened his mouth to answer when a blast cracked the air. Blood trickled from the corner of the assassin's lips, and he fell gape-mouthed to the deck, Charlie half beneath him.

What in tarnation was going on? The scrawny soldier turned, and another blast shattered his chest. He collapsed in a bleeding mess. Behind him, Austen stepped forward, his white captain's uniform a beacon in the smoke. She had been saved.

TWENTY-NINE

T FIRST, CHRISTIE JUST gawked at her commander on the smoking deck of Oceana's warship. His face was cool and his shoulders pulled back with a smoking gun in his right hand. Then relief broke through her.

"Took you long enough," Christie laughed, half with shock, half with relief. Austen had saved her once again, from both bullets and lies. "I've had a wretched day. You wouldn't believe."

Charlie moaned. She rushed forward to clear the dead man off him. Blood seeped through the soldier's uniform, and she kept her bare hand back. Tugging with all her weight, she pulled Charlie free.

Austen stepped forward through the smoke, his gun still in hand, loosely pointed in her direction. "You shouldn't have come back."

"I know; I'm sorry, Commander."

"It's Captain."

She smiled. "Right. Congrats are in order. Sorry, there, *Captain*."

His response was hard. Rigid lips, rigid face, rigid cheeks. Only his eyebrows pinched together.

She composed her face into something more serious. He was clearly in a business mood. "My apologies for bombarding your ship. I had to stop you. I—" She hesitated, guilt spilling into the words she was about to say. "I betrayed you and Oceana. I was hired by Thorton to change the coordinates on your war vessels' itinerary. You're headed toward Britannia with a deck full of weapons. I fear the flaming wreckage on your ship will only make the situation worse. Well, that and you were downing my own bird."

"I already know about Thorton," Austen said. He eyed Charlie who perched on his hands and knees, coughing.

She stepped between them, shielding Charlie from view. Something was off. Something about this had always been off.

She continued. "Let's change course then. Stop the potential war and go take care of Thorton. I am at your disposal, of course." She threw up a smile and took a step toward the Good Baron. She'd feel better with its weight in her hand.

"There's no need to change course for Thorton. He's in my holding cell."

"What?"

"I told you I knew about him. We picked up him up as a traitor when he was trying to escape our waters. He was fleeing like a scared chick, though I'm sure you can imagine why after your little stunt with our ammo stores back at base."

"Yes, but I just told you about Barnes today. You . . . you were surprised."

Austen nudged the dead soldier with his boot. "I was surprised that you were on my ship. Alive."

Shock shackled her thoughts. Her mind ran in a loop. Austen *had* tried to kill her. Why?

"I underestimated you and the number of resources at your disposal. I also failed to take into account that you might have friends or compatriots. Whatever they are." He waved his hand toward Charlie. "You've been busy."

"I don't understand." Blood rushed in her ears, drowning out the crackle of nearby fire. "You let me go on Oceana's beach. Took a bullet for me. Risked your life."

"What I risked was a ruined uniform. But it got me this one instead." He swiped his hand across his white coat. "Worth it, don't you think?"

"But he shot you. I saw the blood. You hit the floor."

"Like Thorton, I've known about Barnes for some time now. I've kept his pistol filled with salt for weeks now, waiting to take control. What you saw was a flesh wound."

She took another step toward the Good Baron. Stopped. She couldn't leave Charlie exposed. Could she grab the pistol before Austen could harm Charlie? Was it worth the risk? She couldn't even tell what Austen's aim was yet. She needed to keep him talking.

"So you used my arrival to stage a coup to take over?"

"Opportunity comes to those who prepare. I've calculated everything, from letting you go on the beach so Barnes couldn't question you to what I'll do with your two friends here. That is, blame them for the impending world chaos." He leered at Charlie, and her stomach lurched.

It still didn't make sense, all his calculation nonsense. "Why keep Barnes' plan to go to war? What good is a country steeped in war debt?"

Austen stepped on the body of the bleeding soldier next to him. His voice rose, "What good is a country that can't expand? Our islands are nearly full, our population a quarter of Britannia's or Americana's. And yet we can't grow, can't expand because our neighbors are pigeon-livered tyrants who fear competition. Their bloody treaty has crippled us."

Christie slipped her foot a few centimeters towards the Good Baron. The rants of ne'er-do-wells never did end well for her or anyone else.

"Our oceanic sisters are ungrateful swells, did you know?" He moved his boot so it rested on the soldier's head. "What would they be without us? Our need for cheap fuel in the middle of the ocean drove the steamvolution outside of Aegyptus, sped up the rise of the machine, and expanded air travel. We've enhanced commerce and created a better place for people to live. How do you think our neighbors grow? Conquering and enslaving populations. I wish to conquer no one. Oceana creates homes for people who are tired of the selfish governments ruling their own citizens. We've created a new power, a new place for those sick of tyranny to live guilt-free. Our dear neighbors need to fall in line."

Christie could listen to this drivel no longer. She dove for the Good Baron. Austen caught her arm and twisted it behind her back. Charlie, still hacking, launched off the ground toward Austen, who thrust him back with a rib-cracking kick. Charlie pooled into a heap on the deck nearby.

"I see you've chosen your side." Austen mused. "I admit, I'm surprised."

He twisted her elbow up sharply, wrenching the nerves around her wound. She gasped.

"I thought you'd choose freedom over the refuse Britannia has heaped on you over the years."

She hung her head. Sweat dripped down her back, and her wound wept afresh. Why *was* she fighting for Britannia? For any of this? She hated society. The people in it. Well, not all of the people. Could one person make the world worth saving? Could two?

"We're already at the rendezvous point." Austen tightened his grip. "Britannia will be here any minute. And now I don't even need the weapons. I can blame Thorton and Blackwell Shipping Co. and Britannia's gentry for attacking my ship. Thanks for the bow-tied man presents, by the way."

Christie lunged forward and broke free. She dove for her gun. Austen smashed his boot on top of it. "I like you Rushing. I could use your grit. I'll give you one last chance. Come to my side and gain an island all of your own."

She froze, heart hammering, shoulder screaming. Her island. And finally with a price she could afford.

"Or, you can die with the other people who got in my way." He leaned over to pick up her gun and paused in front of her, his eyes a few centimeters away. "Your choice. As a loveless spy, it should be easy."

Loveless.

She used to be. But now?

She had Charlie. Even Phillip, though he despised her. They had loved her. And she them. Austen was right, in a way.

The choice was easy.

Christie smiled. Austen frowned. She pushed forward, slamming her head into his. He fell back. She pounced. Clawed for her gun. He flipped her onto her back in a crushing blow. Air escaped her lungs. She couldn't breathe. And then his boot, heavy and black and full of betrayal, came down on her throat. Weight crushed her windpipe. She gasped for air, for life, for a second chance. Her vision sparked. She took one last, shuddering breath.

Then Austen's boot released her. He fell back. She clasped her throat. Struggled to sit. Phillip clung to Austen, his arms wrapped like a wrench around the captain's neck.

"Murderer," he screamed, tightening his noose. "You sent your man to attack Christina. To attack me. You killed my father."

Austen's face burned bright red as he ran out of oxygen. Phillip's teeth clenched in the ugly face of revenge. She did not stop him. She wanted Austen to suffer.

"Phillip," Charlie rasped, pushing to his feet. "Let him go, friend."

"We are not friends," Phillip growled. Lightning flashed in the storm of his eyes. "And this man deserves to die."

"I don't disagree," Charlie said. His voice washed over them like cool water on the beach of a shoal.

How could he be so calm? And why did he want to stop Phillip? Austen was a backstabbing, greedy killer.

"But murder is not the way to right this wrong, Phillip," Charlie continued, hand outstretched, "You don't want this burden, that I know for sure."

How could he know? Unless he had told the truth about the Baron. But how could it be true? All the guilt, the pain she felt over poisoning the Baron. That was real. Painful and ever-present. So how could he have killed the Baron?

Phillip locked eyes with Charlie, a storm brewing on the ocean's horizon. "He deserves this."

Austen's eyes rolled back in his head. His hilly eyebrows sagged.

Charlie took another step. "Aye, but you don't. You can come back from the dark. Anyone can."

Christie held her breath. Was he talking to her? To himself?

"Maybe he's right," she said it first as a whisper, then again, louder. "Maybe this isn't the way, despite everything Austen's done. It can't be. Shadows create more shadows, and I . . ." She looked into Phillip's storm-grey eyes. "I don't want you to live in guilt's shadow, like I do, to be haunted by the ghost of regret."

Phillip's jaw hardened, grinding back and forth, before a softness began to take, first in his eyes, then his jaws and muscles.

Encouraged, she took a deep breath and stepped forward. "I'm sorry, Phillip. For what I did to you and your dad. I really am. I know losing a parent hurts. But this isn't going to help. Let him go," she said, gently, reaching out a hand. "Justice will prevail. On my honor, I promise you that."

Phillip squeezed tighter, tighter. His eyes met hers, hard then soft. He released and kicked Austen's back so he fell forward in a sweaty, ungainly mass. Then, he looked at her, his smile faltering into something boyish and unsure. "Thanks . . . for the apology."

"It's a new trick I picked up," she said, grinning.

"Remind me not to get on your bad side," Charlie stepped forward, punching Phillip's arm.

Phillip offered a half-smile back before it vanished. His eyes widened. "Who's flying the *Ol' Bird* again?"

"The butler's running on auto-pilot punch cards. Why?" Charlie asked.

A shadow darkened the deck. Christie followed Phillip's line of sight over her shoulder. The *Ol' Bird* flew straight towards them, only a dozen yards away, the churning brass gears and flock of metallic birds swirling ominous and deadly. The *Robin*'s crash would be nothing in comparison to this.

She grabbed Charlie's sleeve and pelted across the deck. "Run!"

Thirty

The crack of the two airbirds colliding set the sky aquiver. Raking metal screeched and tore its way down the deck, leaving behind dusty air that smelled like a sawmill on fire.

The *Ol' Bird* would not stop.

How could it? For all Ana's clunking about and unnervingly intelligent eyes, it was just a machine.

The wood beneath their feet shattered into sharp points and flying splinters. Even if they could outrun the point of impact, where would they go? The *Robin* was burning rubble. Its heavy smoke still scratched at her throat and eyes.

Christie picked her way across the deck with Charlie and Phillip in tow, then saw it—Austen's unconscious body rolling toward the edge.

Tarnation and fire, what was she supposed to do?

Despite everything he'd done, she couldn't let him just go down with the ship, could she? He had betrayed her, had tried to kill her. But before that? He'd been her only friend, a sort of father or older brother. And she couldn't have any more blood on her hands. Wood shifted beneath her feet, and she sprinted forward. If she caught him in time, at least she could keep him from going overboard.

"Where are you going?" Charlie yelled after her.

A piece of the captain's box slammed into the decking around her, and a wrenching burst of metal separated her from Austen, from Charlie, from escape. But she had to press on. This was her chance to make something right for once. She gripped the least jagged end of the metal debris with her gloved hand and catapulted herself over the edge.

Austen's hilly eyebrows mushed into the splintering cedar, and his legs were already hanging off the side. She breathed a curse and made a jump. The airship tilted with her. She banged into a pole on the railing and grabbed the cuff of his sleeve. Her blisters pressed into his white coat, smearing black and red. She swallowed hard and looked away.

"Charlie," she cried over the wind. "Phillip. Help me."

Fabric slipped through her glove and across the burnt fingers of her right hand. She couldn't hold on.

Charlie leaped over piles of powder and strands of spilling rope and pulleys. Even Phillip dug his way toward her. But it was too late. They would never make it in time. She could feel it.

"Austen, you must wake up," she yelled. But his hand only slipped further. "Austen!"

His eyes fluttered along with her heart, cracking enough to see her. "Rushing?" He spluttered the name, blood oozing out between his teeth.

"Hang on, we're pulling you up."

"You never were a very good spy."

The starched wool of his sleeve slipped free. Her fingers grasped and stretched, reaching only air. His hilly brows and knowing smile slipped over the edge, and he fell, down, down, down into the tumultuous waves beneath.

Charlie reached her and pulled her away from the edge. "Are you okay?" His ocean eyes scanned her own, and he took her face within his palms.

She nodded feebly.

He lingered a moment, then looked over the side and whistled.

"I lost Austen." The words stuck in her throat but that kept them from sinking to her heart. Heat and ice churned within her, settling to an aching warmth. "I tried. I tried to save him."

And despite the sorrow and horror of loss, she did not feel the weight of his death as crushing darkness. Not this time. She had not wanted this, had tried to save him. But in the end, she could not rescue him from all the things he'd done. From the revenge and justice of all the people, like Phillip, he had also betrayed in his hungry quest for power. Only he could do that.

She hugged herself into Charlie's chest, and Phillip arrived. He stood cooly by the railing, looking down his nose at the choppy water below. "You said he'd get justice. As far as I'm concerned, you fulfilled your promise. We've settled things, you and I."

Her chest squeezed at Phillip's words. "I didn't do this on purpose."

"Regardless, both my father's murderer and conspirator are dead. I couldn't care less how it came to be. It's not for your conscience or mine to worry over what happened to the likes of him." His grey eyes, deep and calm, pierced the discomfort in her heart and released the tension. "I suggest we all move on from this horrible ordeal as best we can."

The airship tilted to the left, knocking them all off balance. They sprawled and fell down the deck. Christie skinned her charred hand on a broken plank and pulled herself up with a wince. Stabbing pain now emanated from the raw burning that lived in her hand. She bit back tears and sprinted after Phillip as the *Ol' Bird* pushed further into the airship they stood on, tearing it to pieces.

"Idea time," Charlie said. He ran with a limp a stride's length behind her. "Isn't that your thing, ol' girl? Working on the fly."

Phillip called back over his shoulder, "Charles has a point."

The situation must be much more dire than she suspected if those two were agreeing with each other. But what did they expect from her? A miracle of bread and fish?

The *Fish*.

She swerved around a falling jumble of tethers. "The *Fish* is still attached to the bottom of this lug. We need to get aft and head over the side."

"Splendid." Charlie managed to sound flippant despite his ragged breath. "We'll just pop overboard and climb down like a pair of spider monkeys, shall we?"

The deck tore asunder beneath their feet. Christie jumped to the side, clasping the railing. Phillip stumbled ahead in the clear. Charlie jumped side to side, managing to secure a precarious footing before it, too, shattered with his weight. He lurched forward and grasped Christie's boot. The shards of wood fileted his hand in a ribbon of red. Sticky blood flowed out around his fingers and into the seams of her boot.

She shuddered as the ooze penetrated her stockings and found her toes. The filth. The red. She fought the urge to pull away, to leave Charlie to his doom. She could not switch hands, the blisters on her left could not grasp the metal railing. But the thought of more blood on her bare skin sent her reeling, twisting. Her mind blackened, no gloves to keep the dark at bay.

"Christina," Charlie's hands slipped down a centimeter. "Help an ol' chap out?" His mouth played into a smile, but fear radiated from his eyes. "You're alright, you know? It's nothin' a bit of soap won't clean up later."

He extended his shredded hand up to her. For her. For her help. She blinked back the dark, the headache squeezing the front of her brain. Charlie pleaded with her, and her gaze held onto his face. His sandy hair, his pooling eyes. She reached slowly, and her sight slipped to his hand, to the red. There had to be another way. Her aigrette? Gloves? Her mother? Not a shred of wisdom could cover up this mess. She must cling to her own strength. It was up to her. She refused to let him tumble into the water like Austen had.

"That's right," Charlie said, his voice edged with urgency. "Just a bit farther. You'll have to grab on tight. Together, even our busted mitts will do the trick. Besides, your hands are clean, remember?" His voice dropped to a beleaguered whisper. "I'm the one who killed the Baron."

Her eyes flashed to his.

The light blue of his eye caught the heat of the sun and shone with unabashed sincerity. Charlie. He was an open book. And he had read her like she was one too. He could see her darkness, and still, he came back for her over and over again. Maybe she was not all darkness. Maybe there was a beacon of hope somewhere in her soul that Charlie continued to find. And if he could find it, maybe she could too.

She tightened her grip on the railing and thrust out for Charlie's mangled hand, grasping with all her might, ignoring the grit and stick and weighty guilt. He clung to her. She pulled; their hands one limb of pain and strength and damaged flesh. He kicked his way up until they both had a footing on the railing. Her stinging hands released. She turned away from

Charlie and rubbed off the blood, back and forth and back and forth and back and forth.

"It's okay," his words touched her ears. "You're okay. You did just fine back there."

Her hands froze. Her heart burned. She turned back to him and rested her forehead on his chest. Breathed in his spice and sweat and perfection, undeterred by the iron and sulfur that plumed in the air around them. Cold wind swirled around her, but Charlie's heat kept her warm.

He pushed her gently back and brushed strands of hair out of her face. She had done it. Fought past the pain before it was too late. And all for Charlie. Because of Charlie. This time, she had come for him. She smiled shyly at the concern in his face. Leaned in. The ship vibrated beneath them, swinging their railing to and fro. Her sweet moment turned violent, and her lips smashed into his from the force.

He pulled away, lip tinged with a droplet of blood. "Oof. You're a biter, eh? I should have seen that coming."

The railing creaked once more, then thrashed about. She was going to be sick. It halted with a jarring rattle.

Phillip held the end, his feet secured against a box of the weapons that started the whole mess. "Come on, you trollop. We haven't time for your pandering. We'll be headed for the locker if you don't hurry up."

Charlie sidestepped his way to the end, tumbling to safe ground. Christie followed. The second her boots hit the deck, she punched Phillip's shoulder hard.

"I'm no trollop, you fusty dorbel."

"Language, Lady Rushing. Besides, I was referring to Charles."

Charlie pulled himself up, dusting off his britches. "That I am. But we haven't the time to gossip about my strong points. Which way is aft? Is it that way?" He pointed over her shoulder.

"No. Opposite."

"Of course. Why would the deck tilt in the direction easiest for me? Where's the adventure in that?"

"Tilt?" Christie spread her boots apart.

The airship continued to list. Her feet struggled for hold as gravity yanked her downward. Charlie was right. If they didn't hurry, they'd be climbing their way aft instead. And heaven knew with her damaged shoulder and hand she would never make it. They rushed toward the other side of the boat, this time Phillip positioned in the back for when one of them fell behind. His long legs and two working hands were just the trick to give her or Charlie a boost. The back railing came into sight amidst shifting debris and brackish smoke. She shielded her eyes and located the ladder she used to climb up from the *Fish* the first time.

"There." She pointed toward the break.

Wind whirled in a torrent about her as the falling airship gained speed. Boxes and barrels tumbled past. One nicked her knee. Another whipped her with a trailing rope. She dug her nails into the tiny cracks between the boards to keep from falling back.

"Almost there. Almost there. Just a little father," she huffed under her breath to keep herself going.

Charlie made it to the metal rails first. He flung himself up and over, so if the ship were straight he would have dove right over the side. As it was, he perched neatly just in time to grab her flailing hand and pull her through the gap. Phillip came last, his lanky arm looping easily through.

They were on top now, at the ship's highest point. It might as well have been the top of the world. The airship groaned its impending doom beneath them. The *Ol' Bird* and its beautiful gears had managed to break free, smoke and steam pluming out in a shimmering grey cloud. It would hit the water eventually, but not in a flaming burst. It might even stay afloat. Either way, it would be far from here, from the scene of the scandal, before it touched down.

Who knew, maybe Ana could even make it back to the manor? Christina had to smile at that. There was hope then, for the brass birds tethered to its side. Even if it came in the form of its only remaining passenger—a machine with glowing red eyes.

A sliver of tension released from her heart. The edges of her shirt and the curls in her hair billowed about her as the ocean grew closer and closer.

She had never felt so free. And there, down the side amongst the exposed barnacles and algae: the *Fish*.

Christie took off down the side, Phillip and Charlie close behind. Her boots slipped in the muck and slime, and she skidded the last few yards to the steamarine, ramming into its coppery side. She shook the smarting pain from her elbows and lifted open the hatch.

They three climbed inside.

They three closed the hatch.

And they three nestled in as the airship hit the water and burst into a million pieces.

Thirty-One

"*Fiery Explosion Over the Atlantic.*" Charlie leaned back against the metal wall of the steamarine and read the headline of the newspaper he had swiped in port. "'*Airship Crashes on Submerged Sand Shelf.*' Ha, well that one worked out nicely. '*Davie Jones' Revenge?*' Can you believe this?" He tossed the paper to the side. "A mythological sea lord gets more credit than I do. It's insulting."

The door to the steamarine hung open, letting a salty spray whisp in with the breeze. Christina inhaled deeply, relishing the cool air under the dock they hid beneath. "You want the credit for downing an Oceana warship, killing its captain and crew and subsequently your business partner?" Christie asked dryly.

"Well, not when you put it that way." He pouted and tossed the paper to the side. "I was referring to the fact that we risked life and limb to prevent a war no one even knew was coming." He held up his bandaged hand. "Not even a thank you. Ungrateful buggers."

She took his hand in hers and patted it lightly, feeling the tuft of bandages. "Thank you, ol' boy." She kissed his fingers.

He grinned. "You're not going to bite, are you?"

"Don't tempt me."

A glimpse of lanky limbs swung from the deck above.

"Hang on a second, okay?" she asked Charlie.

Christie stepped onto the edge of the *Fish*'s doorway and grabbed the planks above. With pain, effort, and a helping hand, she pulled herself onto the rickety dock. Phillip stood before her, copper hair washed and silky, a crisp new suit fitted perfectly across his broad shoulders. She would never have guessed he had been fighting for his life just the day before. It baffled her, the changes he went through. One day a rogue agent in a secret war, and the next back to being one of Briannia's most upstanding gentlemen.

"You coming?" she asked, a part of her aching. She did not want to lose her friend.

The salty breeze ruffled his hair, and the dance of shadows through the overcast sky softened his face. "You know the answer to that."

Of course, she did. It was pressed into his lapel and pinned in with his tie clip. He would stay in Britannia. Take over his father's estate as Earl Sheffield. Live a life away from the darkness.

"I'm sorry... about everything, about your father." She forced herself to look him in the eyes.

He matched her gaze. "At least you didn't try to marry him as I first feared you would. You'd make a terrifying mother-in-law." He flashed her his rare devil-may-care smile, catching her off guard.

She grinned, the ache in her chest intensifying. "I'm no match for you."

Phillip reached out and took her hand in his. She squeezed his fingers, and he squeezed back. Then the whimsy in his eyes faded back into serious-ness. The new hole in her chest pinched, then softened with acceptance.

He let go of her hand. "I imagine you'll be traversing the world making terrible, unplanned choices, but if you're ever back this way, you always have a home at Sheffield Manor."

"Of course." She nodded dutifully. "And...thank you. I've never had a place that felt like home, but now I have two."

Phillip smiled softly, the copper in his hair as gentle as the breeze. "'Til next time, Lady Rushing." He offered her a curt bow.

She smiled warmly at the formal use of her name, at the fact that he no longer thought of her as a Ravensworth. It meant all the world.

"Phillip." She curtsied back, and then he was gone.

She waited until his broad shoulders faded well into the crowd before swinging back down into the *Fish*. Charlie sat back, his feet kicked up against the steering and a pucker on his face.

"He not coming?" Charlie asked. He was trying to play things lightly, but she saw right through that.

"No."

"You kiss him goodbye?"

"And what would you do if I had?"

"Have Ana stalk him in the shadows until he goes mad." Charlie waggled his eyebrows.

"A little heavy-handed, don't you think?"

"You have something else in mind?"

"Aye." She smiled. "Let's raze Ravensworth manor, find where the *Ol' Bird* hit water, and travel the world. I've always wanted to visit Aegyptus or Ascia."

"It *would* be better than traveling in the *Fish*. I know you hate feeling trapped."

Warmth spread across her chest. He knew her so well. He slid his arm around her waist, and chills tickled down her spine. She shivered against the swirl of contrasting sensations.

"Truth be told, it's not so bad when you're around."

"Do tell." He grinned. "Travel it is. Besides, there's something I want to show you." He released her and pulled the door shut. Disappointment pinched at her when, instead of coming back to her, he slid into the thin metal rack that served as the pilot's chair. "Due north."

The water swirled around them in sloshing bubbles as they made their way out of port. The light blue outside the window sunk into deep azure.

"I know it's been non-stop chaos since we started this whole mess," Christie said. She leaned forward so her chin rested on his shoulder. "We haven't even had time to talk, what with Phillip around and all."

"Ah, yes. Fine chap, in the end. Though, I still don't think he likes me much. He is a bit of a wet blanket; I see your point."

"Oh hush," she chided.

She fell asleep like that on Charlie's shoulder, avoiding the question that lingered on her tongue and dreaming other people's happy endings. It was a restful sleep, as far as naps under the ocean went. Charlie woke her in the dim light, jostling her chin with his shoulder. The cool air slipped through her clothes, and she scooted closer to relish his warmth.

"We're almost there, ol' girl. Just a few minutes more."

She studied the angle of his jaw, square and strong, but not too hard. It couldn't be with the grin that always sat atop it. She never wanted him to leave. Never wanted to leave him. But a question—*the* question—still stood between them.

"Charlie?" She pulled away to study his face.

"Hm?"

"What had you to do with the Baron?"

Charlie's shoulders tightened for a moment, then released. "You mean besides the fact that I killed him?"

Those words again. And her doubt. For how could they be true?

"Not exactly, I mean your *insistence* on the fact that you killed him. It cannot be, Charlie. And I don't need you to take this burden because you think I'll feel better if you do. *I* killed the Baron. *I* did. And I need to live with that."

The gentle whirr of the steamarine's engine soothed the silence with a *slugush, slugush, slugush.*

Finally, Charlie spoke. "When have I ever taken the blame for something I didn't do? I rarely even claim responsibility for the things I have done."

"But what you said. About the Baron..."

Charlie's face darkened in the shadows of the *Fish.* "I should have told you sooner. I thought it was the only way. That's why I came back. To explain. To beg your forgiveness. To ask for you back. Since the first time I saw you, I've been trying to find a way to be with you. Do you remember that day, the day we met? My father had business with yours for the first time. I wandered out into the gardens and stumbled upon you climbing a tree in a fancy pink frock."

Christie laid her head on his shoulder once more. "How could I forget? You called me a skirt-wearing lubberwort."

"Aye. And what did you do but turn around, pelt me with acorns, and call me a gobermouch muckspout. And you say I taught you to curse." He tsked through his teeth.

She grinned in the blue light. "Whyever did you come back after that?"

"Why? Because I found you thoroughly enchanting."

Christie's cheeks warmed with the heat in her chest, with the heat from his.

Charlie continued, "Every day I fell more in love with you, but as we got older, things became complicated. And then your parents died, and everything turned into a mess with the Baron. I was a coward back then. You paid the price for that. And, I don't know, freeing you became my new obsession. I was in town one day picking up medicine for my father and saw the Baron. I followed him around like a stalker, trying to think of a way to help. To make up for what I had done. When he stopped for lunch, I watched him eat—so casually, so carelessly. I imagined your pain and... snapped."

He sighed, his whole body bending with the effort.

"I slipped some of my father's opiates into his flask. I thought if I could drug The Baron into a stupor, I could... I could come and take you away. I put enough in his drink to drug a horse, or so I thought, but he just went about his business and returned home."

The cold crept in upon her skin. If Charlie had also poisoned the Baron that day, hers would have been the double dose.

"Charlie—"

Charlie's ocean eyes turned to look at her. "Please, let me finish. I got the news that he had passed that night. I didn't mean to kill him. I've carried that scar with me since. But I wasn't sad when he died. And that made it all the worse. I thought, after what I had done, you wouldn't want me, a murderer."

Those feelings. Exactly. She had lived with that guilt, that shame. The fear of losing the ones she loved. She held her breath.

"I waited. A day. Two. Five. Until a week had passed. Then I decided I didn't care. I wanted to be with you and hoped that would be enough. I came for you then. But you had already gone. I've been looking for you ever since. And then fate brought you to me, and—" His words broke off with a catch in his voice. "And then, dash it all, I lost you all over again."

She took his agony-washed face in her hands. "Charlie, you didn't do this. I did."

He covered her hands with his own, skin against skin. "I'm trying to tell you the truth here. Every word of it. I love you, Christina Rushing. I always have." He dropped his hands and slid his arms around her back, encircling her waist. "Please don't run away again. I don't think I could bear it."

The darkness in her soul began to melt in the warmth of his chest. With the heat of his words. The truth thawed within her and trickled out. "That is not the whole truth, Charlie."

His eyes widened with the hesitation in her voice.

"The whole truth is, I'm the one who did the Baron in. I slipped him poppy-poisoned tea the day he died. Hoping he'd pass out. Hoping for a chance to escape. For a chance to be with you, even when a part of me hated your guts."

Charlie ran a finger up and down her back, tickling her skin, her spine, her thoughts. "You clever little vixen." His eyes looked far away, to some place she was not.

"You haven't called me that since we were kids stealing apples."

His ocean eyes found her once more. "Mmm. Well, seeing as you've stolen my heart, I'd say it's rather fitting, wouldn't you?"

She bit her lip and smiled, snuggling in.

"So what does this make us, ol' girl? Murderers? Victims? A pair of right dolts?"

"All of the above." She waited for the guilt to set in. To weigh her down. But Charlie's nearness kept the darkness away. "And survivors. Which is all the Baron ever wanted me to be. A bit of irony, that."

Charlie pushed the steamarine's handles up so the *Fish* slowed to a putter. The bottom scraped against soft sand, and they came to a halt.

"We're here, my lady," he said with a sweep of his hands. He twisted open the corkscrew lid and climbed up top. His hand, still bandaged, reached down for her own.

She grabbed hold and relished his firm and calloused grip, the strength in his muscles as he hoisted her up. She leaned into him on the metal roof.

He enveloped her in his taut arms. A chilly wind blew grainy sand in baby whirlwinds across an island no bigger than the *Ol' Bird*.

"What is this? Where are we?"

"The North Sea. Shallow waters, these. Took some scouring through maps and travelogs in the Baron's library, but I found a ridge that comes close to where the waves crest. I brought that shipment of sand in the *Ol' Bird* here before we left, dumped it, and voila! Your very own island, just as you always dreamed, minus the warmer weather, of course."

"My own island." The words were barely a whisper. Her voice caught, and she fought to stay afloat. "Do you go around buying islands for all the girls you meet?"

He made his voice gravely serious. "Only for the jammiest bits of jam."

Her heart felt like it would burst. "How did you—Why did you? For me?"

"I knew how important it was for you to have a safe place to call your own. A home. It's a bit chillier here than in the Atlantic, but—"

She twisted around and pressed her lips into his. Softness, warmth, love, surrender. She leaned in, wrapping her arms around him. He pulled her to him and unclasped her aigrette so her hair cascaded down, enfolding them both. He ran his fingers along her scalp and through her hair. She pulled back; he held her close; and they fell, tumbling into the warm sand of the beach, she on top and him beneath. She breathed deeply, relishing the juniper and hint of spice, the shifting sand pressing into her bare hands. She looked deep into his ocean eyes.

"You, Charles Blackwell, are my safe place, my home. You're all a lady could ever need." She traced the smile creases that lined his eyes and cheeks.

"It's because of the island, isn't it?" He grinned up at her. "You didn't know I was a homebuilder."

"My mother always did like you." She yanked him close and kissed him.

The End

(Turn page for more!)

Wondering what trouble Christina and Charlie leave in their wake after traveling to Aegyptus? Get the Rogue Royal's: Book2, *The Pharaoh's Curse* for a mystery adventure that follows Zarina Nefertari, the last descendant of Ra, as she fights fate in the tombs of Egypt while under the constant threat of an ancient assassin.

Want a stream of free books, exclusive content, and info on Kyro's next releases? You can sign up for her newsletter here and be part of the community fire!

Interested in seeing more books by Kyro? Check out her website, or www.eightmoonspublishing.com!

A glimpse inside *The Pharoah's Curse.*

Zarina stepped over the man's lifeless body and peeked her head into the shaft, blinking at the glimpse of sunlight near the top.

A hand grabbed her shoulder tight and pain shot through her shoulder. Fear ran like a fork down her spine.

A fourth robber? Had she been so stupid to miss one?

Zarina dropped to the floor, breaking his hold, and rolled to the side. She scrambled back to her feet, blinked, and took in the green-hued man through her goggles.

Tall, tanned, and muscled, a mammoth to the peons she fought before, and his face shrouded in a thick burlap that covered his head and shaded his eyes.

That must be why he stood despite the pink granules coating the room. The stick of her poisonous dust failed to find his lungs. She released the dagger from the sheath on her braided belt and crouched low. Her only chance with the behemoth would be staying out of reach.

She dodged and bobbed, waiting for him to strike. The man crossed his arms, silent.

"Come on." She goaded him with a flash of teeth. "Fight back."

She had to get him to move. There was no other way she could catch him off balance.

Zarina took a swipe at his shoulder. He leaned back. She pounced, dashing around his back and pulling on his freed arm. He teetered, tipped, then found his feet. She was too close, too slow. He reached out, shoved her back. She toppled to the ground so her hands scraped the roughly-hewn stone. Angry droplets poured from her palm, the blood of her ancestors weeping from her in a family tomb.

How appropriate.

But what was his game? Was he playing with her? Amused by her feeble attempts before he pounded her to a pulp? She pulled herself up and bit through the pain. She would not be made a fool of.

"I said fight back." She ran for him, dagger at the ready.

He caught her, spun her around, and shoved her face-first against the wall. Rock crunched against her face mask. He twisted her elbow behind her back and wrenched it up and up until pain bolted from her shoulder in every direction. She gasped, refusing to let go of the knife clenched behind her back and struggling against his hold.

"You've gotten sloppy," he said, his clear baritone as hard as the metal pressed against her lips.

Zarina froze.

That voice. Those muscles. The sun-kissed skin. She should have known.

Her heart pinched.

"Farak?"

He released her arm, and she spun around.

He pulled the covering from his head. Large brown eyes, creased by the desert sun, stared back at her under thick black lashes. It was him—even with the scarf covering his nose and mouth, he was exactly as she had always remembered.

And his presence meant her doom.

Get the Rogue Royals: Book 2, The Pharaoh's Curse, now!

GLOSSARY OF VICTORIAN AND STEAMPUNK SLANG

*A*ck - AN EXPRESSION of mild alarm or dismay

Addlepate - a foolish or dull-witted person

Aigrette - a headdress or barrette containing the tufted plumes or feathers of an egret

Anamaton - an in-world term for a working robot that has some features resembling humans

Bally - a substitute for a rude word used to express anger with something or someone

Barking Iron - a pistol

Bedswerving - an unfaithful spouse or cheater

Blackguard - a man who behaves in a dishonorable or contemptible way

Bully - a person who habitually seeks to harm or intimidate

Bunkum - nonsense

Cassocks - clergymen

Church Pickaxe - particularly pointy nose

Collie Shangles - arguments or quarrels

Crinolette - a whalebone, cane, or steel framework worn between petticoat and dress

Cumberground - a totally worthless object or person, something/one that is just in the way

Diddling - cheating or swindling

Dorbel - a scholastic pedant, or a dolt

Dulbert - a blockhead, dullard, or idiot

Filk - thief

Fisticuffs - fistfight

Flam - deception or falsehood

Flap Jaw - someone who talks a lot and doesn't know when to stop

Fustilarian - a lowly person or commoner

Fusty - stuffy or old-fashioned

Gigglemug - a habitually smiling face

Gleaming Bulldogs - pistols or guns

Glocks - pistols or guns

Gobermouch - someone who meddles in other people's business, usually unwelcome

Jobbernowl - a stupid person, numskull, or nincompoop

Jollocks - someone who is overweight

Leasing-Monger - a liar or teller of mistruths

Loony - a crazy or silly person

Lubberwort - a lazy, stupid person

Mincing Fops - a dainty, refined, and abjectly silly person

Moke - a donkey or ass

Muckspout -one who swears too much

Nomer - name

Podsnappery - an attitude of complacency and a refusal to acknowledge unpleasant facts

Rakefire - someone who has overstayed their welcome and doesn't realize they're unwanted

Rumbumptious -noisy and lacking in restraint or discipline

Saucebox - a saucy, imprudent person

Scrumpet - a woman who sleeps around a lot

Stay-lace - The lace used to tighten a corset

Steambagger - an in-world term used to describe a low-class person who maintains the balloons on steam-powered airships.

Toff - a rich or upper-class person

Vazey - stupid

Zounderkites - idiots

ABOUT AUTHOR

Kyro Dean has written over 20 novels, including Glister, a familial political thriller about a twelve-year-old djinn girl who has to fight all her siblings to become queen.

She owns and edits for Eight Moons Publishing and for the blog, Vanilla Grass Writing Resources.

She loves to speak and present and has shared her knowledge at many conferences. When not writing, she loves spending time with her delightfully curious children and talking with her plants, though they often give terrible advice.

Check out her website www.kyrodean.com.Or check her out on social media (Twitter and Insta): @kyro_dean

THANK YOU!

A huge thank you to Malorie Cooper for the bally good covers!

Another big thanks to my wonderful Kickstarter chuckaboos! I couldn't have done it without you!

Melissa Brown, Kellen Nelson, Jeremy Kowalski, Adrienne Hiatt, Andrew Kaplan, my darling Dita Bachi, Elesa Hagberg, Thomas 'Kranodor' Hahn, Engineer Ed, Travis Fonseca, Bella's Realm, Michael Hayes, Vixen Rue-Aurora, Derek Egerman, Eron Wyngarde, Tracy L, Nikole, Josh McGinnis, Justin A. Rosenbaum, James Rowland, Coral Hayward, K. Seery, Alex M, M. L. Hutchins, Chris Hubbard, Riki, Golinssohn, Oleksandra, Isaac 'Will It Work' Dansicker, Rachelle Funk, Megan Frank, Michael Webber, Molly Celaschi, Steve L., Richmond, Alison Woods, Mary Ann, John Wesley Dean III, TJ Nichols, Mary Ann, Josh Wilcox, Michelle L, Sergey Kochergan, Jennifer, and all the amazing backers who wished to remain anonymous!

And, as promised, they're written in ink, not blood.

Join my mailing list for updates and free reads:

www.ingramcontent.com/pod-product-compliance
Lightning Source LLC
Chambersburg PA
CBHW061551210726
48287CB00006B/2146